Stealin' From The Neighbors

Written by Ed Ashurst

Illustrated by Mike Capron

Ed Ashurst Publishing Company
Douglas, Arizona

Other Books By Ed Ashurst

Non Fiction
Miracle or Coincidence?

Real Cowboys: Grand Canyon to Mexico

Wagon Boss:
A True Cowboy Story

Mavericks

The Life and Times of Warner Glenn:
A Glimpse into the American West

Alligators in the Moat:
Politics and the Mexican Border

Fiction
Stealin' From The Neighbors

There has been stealing since the world began, and it will probably go on to the end. On the range it was easy, and somewhat pleasant work, to appropriate your neighbors' goods or chattels. In the old Texas days, when might was right and the big owners covered their vast tracts of land, sweeping up everything before them, their cowboys had a bad example. Their morals were corrupted, and many of the men, coming up on the trail with the idea that a horse or a cow was a sort of public property, soon commenced to put their ideas into action.

Quote by John Clay *My Life on the Range.*

This book is fiction, any resemblance to a character or event in real life is purely coincidental. And yet it is reality. It is a story about a subculture that I have been a member of for longer than I can remember. I will be accused by some of exaggerating: the bucking horses, the wild cattle, and the meanness. There are no exaggerations here. There are no six-guns with seven bullets. I know what I'm talking about. I've eaten the dust and drank the dirty water.

Red Ram jumped into a dead run.

Chapter One

I guess it's safe to tell the story now, they're all dead after Ray killed hisself. It's odd how Pete outlived most of 'em, actually outlived most of 'em by a long time; and he was the rottenest one of the bunch. Looking back I have good memories of the rest and don't see that they were any worse than I was. But Pete, he was one bad individual, and though I didn't think it at the time, there was no good in him. At least that's how I see it now, looking back. The truth is, I was just a kid, and I suppose that's no excuse because the preachers say we are all without excuse, but a kid of eighteen shouldn't have to get mixed up in stuff like that.

I first went there to the Cow Creek outfit when I was seventeen, about a month before my eighteenth birthday. I was supposed to break horses and help with the spring roundup. It had been dry that spring of '69, and Pete had decided not to start branding until late, around the middle of May. I got there early in the morning the day after I graduated from high school. I think it was the twenty-fourth of May. That's when I first met Ray Lewis, Dale Scott and Ben Favor. That's who the crew was, the four of them: Pete, Ray, Dale and Ben; and I made number five. Pete's wife Mitzi was cooking when we were camped at headquarters; but then when we moved to Black Creek where Ben lived, his wife Sharon cooked. Later, toward the end of roundup, we camped at Badger Flat and we cooked for ourselves. At least they cooked and I did all the dishes.

Pete had given me five horses to start with, all of them three- and four-year-olds, and nothing but green broke. It was dry and droughty, but the remuda had been fed good, and because of that the five colts he gave me to ride were stout and feeling good, and everyone was anxious to see if I could get along with them. I wish now I had known more about life's other challenges than I knew about broncs, and maybe I would have gotten out of there the first day and never been involved in that mess. But the truth is, broncy horses was about the only thing I had much understanding about, and the three- and four-year-olds Pete gave me to ride fit right into what I had been doin' since I was eleven or twelve. The other stuff would come soon enough.

The Cow Creek Ranch headquarters was forty miles or so southwest of Seligman and lay at about forty-eight hundred foot in elevation. It was a country with considerable cedar and piñon trees scattered about with some chamisa and cliffrose mixed in with the trees. There were several big springs at the ranch headquarters that ran enough water to irrigate about a hundred acres of permanent pasture. But farming wasn't in the forefront of Pete's style of management, and the irrigated fields were turned over to an old Mexican man named Luis who kept enough water running on the fields to make something grow. The main house was an old two-story structure made out of native limestone, and it resembled a stone fort. There was a bunkhouse down by the horse corral and a saddle house which lay south of the two-story rock house.

This was where my first morning on the Cow Creek outfit started, down at the horse corral and saddle house. Pete caught me a big roan four-year-old he called Red Ram. The horse was Three Bars bred but the name was also a play on words that honored the favorite local saloon in Seligman forty miles away. I knew through legend that every cowboy worth knowin' had spent time in the Red Ram. Red Ram, the horse, supposedly had outlawed on some gunsel kid twelve months earlier and had not been ridden since.

It was barely light in the east when we led our horses outside the picket corral and everyone else was mounted quickly and began to let me know that they were waiting on me. "Get on, kid, time's a wastin'!" Pete said. Actually, I was the last one out the gate, and I had to latch it and was still only seconds behind them.

"Hell, he ain't never been with a woman before, let alone a fresh four-year-old!" Ray hollered.

I gathered up the leather reins attached to the snaffle bit and got my left foot in the stirrup, and then Red Ram let out a huge expulsion of wind and whirled sideways, and my toe came out of the stirrup and Red Ram almost jerked away.

"By golly! I thought you could get on a horse better than that, Tommy! Get a holt of that sorry ball of hair and get on!" Pete was now talking in his low tone of voice, low on the octave level that is, but not low in volume. When he talked like that his voice resembled the sound of a big cedar post being drug across a gravel road.

"Heck, I never seen anyone from Wickenburg, the dude ranch capitol of the world, that could ride a bronc, or anything a cowboy is supposed to do!" Ray jeered, feeling certain that everyone was enjoying his intelligent comments.

Dale Scott rode over, and when I was about to get Red Ram gathered up again, he sidestepped his big black horse up close to Red Ram's offside and created a wall to hold the bronc in place. This time I put my toe in the stirrup and my left knee in Red Ram's shoulder and was on before Ray could open his mouth again.

Pete turned his horse south toward Cow Creek and whipped him down the right hind leg. Everyone was in a lope in one stride including Red Ram who went about three strides before he set up and took his head. He was big and stout and fresh, but the bucking wasn't hard to deal with. He put his head right down between his front feet and jumped straight forward. Red Ram bucked about four good jumps, and then Ray ran his horse around behind him and hollered, "Let me help you, boy!" He doubled his nylon rope and went to whipping Red Ram across his rump, raising his swings more with each lash so after the fourth stroke his rope was beating me across my back and eventually the top of my black hat.

"Yee Haw! Yee Haw! Look at him ride, boys!" The whipping Ray gave me wasn't pleasant but it did in fact prompt Red Ram into a run, and after eight or ten big jumps, the bronc picked his head up and went to running. Pete, Ben, and Dale were impressed enough with the fact that I had not fallen off that they kept my out-of-control horse hazed into the column, and so without further adieu, we proceeded on into the morning's work. I had passed my first initiation, but even though I was clueless about a lot of things, I knew there would be more of these to come.

With Pete in the lead, the five of us trotted south on a primitive road that soon began losing elevation as it dropped into the canyon where Cow Creek ran, the same Cow Creek that the outfit was named after. In a couple miles we had descended down a side canyon, or tributary of the main canyon, and continued traveling downhill with the country becoming rougher and steeper as we went. Eventually we slowed down to a fast walk with very little said between the men, including me. It seemed that at any given moment at least one man in the crew was smoking a cigarette. When one got the last pull of fiery smoke out of his cigarette, someone else would be striking a match against the button of his Levi jumper and lighting up a fresh one. Ray, Dale and Ben all smoked Bull Durham and could roll a cigarette with ease without stopping their horses. Pete smoked tailor-made Camels. As we rode along, I wondered if he liked tailor-made smokes better or his position as manager, or cow boss, of the outfit gave him the luxury of being able to afford the Camels in place of the cheaper roll-your-owns.

Presently, after riding south about five miles, we found ourselves about a thousand foot lower in elevation and in the bottom of Cow Creek. When the trail we had descended hit the bottom of Cow Creek proper, we turned upstream, or to the east; and the country opened up into a very large basin. This basin was made up of many steep and rocky canyons with high ridges in between and a considerable amount of good cow feed amidst the unending supply of rocks and boulders. Occasionally there would be a gentle flat spot a couple acres in size, but for the most part, everything was on an incline rising upwards in every direction. The main course of the canyon flowed downhill toward the west and uphill toward the east with tributaries flowing into the main canyon from both the north and the south. I had been told that the Cow Creek Ranch owned around fifty square miles of the Cow Creek Basin plus another hundred square miles of country that lay on the high, cedar and pinion-covered plateau north of Cow Creek Basin.

We rode upstream to the east several miles and then started up a good trail that ascended up a steep rocky ridge toward a visible malpai rim rock far above us. When we had traveled upward about half the distance from the creek bottom below and the rim rock high above, we came upon a small flat spot on the top of a ridge. It was obviously a place where cattle congregated, and there were four blocks of salt on the ground that someone on the crew had recently packed in on a horse or mule. There were well-used cow trails coming into this salt ground from several directions.

When we reached the salt ground, Pete pulled up and dismounted, and the four of us followed in kind. We all hobbled and unsaddled our horses that were breathing heavily and sweating. Every man on the crew lit a cigarette except me. "What's the matter, kid? You don't smoke?" Ray asked sarcastically.

"No, I haven't learned yet." I replied.

"Don't smoke and don't go with girls that do!" Ben interjected.

Pete was staring upward, his eyes following the trail to a gap in the rim rock that was still five hundred foot higher in elevation and a mile and a half to the southeast. "You been out there, haven't you, Dale, up to the top in that O R O pasture on the mesa? What do they call that pasture anyway?" Pete said as he continued to look upward.

"Cow Creek, they call it the Cow Creek Pasture." Dale was now looking uphill toward the mesa above. "Same name as this outfit. Yeah, I helped gather it a couple times when I worked there for old Skeet."

"What do they usually run in there, cows or yearlings?"

"They always ran yearling replacement heifers in there when I was there. They would put about four or five hundred in there in the winter and leave them most of a year, and then they gathered them and scattered them all over the ranch." Dale said. He had now sat down and was resting with his back against his saddle that was laying on its side on the ground.

"If a feller went through that wire gate at the top of this trail, how far would he have to go to the nearest water?" Pete asked.

"Oh, I reckon it's about a mile and a half over there toward the south to a big dirt tank. They call the dirt tank Cow Creek also."

I was standing next to Red Ram scraping dry dirty sweat off of his hair with a smooth stick I had picked up off the ground. As I listened to the two men talk, I thought there was sure a lot of places around there that were called Cow Creek.

"I suppose a feller could go out there and find a bunch of yearlings and have them held up right against that wire gate without much trouble." Pete was now talking in a low voice, more like a man talking to himself than to another person.

"Yeah, hell, you could probably get more than you wanted real quick if you knew what you was doin'." Dale answered back in his own low tone of voice. Dale and Pete suddenly looked at each other, reading each other's minds. Pete turned and gazed up the trail toward the gap in the rim rock where the wire gate was located. "I reckon four or five good cowboys could drive a hundred yearlings or so right down this trail. I mean, you know, if for some reason they wanted to."

"By golly, Pete, you old rascal! If I didn't know better, I'd think you was planning somethin'!" Ray blurted out. He was grinning as he looked at Pete, and he obviously thought that his remarks were simpatico with Pete's imaginations.

"No, I was just thinking. Just thinking, you know, about the future and its possibilities."

Suddenly Pete stood up and threw his saddle blanket on his horse and then the saddle and began cinching up without saying anything. The signal had been given, and obviously the short period of rest was over. Our horses were now all cooled off and the sweat dried off their backs. We threw our blankets and saddles on, and when we had cinched up, we stepped on the horses.

"Ben, you and Tommy stay here and set us up a holdup here on this salt ground. We'll climb on up to the rim and split up and drive to ya." He addressed Ben, giving orders for him as well as for me. He never looked at me or acknowledged my presence except including me in the orders he gave to Ben. The fact that I was the kid on the crew, I was riding a green horse, and perhaps the fact that I was the new guy all added up to Pete giving me my orders secondhand through another man. The lack of not being addressed directly by Pete didn't bother me, but I began to determine that I would prove I was equal to anyone in the crew, at least in cowboy skills.

Pete, Dale, and Ray rode off continuing to ride upward on the cow trail that followed the top of the ridge we were on. Ben and I sat on our horses watching them ride upward for several minutes and then Ben broke the silence, "They'll be gone for a spell, I reckon. It's gonna take 'em a good while to get up there under that rim rock. And then it'll be longer yet to get back here after they split up. I reckon we just as well take it easy 'til some cattle start driftin' in."

Ben stepped off his horse and sat down with his back against a big boulder, and so I, thinking that I should do whatever it took to fit in, did the same. We stared upward watching the other three men, and presently we could tell they had reached the rim rocks at the top of the trail. I surmised that it was there that the wire gate was located that when opened would allow a rider to enter the neighbor's pasture, the pasture that Pete and Dale had discussed earlier.

"They'll be splittin' up now." Ben told me as we watched from a mile and a half away. "Pete will probably go to the right, and after a ways he'll drop down and come around this right side of the ridge. His cattle should come drifting in on these trails over here." He motioned with his right hand towards several trails that came into the salt ground from that direction. "Pete will send one of them other guys off to the left, and he'll be gatherin' the north side of the ridge, and the other man will come back down the top and may fall off to either side if he needs to."

We could see a few cattle scattered out in all directions and had passed several small bunches earlier in the morning as we rode to our present position. The area was a series of steep canyons and ridges, and in places visibility was limited because of the thick vegetation that grew as well as the abundance of boulders and the general roughness of the terrain.

Pete disappeared out of sight, riding to our right in a generally southern direction just like Ben had predicted. Dale was now the only man in sight because Ray had ridden to the north and disappeared behind a ridge. We could tell it was Dale in the middle because of the color of his horse. Soon he rode out of sight going north toward Ray, and so we sat and watched.

"What about that horse, kid; you think you could rope somethin' on him? He looks pretty green to me." Ben asked, giving me a sideways glance. Before I could answer he continued, "Before too long cattle are going to start driftin' in here, and we're gonna have to stop 'em one way or the other. Probably won't be no need to catch anything, but we might need to ride like hell to get 'em held up." Ben's voice had now changed into a full-scale lecture tone. "I suppose if something needs roped I'll be the one doin' the ropin' beings I'm the one mounted on a broke horse!" Now he sounded like he was complaining.

"I'll try to whip up and do my share." I answered. I decided to get up and cinch up and then ride off to the north 150 yards and wait for the wreck to commence. Ben had convinced me by the tone of his voice that I needed to wake up and be ready.

Finally Ben got up and mounted and rode to the south fifty yards, and we waited. After twenty minutes or so, a small bunch, three crossbred cows and a couple calves, came walking down the top of the ridge, and they stopped two hundred yards away from the salt when they saw us. Nothing wild about these, I thought to myself. A couple minutes later, a cow and a yearling and a bull came walking toward the salt ground from the south side of the ridge. They paused for a moment but then walked on in, and the cow and bull commenced to licking salt.

Several more cows with small calves came drifting in, and so far everything was quiet. And then we heard someone holler from a great distance off to the north. The voice was faint, but it was an obvious call for some cow brute to stop or turn. We then saw Dale, about a quarter-mile above, following a couple gentle cows down the trail, and then he left them and rode off quickly to the north and the direction of the voice we had just heard. Then we heard more hollering that was closer, and I could tell it was Ray who was cursing some critter for not cooperating. More cattle started coming in from the north and south, and the ones coming from the north were in a trot and a lope. Ben and I now had our hands full trotting and loping back and forth in an attempt to get all the cattle bunched up and stopped at the salt ground.

I looked to the north and could now see Ray who was riding wildly trying to keep several cattle turned toward our holdup. One of them suddenly turned downhill off the trail in an attempt to escape. Dale came into sight flanking for Ray, keeping the rest of Ray's cattle, about eight head, coming toward Ben and me and the salt ground. Ray crashed down through the brush and boulders to turn the escaping critter that appeared to be a bull that weighed around seven hundred pounds. Ray and the bull were now about three hundred yards away from the holdup and had become separated from the rest of his cattle.

Four or five head of cattle were now coming in from the south with Pete following them and everything seemed to be working out fine except the difficulty Ray was having. Ray and the bull were over a little hump and out of sight from where Ben and Pete were. Dale was bringing up the drags of the bunch that Ray's bull had escaped from, and I was in the front of it all trying to keep everything turned into the salt ground.

Ray whipped his horse downhill and managed to get up toward the bull's neck, and he turned him uphill toward the holdup. For a second it looked like everything was going to work out. Ray had his rope down and had built himself a loop, and so had Dale. I had, about twenty minutes earlier, tied my rope to the saddle horn and had been holding a loop in my hand. My latigo bridle reins were tied together because I figured if I did catch anything I might need both hands to control Red Ram whom I doubted had ever been roped off of. The bull came toward the holdup for a ways, but then when he was about fifty yards from where Red Ram and I sat waiting, he suddenly took a right turn and started running downhill.

Ray was in a perfect position, and he was on the bull as he made his turn downhill; and taking two swings, he roped the maverick bull around the neck. From where I was it all looked perfect until Ray jerked his slack and tried to dally. His horse, that was obviously winded, set up and turned slightly to the left, and Ray got into a fist fight with the saddle horn but finally got a wrap around the horn but it was way out at the end of his rope. I could hear the rope running and the flesh on the palm of his callused hand burning, and then Ray cut loose with as loud a string of profanity as I ever heard. He lost his rope, and in doing so the tail of it whipped around his slick saddle horn and popped him right in the fly of his Levis. He leaned forward acting like something below his belt had been injured. Then he really went to cussing, and the bull went running downhill dragging the rope.

I jumped Red Ram into a run and took out after the bull who was now determined to get to the bottom of the canyon in a hurry. The bronc and I got to him quick, but we were going downhill and pretty much out of control, so I waited, more out of fear than wisdom. But after a couple hundred yards the trail turned slightly uphill for just a short spell, and the bull slowed down because he was running out of air. I managed to swing my rope one time, and I cut her loose and roped the bull around the neck with one front leg in the loop also. I pitched my slack and turned Red Ram slightly to the left, and it turned out I was lucky when we forked a cedar tree. Red Ram and I were about fourteen feet to the left of the tree, and the bull was fourteen feet to the right of the tree, and we all stopped because we were anchored by nylon rope and a stout cedar stump. My horse whirled and faced the tree with his sides heaving from his heavy breathing. The bull fell down, and I jumped off and ran to him and grabbed his hind legs and went to wrapping a nylon pigging string around his legs. I wrapped the string around his legs between the hoof and dew claws on one leg and above the dew claws on the other, and after making several wraps, I pulled everything very tight and tied several square knots.

Quickly I got back on Red Ram and rode up close to the bull who was still laying on his side breathing heavily and took both my and Ray's lassos off of him. I mounted up and hurried back uphill toward the holdup that was now several hundred yards above me.

I rode up, and when I came into view, Dale hollered at me, "You got him, huh, kid? Did you get old Ray's rope back for him?" I decided to keep my mouth shut and not respond as I rode up and handed Ray his nylon rope. "Not a damn word out of you, you understand, Peckerwood?" Ray hissed at me as he took his rope. He didn't thank me.

Pete hollered at me from the other side of the holdup that had swollen to about twenty-five head of cattle. "So where's the bull, Tommy?" His voice sounded like gravel or sandpaper rubbing against a hard board.

"He's down the trail a little ways."

"So you got him tied down or what?" Pete asked.

"Yes sir. He's tied down in the middle of the trail." I wasn't sure I had done the right thing because I had never worked with any of them before. I had simply reacted, relying on past experiences with my dad gathering cattle on the Hassayampa River.

"Good job, kid! Heck, you might be all right after all. What you think, Ray?" Pete rumbled. Dale let out a war whoop, and Ben turned his horse's backside to Ray and rode off, obviously afraid to let Ray see him smiling. I started to ride around behind Ray and get back in what I thought was my spot between him and Ben, but Pete ordered me in his gravelly voice, "Get out in front, kid, and lead us off of here and down to that bull you tied down."

So I turned my horse around and down the trail, but as I passed Ray, he wouldn't look at me but instead looked at the palm of his right hand that had a long white spot on it that looked a lot like melted skin.

Pete and the rest of the crew followed me down the hill to where the maverick bull was tied down. As I led the way, they drove the cattle that had been gathered. When we reached the bull, I stepped off of Red Ram and took my nylon catch rope and put a loop around the bull's hind legs and then took several wraps around the saddle horn pulling the rope tight. The tight rope stretched the bull's hind legs out behind him causing him to lay on his side, and I untied my piggin' string and took it off his hind legs.

Then I stepped back on Red Ram, and when my feet were in the stirrups, I turned my dallies loose and released the pressure on the bull's hind legs, and he jumped up. He shook his head and took a run at Red Ram's shoulder blowing snot and bellering as if he intended to kill all of us, but his bluster soon played out, and he turned and ran into the middle of the small herd of cattle that everyone was holding.

Pete now gave Ray orders to take the lead, and we drove the small bunch of cattle down the trail about another quarter-mile where a natural rock hole in the creek bottom held a considerable amount of water. It was evident by all the cow-sign laying around that the waterhole was frequented on a regular basis. This time Pete had Ray and Dale hold the herd, and he took Ben and me, and we rode up a trail in the bottom of the canyon about a mile or a little better. Pete gave orders to Ben to rim out of the canyon bottom and go north, working the north slope, driving cattle forward and preferably downhill in front of me. Pete himself rode out and toward the south, but before he rode off he instructed me to not move for at least fifteen minutes, which would give him and Ben a little time to get ahead of me. We were all heading back to the holdup and the herd of cattle that Ray and Dale were holding, and hopefully we would be adding to it with the cattle that we would try and find on the second drive of the day.

We repeated this process of moving our small herd that increased in numbers with each new drive we made. We moved the herd to a new holdup ground about three times, and with each new drive, we gathered a new chunk of country that was always adjacent to the country we had gathered on the drive before. Although Pete's way of doing things or explaining things was different, the work was much like work I had been doing my whole life, and I understood and was comfortable with what Pete was trying to accomplish.

About eleven o'clock or so, we drove our small herd to an old corral that was located in a side canyon that ran south out of the bottom of Cow Creek. The corral was actually two corrals: one was round in shape and about ninety feet in diameter and was made of stones that had been laid by hand many years before. There was no mortar holding the rocks in place, but the wall they made was wide, about three feet, and the expertly laid stones made a barrier close to five feet high and impossible for a cow brute to jump over.

This stone corral lay up against a rock bluff on its backside and had one opening with two large cedar posts that were not only buttresses to lay the ends of the stonewall against but also posts from which hung an old wooden gate. The other corral, which was actually the first corral and the one we entered when approaching the place, was much larger, about 120 feet in diameter and also round in shape. It was made of cedar pickets at least six feet high that were held in place by an old piece of steel cable about a half inch in diameter. The cable was tied solidly to a few large cedar posts that were set deep into the ground. All the rest of the cedar staves were also tied with wire to this cable, with the bottoms of the pickets being buried in the ground. There was one wide gate made out of barbed wire and cedar staves, and it was through this gate that we drove our morning's gather. The herd now numbered about sixty head of cattle including bulls, cows with unbranded calves, and numerous yearlings, some of which were needing to be weaned.

When we got the cattle through the gate and captured in the big picket corral, Pete gave instructions to Ray and Ben to stay outside and rest while he, Dale and myself entered the corral to sort the cattle. He gave me orders to open the gate into the stone corral and then position myself inside the stone corral and off to the side of the gate. Pete was going to cut the yearlings out of the rest of the herd while Dale turned back the other cattle, and the two of them would push the yearlings Pete cut through the gate and into the stone corral. My job was to sit on Red Ram where I could make sure the yearlings did not run back out the gate and reenter the herd they had been separated from.

The cutting and separating of the cattle went smoothly. Pete was a consummate cowboy as was Dale, and they were both mounted on good horses. To watch this process was a joy to me because I knew enough to recognize that the two men were only moving their horses enough to get the work done. There was little wasted motion and very little said as they expertly removed the wild yearlings from the herd like the wind separating the chaff from the grain. I was sure to pay attention and not let any of the yearlings bolt, then run back out of the gate; but in truth, my job was easy.

About the time we got the yearlings separated and locked in the stone corral, old Luis, the Mexican who took care of the small farm at headquarters, showed up riding an old gentle horse and leading a mule. The mule had a pack saddle on his back and was loaded with a lunch. There was also a coffee pot and several large canteens of fresh water. Soon Luis had a fire built a few yards from the corral and a pot of coffee was quickly brewed. We all drank coffee from some porcelain-covered metal cups that were included in the pack and lunched on some simple sandwiches we made out of steak and bread that had been packed tightly along with the rest of the mess kit Luis and the mule had borne to us. After our sandwiches were eaten, the men sat and drank coffee and smoked cigarettes. The smoking was done with such visual expressions of pleasure one would have thought the crew had been on a tobacco-fast for a month. Actually, they had all been smoking all day. I thought surely I must take to this smoking soon as it appeared to give its participants such pleasure. I sat and drank coffee and kept silent, feeling pleased that I was making a hand, or at least I wasn't being hollered at constantly.

After everyone had eaten their sandwiches and drank several cups of coffee along with their smokes, Pete stood up and walked over to the corral and built a fire just inside the gate of the big corral. Old Luis had brought a bottle of Blackleg vaccine in the panniers on the mule's back, along with our lunch. There were several old branding irons hanging from a wire on the picket corral fence, and they were laid into the fire. The irons had long handles, close to forty-eight inches, and Pete took the palms of his big hands and shoveled sand and covered up the ends of the handles. There was plenty of wood laying around that someone had obviously drug up to the spot and piled at some earlier date, I figured maybe that was a chore someone would do on a day when they were packing salt and depositing it at the various salt grounds. Luis packed up what was left of the lunch and utensils and pulled out for headquarters leading the mule while the rest of us stood around waiting for the irons to heat. Presently Pete said in an off-handed way, "Come on, Dale, let's me and you catch 'em." Nothing else was said and the two men stepped on their horses and proceeded to rope the calves that were not branded.

A good number of the calves, about a dozen, were fair sized, being four or five months old and weighing perhaps as much as 350 pounds. Pete and Dale took turns with the heading and heeling of them. The man who had roped the hind legs continued to hold the legs tight with his lasso rope dallied off to the saddle horn during the ground work. After a few were branded, they switched ends with the man who had been heeling taking a turn at roping the calves around the neck. Without being told I knew that my main job was to hold the calves down by a front leg after the head rope was taken off.

Both Pete and Dale were expert hands at roping in a branding corral, and occasionally Ray or Ben would let out a warwhoop when one of the men made a spectacular shot. Soon I was joining in and hollering at the good action I was watching. It seemed to me the mood was softening for the first time that day, and everyone seemed to be enjoying the work. I was agile and quick and made sure that I was the first to get my hands on the calf's tail when the roper had dallied and got his rope tight after getting a calf heeled. I jerked on the tail while either Ray or Ben pulled in the opposite direction with their hands on the rope, and we laid the calf on its side. Then I grabbed the left front leg while sticking my right knee in the calf's neck, and in a sort of wrestling maneuver, I held the critter still while Ray and Ben did the branding, vaccinating, castrating and earmarking. I enjoyed the work and enjoyed the fact that Ray didn't make any negative comments. He didn't call me Peckerwood one time all afternoon.

We branded about twenty calves and did so in short order, or at least I thought so. No one seemed to have a watch or care about time, but I supposed it took us an hour or maybe a little longer. When we finished branding, we kicked and scattered what was left of the fire, laid the irons against the fence, and put what was left of the Blackleg vaccine along with the gun in the shade of a nearby tree. Pete gave instructions to Ben to ride into the corral while the rest of us mounted up and rode a short ways off in the distance. Ben pushed the cattle out of the corral gate while the rest of us held them up outside and waited, making sure every freshly branded calf found its mother.

We left the yearlings we had separated in the rock corral and checked that both gates were tied shut and rode off heading up the canyon toward headquarters. I supposed it was about two or three in the afternoon. Nothing was said, but I surmised that the yearlings we left in the corral would be trailed out of the canyon the next day after adding a few more to their numbers. The maverick bull that I had roped that morning was among that bunch, and we still had not branded him.

Chapter Two

Pete turned his horse north toward the trail and waved at all of us, motioning us to follow, and we headed toward the headquarters. The trail we took was the same we had ridden down that morning, and our horses, being tired from a good morning's work, were not nearly as fresh acting as they had been earlier. Pete led us upward on the steep and rocky trail in a walk, and everyone seemed content to ride at that pace, not pushing their horses too fast.

Dale Scott, whom I had decided was the most genuinely friendly fellow on the crew, rode alongside of me as we rode up this steep incline. He told me, while riding along smoking a Bull Durham cigarette, that the corrals where we had branded and left the yearlings was called the Cienega Place after a good spring located nearby. He said that there was a foundation of an old homesteader's cabin nearby, and he promised to show it to me sometime. He pointed out several other landmarks as we rode by them, and we made small talk. He put me at ease, and I began to feel like he was a friend.

It took us probably an hour and a half to reach the horse corral at the headquarters, and as we rode up, old Luis, the Mexican, was wrangling horses, which I found out was part of his job; at least, that was when Pete told him to.

We all unsaddled but held on to our horses until Luis had run the remuda into a large picket corral next to the barn, and then we led the tired horses we had ridden all day and turned them loose outside the corral, and they walked to a nearby water trough and drank and then rolled in the dirt. I noticed that Red Ram rolled completely over from one side to the other, which according to my dad was a sign of a good horse.

Everyone threw his catch rope to another man, and we quickly formed a rope corral, holding the horses in a bunch. Everyone, that is, except Pete who started roping horses for the next morning's work. Pete roped a big stocking-legged, bald-faced sorrel and led him out to me. The bronc rolled his nose making scary sneezing like noises with his nostrils, and he held his head high. "Put you a halter on him, kid! When we are done catching horses, you need to shoe him. His name's Dollar," Pete ordered me.

I slipped my snaffle bit and headstall onto his head. The bronc wanted to run backward and not cooperate. "What's the matter, Peckerwood? Get a bridle on him, we want to get to the house!" Ray chided me in a caustic voice.

I finally got Dollar bridled and realized I would soon have to take the bridle off and exchange it for a halter. But I would hobble him before I did that. I quickly took Pete's lasso off of Dollar's head and took my end of the makeshift rope corral out of Pete's hand, allowing him to go and rope another horse out of the remuda. Pete turned and took about six steps to my right and suddenly turned around and stared at Dollar, or was it me he was looking at me? "You are a miserable bastard!" He made the blunt statement and turned and went about his business. I thought he was talking about Dollar, but I wasn't sure.

When Pete caught everyone a horse, we dropped the end of the other man's lasso and coiled up our own, turning the remuda loose. Then we let them out the gate into the horse pasture. I led Dollar over to the side of the corral where I had my saddle and what little gear I had draped over the top of the fence. I got my good stout stake hackamore and put it on Dollar's head replacing the snaffle bit, then tied Dollar up good and solid to a big cedar post and proceeded to shoe him. Everyone except Dale walked toward the bunkhouse. Dale offered to help, which at first didn't amount to anything except standing by Dollar's head and petting his neck. Nailing front shoes on him wasn't hard.

When I got the bronc's front end finished, I hobbled him and tried picking up a hind foot, but he wouldn't let me hold it and went to kicking and proceeded to get mad. So I got a cotton rope about an inch and a quarter in diameter and wrapped it around the backside of the big cedar post, and then with Dale's help, I ran both ends out and tied them to the horse's hind feet between his pasterns and hooves. There was about twelve foot of rope from the post to the horse. I led the bronc forward until he took out the slack in the rope between himself and the post. When he hit the end of the rope, he jumped into it and threw a fit, jumping and kicking and then jumping and kicking and hitting the end of it again and again. The post holding the cotton rope never budged, and the horse could not break the rope and go any farther than the rope secured to him at one end and the post at the other allowed.

After fighting the situation for a minute or so, Dollar began to give it up, realizing he couldn't go forward or kick the cotton rope free. I hobbled his front legs with a piggin' string and then tried to pick up a hind foot. He jumped and kicked and then fell down but jumped right up after a slight struggle. This process was repeated several times with Dollar fighting a little less each time. Finally after several attempts, the horse allowed me to pick up his left hind foot. Dale, throughout this process, had been holding the lead rope and keeping the horse facing straight away from the fence. Dollar was tired and quit fighting and realized that me picking up a hind leg and holding it was less painful than jumping and kicking. Before long I had shoes on his hind feet also.

When we were through shoeing Dollar, we turned him loose to eat hay with the rest of the horses we had kept up for tomorrow's work, and we walked toward the bunkhouse, which was an old building made out of native limestone. I had showed up on the outfit that morning

Finally after several attempts the horse allowed me to pick up his left hind foot.

at four and had not unloaded my bedroll or any other particulars of my plunder, so I packed my bedroll into the bunkhouse, and as I entered I dropped it on the floor in what appeared to be a vacant, unclaimed spot.

The bunkhouse was long and narrow with a very large common room that was big enough to accommodate six or eight bedrolls. On the other end of the rock house was a kitchen big enough to hold a very long and narrow table where six or eight men could sit and eat a meal. I found the bathroom and washed the dust and sweat off my face and hands and then drifted toward the voices coming out of the kitchen. The crew was seated at the table and acting quite relaxed while Pete's wife Mitzi, whom I hadn't been introduced to but knew of from stories told around, stood at the cook stove stirring gravy. Ben was drinking coffee but it appeared that Pete and Ray were drinking Old Crow whiskey out of large glass tumblers that rested on the table in front of them. Dale, who had entered the room only minutes before me, had a cup of coffee in one hand and proceeded to add some Old Crow to it.

"Get you a glass and have a drink with us, kid!" I had stopped in the doorway and suddenly felt awkward when I heard Pete's offer to share a drink. I wasn't sure if he was being genuine or if he was kidding me. Ray looked at me and grinned and his glass eye looked off to one side about ten degrees. I faltered.

Mitzi turned and looked at me, "Drink whatever you want to. There's coffee, or water in the faucet... but don't drink somethin' because you think you have to." She smiled and turned around and tended to the gravy.

"That's right! Drink whatever you want, kid! But you are welcome to share our Old Crow if you want to." Pete picked up the bottle and held it to my face and slammed it down on the table.

"Take a drink and try to fit in around here!" Ray bellowed.

"Well, the way I recall it, he fit in pretty good this morning when he roped that bull yearling and brought your rope back to you!" Dale looked at Ray and grinned.

Ben hung his head and muffled a slight chuckle, and Ray whirled and glared at him. Ben seemed to melt.

"Yeah, you done alright today, Tommy! Glad you're here. Yeah, real glad, I got plans for you." Pete said. He stood up, all six feet two of him, and walked to a cupboard hanging on the wall to the right of the cookstove. He got a coffee cup and walked back to the table and sat back down and poured the cup a quarter full of Old Crow. "Sit down, kid, and have a drink, you're making me nervous."

I sat down and took a sip of Old Crow, and it tasted hot. My dad always said Old Crow was cowboy whiskey because it was cheap and a cowboy could afford it. He also said nobody with money would drink rotgut stuff like Old Crow. I was puzzled why Pete would drink cheap whiskey but smoke tailor-made cigarettes.

About then Mitzi hollered chuck and walked over and sat down in a chair next to Pete. The supper she had fixed was left sitting on the stove: baking powder biscuits, round steak rolled in flour and fried with lots of salt and pepper, and gravy made in the pan the steak had been fried in. For dessert there was honey to put over the biscuits.

It was good, real good, and I told Mitzi that it was. She smiled, and I could tell she was grateful for the compliment. Mitzi was a good looking woman with sandy-colored hair, shoulder length, and sort of curled under at the bottom. She had thick hair, and it was combed and immaculate as was all her personal attributes. But she seemed to me to be tired like a horse that had been rode hard and put up wet too many times. Folks said she was older than Pete by six years. I knew lots of stories about Pete and Mitzi. They had caused a stir more than once in northwestern Arizona, and everyone in the cowboy world had heard the stories. Actually, Pete was the one who authored all the excitement that led to stories and rumors. Mitzi was just his wife, and because of that she was along for the ride wherever the ride might lead.

Mitzi sat next to Pete and drank a glass of water and smoked a cigarette while all of us men ate beefsteak, biscuits and gravy. Suddenly Pete looked at Dale and asked in a low gravelly tone. "Who takes care of that O R O pasture on top of that mesa? Does old Skeet send someone from the headquarters over there to ride on them heifers?"

"Hell, this time of year I doubt if anyone's watchin' 'em. They always take the whole crew with the wagon when they're brandin' or workin' in the fall, so I doubt that anyone is ridin' up there at all. I imagine the O R O wagon is camped at Triangle N or Mohon about now, or maybe down at Cabin Dam, but I know they're busy brandin'. They got an old crazy guy at headquarters named Ernie that cuts wood and fixes a little fence. He might mosey over there with some salt in a pickup, but I doubt it. I bet that nobody will be ridin' in there at least 'til after the Fourth of July. They might send someone over there to prowl around a little during the summer."

Ray had been listening, and it seemed to me that he was worried he was going to be left out of the inner circle of the conversation. "That's too damn easy!" He said in as intelligent a tone as he could muster.

"What in the world are you guys workin' up now?" Mitzi asked in a voice almost as raspy as her husband's. Raspy from years of inhaling barroom smoke and her husband's dust.

"Oh nothin', honey. We're just talkin' about a little idea I've got. Some work for us in the future." His words came slow. Mitzi stood up and headed toward the stove, and in her own version of a low, gravelly voice she commented, "I never saw you when you weren't thinking of something."

I had sat through supper saying nothing, aware of my position as the new man on the crew and a kid at that, so

I had my mind wrapped around my own existence. It was like I was treading water and trying to learn how to swim, and so the innuendo about the neighbor's cattle and what might be done with them someday was too much from me to think about. The meal was finished and Pete ordered me to do the dishes, and he and Mitzi left to go to their own house. Dale, Ben and Ray retired to the large bedroom, and I followed when the dishes were done. I cleaned up in the bathroom and then unrolled my cowboy bedroll and crawled inside of it. I had been awake for twenty hours.

About four the next morning, I woke up to the sound of meat frying, and it took me several seconds to remember where I was, and then I heard Ray talking to Mitzi on the other side of the kitchen door. She was saying very little other than an occasional yeah, or oh really, or I didn't know that. Ray was going on and on, and as I listened for a moment, I realized he was talking about his childhood in Wyoming. I couldn't hear Pete's voice so I figured he wasn't there, and then suddenly he and Dale and Ben came through the door talking. When Pete walked into the kitchen, Ray ceased to talk, at least for a moment, and when he resumed, his dialogue was aimed at the men. They had been down to the horse corral throwing the horses some feed while for some reason Ray stayed in the kitchen. I made haste to get up.

Breakfast was steak and biscuits and gravy. Biscuits with honey was for dessert. I drank coffee and put Carnation canned milk and sugar in it. Dale and Ben were drinking theirs black. Pete was drinking his mixed with Old Crow whiskey and Camel cigarettes.

By a quarter to five we were walking to the horse corral, and everyone except Pete took lasso ropes and threw up a rope corral around the horses that we bunched in a corner of the picket corral. Pete roped my bald-faced sorrel bronc first, and when I had my snaffle bit and headstall on him, he told me to go ahead and get saddled up. I took this to mean that he thought the horse might give me some trouble, and he didn't want to wait on me.

I hobbled Dollar and rubbed the dirt off his back with my hand and eased the saddle blankets on to his back and then lifted my saddle and laid it on the blankets. Dollar snorted and wiggled a little but really gave me no trouble. I was saddled and cinched up before anyone else, and so I stood there waiting for them to get ready. When Dale and Ray were saddled and leading their horses out the gate, I unhobbled Dollar and led him forward, but he didn't untrack real good because of the hump in his back, but I whipped him around in a circle and he moved. I thought about stepping on him right where we stood in the corner of the picket corral, but Pete must have read my mind because he said, "Lead him outside away from the fence before you get on him." It wasn't a suggestion, it was a command.

I led the sorrel bronc forty feet out from the horse corral gate, and by then everyone else was mounted and watching. In his lowest gravelly voice, Pete said very slowly, "That bastard is going to buck, and when he does you better not pull on his head." I looked at him staring down at me in the pale light of dawn. Was there some kind of rule around here that you couldn't pull on your bridle reins if a horse bucked? Nobody explained or commented, they only watched. Evidently Dollar bucked high in the front end and might flip over backwards. That must be what he was trying to tell me. Trying to tell me without telling me.

I gathered up my latigo reins and stuck my left foot in the stirrup and was on Dollar in a flash. I slipped my right hand under the piggin' string night latch tied through the fork of my saddle and Dollar stood there as tight as a drum. Pete started to ride off and everyone turned to follow, and

Dollar stood like a rock. I picked my right foot up and stabbed Dollar in the ribs and sunk a spur as deep as I could get it. An instant sensation of upward movement was all I felt, and I tossed as much slack in my bridle reins as I could. I realized that Dollar's face was looking straight up into the sky and his back was at a right angle to the ground. Somehow he came down face forward, and the next jump he made a little forward motion with his back only at a sixty degree angle from the earth. The third jump, he took his head and bucked forward, and I could pull on him all I wanted to; and then I went to spurring him in the ribs as hard as I could. He farted and squealed, and I spurred and rode and thought to myself, *If this is all you've got, I can handle it.* In about twelve jumps he broke into a run, and we were all on our way down the same trail as the morning before, descending into Cow Creek Canyon.

When we hit the bottom of the canyon and passed the stone corral where the yearlings were penned, we turned east and up the creek like the morning before. We made several drives that morning, working canyons and ridges that lay west of the country we had gathered the day before. We made several drives into the first holdup and gathered about forty cows plus bulls, calves and yearlings. Then we moved the herd a mile and made several more drives and eventually accumulated close to a hundred head of cattle. Everything went smoothly, and I had no trouble with Dollar. He was awful green and grabbed himself, as the saying goes, on several occasions and acted like he might blow up and buck, but I managed to keep him under control. I felt that he was like Red Ram, being a very green bronc that just needed lots of miles and work. But he was definitely not a kid's horse.

We drove the bunch of cattle to the rock corral and penned them, and like the day before, we cut the big yearlings into the round stone corral and mixed them with the cattle that had been left there the day before. About the time that was done, Luis showed up leading the mule and packing us a lunch and coffee pot. We hobbled our horses and made a fire to brew coffee and ate sandwiches made out of biscuits and cold steak. After the proper amount of coffee had been drunk and cigarettes smoked, Pete announced it was time to brand calves. He told Ray and me to do the roping, and so we cinched up and led our horses through the corral gate.

I had taken my rope down and built a loop on several occasions during the morning, but I had not actually caught anything, and I doubted that Dollar had ever had a critter caught on him. He was green and definitely needed to be plow reined around and would not neck rein at all; but I could get him stopped and he would back up a little.

When Pete motioned to us that the branding irons were hot, Ray looked at me and told me to catch one around the neck. I slipped into the middle of the cattle and pitched a loop over a 250 pound bull calf's neck. I dallied up short and drug the calf out into the middle of the corral, and Ray rode up to the right side of the calf and threw a loop toward the calf's heels but missed. Being on the right side of the calf drove him behind Dollar's hind quarters, and when the rope rubbed against the bronc's rump, he grabbed himself and lunged forward. Good way to sack one out, I thought, but I wondered why Ray couldn't approach the calf from the left side which would drive him away from the bronc's rump instead of toward it. Ray built another loop and this time was successful, catching the calf's hind legs. Ben, Dale and Pete had him branded, castrated and earmarked in short order.

Ray wanted to catch the next calf around the neck and let me heel him, so I let him do so, and he roped the biggest heifer in the herd, weighing about 450 pounds.

Ray let a lot of rope run across his horn and ended up with the heifer out on the end of thirty foot of rope. The heifer was bouncing and bellering and jumping about like a wild rabbit, and I couldn't get Dollar anywhere near the calf's hind legs. Ray and the heifer ended up at one end of the corral, and I followed the calf around the right side of Ray's horse in pursuit of her. She bounced out of the corner and continued circling Ray's horse, and Ray let another ten feet of rope slip around his horn and stopped his horse, and the calf bounced and windmilled into the same corner on a second revolution. She was now on forty feet of rope and getting wilder. She ran into the corner with me whipping and spurring Dollar in pursuit, and when she came out of the corner, Ray jumped his horse into the fence and turned her back in my direction. She whirled and ran, having a considerable amount of slack in the rope, and then Ray started following her, and I was suddenly caught on a green bronc with no steering and a 450 pound calf bearing down on me dragging a lot of loose rope.

I pulled Dollar to the left and spurred him in the right ribs in an attempt to get out of harm's way. But before I knew it, the calf had run by Dollar's right side, and then the fence corner forced her to turn behind Dollar's hind end. Ray then, for whatever reason, stopped and dallied, causing the rope to come tight around my horse's hind end. Dollar blew up and jumped three foot in the air. When he came down after the first jump, the rope was now between his front and back feet, and then he really went to bucking. Around the third jump, Ray's rope got tangled up in Dollar's front legs and jerked the horse sideways while in midair. The sideways jerk was enough to rip me out of the saddle, and like a falling star, I went to crashing toward the earth. Right before I hit the ground, my neck and shoulders crashed against Ray's rope that was tight and two feet off the ground, with one end being connected to Ray's saddle horn and the other end to the heifer and wrapped around Dollar's legs in between. My body was slapped against the ground like the end of a whip, and it seemed like time stopped. I gasped for air but couldn't suck any in. I turned my head and saw Pete and Dale staring at me. I wanted to tell them I couldn't breathe. I wasn't scared but lay there with the realization that my lungs would not work.

What seemed like minutes was no doubt only seconds, and suddenly the spasm that had been pushing my diaphragm up into my chest cavity relaxed, and I took in great expanses of open space into my lungs. Air, dusty air, I sucked it in and became aware that men were hollering. "Damn it, Ray, shorten up! Get that darn calf out of the corner and away from the kid!" It was Pete hollering.

"Well, Ray, you've been wantin' to get the boy in a wreck; you ought a be happy now." It was Dale talking in a normal tone of voice, sorta to himself.

"Well, old Peckerwood should'a drove some iron in old sorely and got him outa the way." Ray observed.

"Maybe you could show him how." Dale said.

"You bet I can!"

"Shut up and get the damn calf down on the other end of the corral!" Pete was now walking toward me. I was still laying on my stomach on the ground. "You all right, kid?"

"Yeah, I just need a little air for a minute." Dollar had got himself untangled, quit bucking, and run off toward the opposite side of the corral. Dale walked over to the side of the corral and caught my horse who was standing there watching everything. My rope had somehow stayed draped over the seat of my saddle with fifteen feet or so hanging off of both sides. Dale got the end of my rope and coiled it up and hung it over the saddle horn and then led the horse forward a step or two and held him. I gathered myself up and stood for a few seconds while everyone looked at me skeptically. After a minute I decided that I was going to live, and I walked over and took my bridle reins from Dale. I thought that perhaps Pete would tell me to sit down and take it easy for a while. I hoped that maybe Pete would order someone else to finish roping the calves, but neither he nor anyone else said anything. If I sat down and rested and regained my strength, it would have to be my decision. I gathered up my bridle reins in my left hand, holding them tight against the top of Dollar's neck, and I saw my left hand trembling. I realized anyone who saw it would think the trembling was a result of fear, but I wasn't scared, I was in shock. I stepped on the sorrel bronc, and then I built a loop in my rope. Now both hands were trembling. "Get that blasted heifer dallied up on a short rope, Ray!" Pete hollered.

Ray said nothing but jumped his horse up and got closer to the calf the best he could, which wasn't much for he really had no feeling for a horse. He came out of the far corner of the corral pulling the bucking and bawling calf, and somehow I managed to rope a hind foot. I dallied and got Dollar stopped, and then Ray spurred his horse and hit the end of his rope hard enough to jerk Dollar forward several steps. I pulled on my bridle reins and hoped I could keep Dollar's head up. For the first time I got mad and dreamed of roping Ray around the neck and pulling him off his horse and then claiming that it had been an accident. No one would have cared, they probably would have laughed, but I knew that Ray would beat me half to death in retaliation, so I told myself to try and concentrate and maybe my hands would quit shaking.

Ray and I mucked around and got a half dozen calves roped by the head and heels, and Pete, Dale and Ben did the work on the ground, but it was ugly. Ray was an average roper at best, and that day he was at his worse.

My horse was green as grass, and I was having a hard time catching, especially when it was my turn to heel, so things were going slow. "Well, your old bronc done pretty good, wouldn't you say, Tommy?" Pete said after the seventh or eighth calf. "Don't want to overdo it. Think maybe you oughta give him a break since he's doin' so good. What do ya think, kid?"

"Sure, you're the boss."

"Why don't you and Ray trade off. We'll let Dale and Ben finish 'em." Ray and I rode out of the corral and hobbled our horses while Ben and Dale cinched up and led their horses into the corral. Pete was nice to use my green horse as an excuse to change ropers, and I appreciated the kindness; but I knew the truth was he was worried he wouldn't get through before sundown if he didn't get Ray and me out of the corral. Actually, more getting jerked around by the saddle horn would have done Dollar a lot of good, but he had made great improvement in spite of the fact he had bucked me off and come close to killing me, or at least making me wish I was dead.

We branded about thirty-five calves that day with Dale and Ben doing the rest of the roping. By the time we were finished with that chore it was about two in the afternoon, and we still had to drive all of the yearlings we had been accumulating to the headquarters five miles to the north and a thousand feet higher in elevation. Dollar was pretty much mucked out by that time and was not wanting to buck, and I was sore and hurting from getting slapped hard to the ground, but no one asked me how I felt or if my bronc was too tired to carry on. Dollar and I had no choice, it was do or die.

Pete instructed me to stay in the corral while he and everyone else positioned themselves outside in preparation to hold up and control the yearlings, a dozen of which were unbranded, when they came out of the corral. When Pete gave me the nod that they were ready, I rode out from in front of the open corral gate and put the forty-five yearlings outside. They hit open ground in a trot, and the leaders were soon running. Pete stayed out in front of them slapping his heavy chaps with his coiled rope and working hard at slowing the cattle down. Ray was on the right side up near the leaders and Dale opposite of him near the front of the herd also. Ben and I brought up the rear, and for a quarter of a mile, we whipped on the drags making sure they kept up with the leaders so the herd wouldn't get too strung out, which would create too large of a hole to block should one of the yearlings want to break out on one side or another. Within several hundred yards the trail turned uphill and soon the cattle slowed down. There was no doubt that a bunch of inexperienced riders would have immediately lost control of the skittish herd of young cattle, but Pete, Dale and Ray were on their game, and we traveled uphill through the rocks, mescal and cedar trees making it look easy. I forgot about the fact that I was sore and aching, especially my ribs on the left side and my left wrist that was somewhat swollen.

When we got to the headquarters, we turned the yearlings loose in a well-fenced field that Luis kept irrigated with the free artesian water, then we rode to the barn and horse corral, and caught horses for the next day. Pete roped me a big buckskin four-year-old for the next day's work. The buckskin had no shoes, but his feet were big and black. While I was putting my bridle on him and taking Pete's rope off of the buckskin's neck, he commented, "He don't have any shoes, kid, but ride him barefoot. It's late and you can shoe him tomorrow afternoon." We started walking toward the bunkhouse as the sun was going down in the west.

Chapter Three

I had been on the outfit about two weeks when Pete announced he was giving everyone Sunday off. He told us that he had important business that he needed to tend to down in Kingman on Saturday afternoon, which was June the seventh. He looked at Dale and Ray, as if they knew what he was talking about, and said he needed to talk to a cattle trader who would be in Kingman Saturday, and so he was going down to visit with him.

"So you think you can find a home for those cattle out in California?" Dale asked.

"Yeah! I think so." Pete replied. "Might find a home for more than we've talked about. I'll know more after Saturday night." I overheard the exchange of words but it meant nothing to me. I didn't know what cattle needed a home, or how many anyone had talked about, so at the time I didn't think anything of it. I was wrapped around my small world that consisted of trying to stay mounted on the string of broncs Pete had given me to ride and every other aspect of making a cowhand. I wasn't interested in management talk like buying and selling cattle or driving to Kingman to visit with cow traders.

We had heard rumors that there was going to be a live band at the Black Cat Saloon in Seligman on Saturday night, and now that we had Sunday off, we made plans to be there. A real band in Seligman, Arizona, only happened maybe once a year, according to Dale and Ray. I hadn't reached my eighteenth birthday, but there was no talk among the older men that I wouldn't join them in their trek into town and everything that went with it. I figured if I was big enough to rope and ride and bust my backside along with everyone else on the ranch, I was certainly big enough to go to Seligman and hang out in the Black Cat bar.

We had a short day of work on Saturday, moving a few cows away from a dirt tank that was drying up; and Ray, Dale and I did that by ourselves. Ben had gone home to his cow camp at Black Creek the night before, and Pete and Mitzi had loaded up in their Ford pickup and had taken off for Kingman early in the morning leaving orders with Dale and Ray to catch horses for everyone on Sunday night.

We took turns taking a shower and shaving and putting on our newest Levis and ironed shirts. I polished my black Tony Lama dress boots, and Dale polished his nice Paul Bonds. Ray put some kind of black grease on his high-heeled work boots that were made by Champion Boot Company in Colorado. They were what Champion Boot Company called their Old-Timer style and the vamps and the front of the tops, that were eighteen inches high, were made out of one piece of roughout waxed French calfhide. They were the crudest-looking boots I had ever seen. He bragged to Dale about having blacked his boots. He was right, he hadn't shined them, he had blacked them; and they looked like something a grease monkey would wear around a diesel shop. Ray had showered and shaved but he had on a course work shirt that had never been ironed. The shirt and the Levis he wore were clean, but they had permanent stains on them from the blood of castrated bulls. His knuckles were cracked and bleeding, and the black grime under his fingernails was a permanent fixture.

We loaded up in Dale's Chevy pickup that was a nice shiny rig, and we headed toward Seligman forty miles to the east. Dale was driving and was going fast enough we were only hitting the high spots. I was riding in the middle and Ray sat in the shotgun position. "I'll tell you what, Peckerwood," Ray explained as we floated along doing sixty on a dirt road, "tonight I'm going to show you how to chase women!"

"You've got that right." Dale said dryly. "Every one of them will be running like hell when they see you coming!" I couldn't help but chuckle.

"Yeah, I know it! I know it! And I'm going to chase me one down and catch her, just like Tommy Lee chasin' a wild cow on old Red Ram! Yee Haw!" Dale drove on smiling, and he winked at me sorta on the sly. Ray was whooping and hollering like he had already drank a half pint of joy juice, but I hadn't seen him drink anything. But he was boisterous and happy, and I was glad he wasn't picking on me.

We roared past a place Dale told me was called the Black Tub on the Double O Ranch and waved jubilantly to four Double O cowboys who were trailing some Mexican steers toward a water lot a quarter-mile distance. Dale honked the horn on his Chevy pickup loud and hard, and Ray leaned out the window and gave them a loud Yee Haw! They waved back, and we roared on toward our destination. Soon we passed Markham Well and then Twin Buttes, and Seligman came into view a few miles ahead. The way we acted it could have been Las Vegas or Paris, France.

We hit town about five o'clock in the afternoon and drove east on Route 66 and passed the Black Cat on the left and the Copper Cart Café on the right. Across the street to the east of the Copper Cart Café was the saloon called the Red Ram, but we continued on driving east. Dale informed us that he needed gas and wanted to get it now instead of later when he might not have time.

On the east of town, Dale pulled into a Conoco service station and stopped the truck in front of one of only two pumps. He got out to pump the gas because it was a self-serve, and so Ray and I got out to stretch our legs. He went around back in the direction of a sign that read restrooms. I walked into the small building that was an office, and there she was, sitting behind the counter and cash register. She looked at me and asked if she could help me.

"No, I'm just killin' time."

I looked around and pointed at Dale who was holding onto a hose and gas nozzle that was stuck into a pipe on the side of his pickup. Her eyes followed my glance at Dale, and she gave me a sort of, okay, I understand, look. She had the most beautiful emerald green eyes I had ever seen and red hair that fell to her shoulders and was faintly streaked with different shades of carrot-colored red. I stared at her. She was reading a paperback book while perched on a stool making herself available to take money from customers.

I wanted to talk to her. "You comin' to the dance tonight?"

She looked up from her book. "There's a dance? Where?"

"There's supposed to be live music tonight down at the Black Cat Saloon. I thought I might see you there." She looked at me with no expression, just staring. I thought to myself that this wasn't going real well.

And then she kind of smiled, very slightly, mostly with her eyes. "You going to be in church tomorrow morning?" I didn't know what to say. She knew I didn't know what to say, and she was enjoying it.

"I didn't know there was going to be church tomorrow morning. Ah... I mean, is there church tomorrow morning?" I told myself, *You are an idiot! Of course there's church somewhere tomorrow morning. There's always church somewhere on Sunday morning and—No! You won't be there!*

Ray had not said anything since I had walked back into the bar.

"Two blocks behind the Black Cat at the Foursquare Gospel Church. You going to be there?"

"No. We're going back to the ranch tonight after the dance."

Dale walked in and gave the redheaded and green-eyed girl a five dollar bill. She counted out $1.29 in change.

Dale took the money and looked at me. "You ready, Bronco Billy, or you got business to tend to? Maybe you want to catch up to us later on."

"No, I'm comin'." I followed Dale toward the door but halfway there I turned. She was looking at me and she said, "Bronco Billy, eh?"

"My name is Tommy Lee. What's yours?"

"Bevin. You're going to be late to your dance."

I ran toward the truck were Ray was waiting with the door open because he was not going to ride in the middle. "Man, that was the best looking girl I ever saw!" I said.

"No, she ain't. You been out at the ranch too long. The best looking girls you ever seen are at the Black Cat bar." Ray said loudly, and as we pulled up to the entrance of the Black Cat Saloon parking lot, he added, "Besides her daddy is one of those fire and brimstone religious nuts, and he'll kill you deader than a doorknob if you get near her! Especially when he finds out you're hanging out with me!"

The parking lot looked pretty empty to me, and I doubted that there were bunches of good looking women inside the bar. But Dale and Ray were anxious. I was wondering how I should act since I was only seventeen. I figured they would probably throw me out for being too young. I pulled my cowboy hat down low in front and hid my eyes under the shadow of the brim. I figured I would put on my tough guy face, but then I realized I didn't have one. We strode into the dark interior, Dale first, then Ray and me bringing up the rear. There were three people inside plus the gal behind the bar.

A lady in her mid-thirties turned toward the door when it opened letting in the last rays of the setting sun. "Hey, look who's coming in! If it ain't the king of the cowboys, Dale Scott! Cowboys in town, trouble expected! Yee Haw! She jumped off her barstool and ran, throwing her arms around Dale.

"Wanda! Sweetheart! How are you?"

"I'm rip snortin' and ready to start the roundup, Dale!" She laughed and threw her head back and showed a mouthful of white teeth framed in dark red lipstick. Her voice was loud. She had on bell-bottomed Wranglers and pointed-toed kangaroo skin boots and a low-cut red blouse that was bursting with her voluptuousness.

"Wanda, what about me? How come I don't get a hug?" Ray asked, obviously trying to be as loud as she was. She turned and looked at him for a second, her face was straight and unsmiling and then, "Ha! Ray, you old son of a gun, I thought you was a prospector or sodbuster or somethin'! Ha! Ha! Ha!" She slapped Dale on the back and laughed uproariously at her own sharp tongue. "Ha, no, I'm not going to hug you, but I'll let you buy us all a drink! Ha! Ha!!"

Dale sat on a barstool to the left of the corner stool where Wanda had been sitting. I sat down to Dale's left. Ray bellied up to the bar on Wanda's right and told the barmaid to give us all what we wanted. "But first give me a Schlitz." Ray said.

"Ha! Ha! Give him a Schlitz! He's always got to be different! Ha! Give him a Schlitz, Rita! But bring me another Coors!" She said as she laughed and flashed her smile incased in the heavy red lipstick.

"I'll have a Coors, Rita, thank you." Dale said.

Rita looked at me hiding under my hat brim. "Kinda young to be in here, aren't you, kid?"

"He ain't too young, Rita! He's just awkward. Sort of a halfwit." Dale slapped me on the back so hard I started to cough. "He'll take a Coors also!"

Rita looked at Dale with her eyebrows raised. "Tell him to push his hat back a little." Looking at me she added, "Hiding under your hat brim don't make you look any older." Then turning back to Dale she observed, "Well, maybe he is a halfwit."

"Actually he's only a quarter wit, or perhaps an eighth." Ray said as philosophically as he could.

Rita brought our beers, and I pushed my hat back and tried to be somebody while Ray waxed eloquent about my intellectual capacity and Dale made small talk with Wanda while she burst out in loud laughter every minute or so.

After a few minutes, Rita came strolling back down toward our end of the bar to check on us, and Dale asked her, "When is the band going to show up, Rita?"

"Band? What in the world are you talking about? There isn't going to be a band in here anytime soon."

"You've got to be kidding! That's why we came into town tonight; we heard there was going to be live music and a dance."

"For heaven's sake, Dale, who in the world told you that? There was never any talk around here about having live music."

"Well," Ray announced, "we will just have to entertain ourselves some other way, won't we!"

"Ha! Ha ha ha ha! Nobody was going to dance with you anyway!" Wanda laughed at her observation.

I finished my Coors beer and told Dale I would see him later. He asked me where I was going, and I told him since there wasn't going to be any music I thought I might try to go back to the Conoco station and talk to the redhead. He offered me the keys to his pickup but made me promise to be back in an hour or so. I promised.

I drove the Chevy pickup to the gas station and all the while wondering if she would still be there. I parked off to the side so I wouldn't be blocking the two gas pumps and walked toward the little office building. She was still sitting behind the counter reading her book, but when I entered she stood up. "Bronco Billy, you're back! No, I'm sorry, your name is Jimmy not Bronco." She laughed slightly.

"Tommy, and your name is Bevin." She stared at me, so I stared back, for a moment anyway, and then I tried to smile. She allowed a very faint trace of a grin to show. There was a display of various brands of candy bars and chewing gum against the wall below a plate-glass window opposite of the counter where she stood. I chose a pack of Juicy Fruit and a Mr. Goodbar and laid them on the counter. "You came all the way back here for gum and a candy bar?"

I thought I detected sarcasm in her voice. "Actually I came back to see you. Figured I would get throwed out if I didn't buy something."

"You will if you don't give me twenty-five cents."

I laid a quarter on the counter and tore open the gum wrapper and put a stick of Juicy Fruit in my mouth.

"Trying to hide the whiskey on your breath?"

"I didn't drink any whiskey." I offered her a stick of gum, and she declined my offer, so I offered her the Mr. Goodbar. She surprised me and took it and started eating it by breaking off very small pieces with her fingers and depositing them into her mouth. I noticed she had freckles and I stared at her thick red hair. "Is this your dad's gas station?"

"Yeah, and he'll be here in a minute to take me home. Then someone else will come in and work until midnight when we close down."

"Will your dad be mad because I'm in here talking to you?"

"Yeah, maybe. He might take after you with a tire iron or even pull a gun on you. He killed a young boy in here a month ago because he was just hanging out. Told the cops the boy was trying to rob the place."

"Yeah, and you watched him do it?"

"No, my older sister was here. She's really good looking, but she's an old maid. Doesn't like men but she attracts them."

"What about you, do you attract them?"

"That's a stupid thing to ask a girl!"

"Sorry, but it's not very smart to tell me your dad killed someone a month ago. I bet your good looking sister isn't an old maid either."

"You're right! I don't have an older sister. But I do have a dad and he's driving in here right now."

I glanced out the window and saw a man driving up in a pickup. I started to get nervous, and I figured I better give it my best shot. "Is there any chance you would ever go out with me? I mean like on a date? I could take you out to dinner or down to Prescott to a movie or whatever you wanted to do." Now he was halfway from the truck to the door.

"Next weekend is Seligman Days and there will be a street dance. I might be there."

"See you then!" I turned and walked toward the door meeting Bevin's father as he walked in. We both stopped, he on the outside and me on the inside, and then he motioned me with his hand to come outside with a polite gesture. "Thank you, sir." I said as I stepped out.

"Certainly," he replied and then I escaped to Dale's pickup.

I pulled into the Black Cat parking lot, and noticed that there were several more cars parked in the lot than when I had left a short while earlier. When I walked up to the front door that opened up on Route 66, I could hear a lot of noise coming from the inside. The jukebox was blaring away with the sound of Charlie Pride singing "The Snakes Crawl at Night" mixed with loud voices and laughter that found its way out of the door. I opened the door and stepped inside, and the first thing I saw was Wanda who was in the process of standing up on her barstool. As the door closed behind me, she straightened up with her cowboy boots resting on the bright red naugahyde-covered cushion of the barstool. Her black hair waved wildly as if she was a barrel racer streaking toward home stretch in some big rodeo arena. Her bright red lipstick glistened, reflecting the light that hung over the pool table. Her tightfitting bell bottom Wranglers looked like they might burst at the seams, as did her blouse that was straining to capture her pointed breasts.

"Hey! All you gunsel brakemen and conductors, listen to me! I'm fixin' on cullin' the herd! You better find your holes and look out cause I'm gonna rope and drag you outa here!"

Rita came running down toward Wanda from behind the bar where she had been mixing someone a drink. "Wanda! Get down and behave yourself! I don't want any trouble in here. Get down!"

Wanda ignored Rita and turned and grinned at Dale who was slyly cheering her on. And then she saw me standing inside the door. There were now about twenty men in the bar and several other women. "Tommy!" She screamed. "You're back!, Come and help me, we're going to cull the herd!" Everyone in the place turned and looked at me.

"Wanda! Get down or I'm calling the law! Now get down and shut up!"

She began lowering herself down, but she was weaving as she did so. She laughed continuously at her own cleverness. "Now, there ain't no lawman this side of Chino Valley! Ha! Ha! Go ahead and call them! When they hear I'm in here, they'll be afraid to come!"

Seligman was a turnaround for crews on the Santa Fe Railroad. Crews consisting of engineers, brakemen, and conductors drove trains from Winslow to the east, or from Needles, California, to the west, and they got off at Seligman and turned the train over to a different crew. Then they spent the night in a motel and got on a different train the next day to take it back to where they had come from. Seligman businesses made a lot of money off of the train crews while they were held up in town for a few hours. About a half dozen railroaders from Winslow and some other regular customers had come into the bar while I had been down at the Conoco service station.

Wanda continued to laugh at her own wit, emboldened by the fact that the crew of men she wanted to cull had not so much as made a peep, let alone a smart remark back to her. The fact that she was female was what kept them from coming at her with clenched fists never crossed her mind. She obviously had consumed a heavy quantity of alcohol during my short absence.

Several of the Winslow railroad workers were chuckling at her outrageous drunken behavior, but several others were overtaken with a sullen appearance. They stared at her in blatant dislike and were obviously talking about her. She stared back and laughed out loud and slapped Dale on the knee. "Look at 'em, they are scared of me!" I walked up to the bar and stood to Dale's left on the opposite side of all the action. Wanda motioned to Ray who was standing to her right and closer to the railroaders. "Ray! What do you think? They're worried, aren't they?"

Ray had not said anything since I had walked back into the bar. He was leaned with his back against the bar and both elbows resting on it and his left boot heel resting on the top of a brass rail that was there for that purpose. He was giving the railroaders his toughest look. "No, Wanda darlin', you don't have anything to worry about from that bunch."

"Oh, shut up, you guys! Shut up! You Cow Creek cowboys aren't happy unless you are shooting up the town. I don't want any trouble!" Rita was acting nervous.

I stood watching and I knew enough about fighting to see one was brewing. I wanted to tell Rita to bring me a Coors, but I thought in a minute I might need to be running out the door. There were four of us if you counted Wanda, and she was a woman and drunk to boot. Ray and Dale had to have consumed four or five beers. There were at least six railroaders in the bar, and maybe more.

Ray hooked his can of Schlitz beer with his cracked and calloused left hand and lifted it to his chapped lips. "Don't worry, Rita old girl, there won't be much trouble in here tonight." He looked at the Rails and grinned with a little tobacco juice mixed with beer dripping down his chin. One of the Rails stood up. He was identical to Ray in size, but a handsome young man and very athletic looking. "I won't do nothing to that goofy looking cowgirl with the red lipstick, but it won't bother me any at all to kick your ass, Cyclops."

Rita stared and screamed louder, "Settle down, you guys! Settle down!" But nobody was listening to her.

Ray stood straighter and stepped away from the bar and faced the Rail. A pool table was to Ray's right and the Rail stepped forward and around the corner of the table and up to Ray's side of it. The light hanging over the ceiling above the pool table illuminated the Rail's face. He grinned and said, "I'll tell you what, Cyclops, I don't know which eye I should be watching. That one seems to roll around in your head like numbers in a slot machine. You are the funniest looking thing I've ever seen!"

Ray started for him, putting his fists up like a boxer as he stepped forward. The Rail stood in his place but crouched slightly, and he kept his hands down by his sides and open. When Ray was a step and a half away, he lunged and took a big swing with this huge right fist clenched. The Rail moved his head like a cat and let Ray's fist pass in front of his nose by an inch. And then in a flash he brought his left hand up, closing his hand as it moved upward, and he smacked Ray on the chin. His right hand moved up, and like the left it closed as it came forward and cracked into Ray's rib cage. When his fists connected to Ray's body, they made a sound like a .22 caliber pistol being fired.

Ray staggered back two steps but regained his footing, spreading his legs far apart. The Rail grinned. Ray again put his fists up like a boxer, and this time he led with a left jab toward the Rail's chin and then a jab toward the Rail's ear, both of them missing the man who bobbed his head like a ball on the end of a string. Ray moved forward and jabbed with his left again, and then like before he sent his right crashing forward putting all of his weight into it. The Rail was crouched with his hands dangling low and open, and he moved his head one way and then the other anticipating Ray's roundhouse swing. As Ray's right hand passed in front of his face, the Rail closed his left hand and smacked Ray in the ribs with a crack of lightning, and then the right hand closed and connected to Ray's nose as if it was a target nailed to a cedar post. Ray's head popped backward, and blood began to run down the only clean shirt the man had, and it started to puddle on the floor. He cursed the Rail and muttered some indistinguishable oaths. And he moved forward again, but this time the Rail didn't give him time to swing. He brought his hands up quickly, closing them as they moved toward Ray, and he smacked him with punches that made cracking sounds. Ray stood there like a great bull that was being shot by a gun that was of too small a caliber to kill but only to wound. The floor became bloody, and then it happened.

The Rail, who was now slugging with no opposition, hit Ray hard on the left cheekbone with a right hand, and Ray's glass eye exploded out of his eye socket and landed on the felt of the pool table where it rolled and banked off of the far end and came to rest, the pupil staring up toward the light hanging from the ceiling. AAAHHHH!!!! You knocked my eye out! AAAAHHHH!!!! My eyeball! My eyeball!"

"Holy crap, Donald, you knocked the guy's eye out!" one of the other Rails shouted, jumping to his feet and staring in horror. Donald, the man whom Ray was fighting, looked at the eye in disbelief! Ray staggered backward holding his hand over his face momentarily.

The place erupted into pandemonium with the exception of Dale and me. Dale was unconcerned and I was unable to focus. Wanda started laughing uncontrollably and Rita was screaming, "You've knocked the guy's eye out! He's bleeding all over the damn place! He's going to bleed to death right here in the Black Cat! Holy Cow!" All the other people in the building were now on their feet and had walked over to the pool table and were staring at the eyeball in amazement. Donald, the nice young man who had just whipped his opponent, appeared to be wondering whether to apologize or run home to Winslow. He acted as though he had never before removed a body part from an opponent in a fist fight even though, by the skill he had exhibited, there must have been many of them.

Ray had been leaning backward with his head tilted back over the bar and moaning in pain while holding his hands over his face. Suddenly he lunged forward toward the crowd that surrounded the pool table and threw his hands down toward his waist and exposed the empty and ghastly looking eye socket. "OOOHHH! NNOO! My eye is gone! AAAHHHHH!! He stumbled forward and wailed piteously. "I'm ruined! I'm ruined!"

Donald stared in disbelief at the hole in Ray's skull, and one of his friends grabbed him by the shirt sleeve and screamed, "Let's get out of here!"

All of the people except us three cowboys and Wanda

and Rita started running toward the front door, and Ray staggered behind them moaning, "I'm ruined! I'm ruined!"

Wanda rocked back and forth on her barstool and laughed and slapped her leg. "You culled the herd, Raymond old buddy! You culled the herd!"

Rita came from behind the bar packing a mop and wet towel and muttering to herself cursing Cow Creek cowboys. She leaned the mop against the pool table, picked up the glass eyeball, and walked back toward the back wall where there was a wastebasket. She started to pitch the prosthesis into the garbage as Ray came up behind her. "Hey, give me my eye back! Give me my eye, Rita! What are you doin'?"

Rita whirled around on her feet and shouted at Ray who stood there with his shirt all bloody and his face looking like a freshly butchered quarter of beef. She thrust his glass eye at him and shouted. "Here, take it! Take it and get out! All of you, get out, I'm closing up! The bar is closed!" Ray took the eye from her and deposited it into its correct place, and Rita walked back to the pool table and picked up the mop and shoved the wet end of it into Ray's chest and moved the wet strings toward his chin. "Get out!"

She didn't need to tell me twice. I headed toward the front door with Dale, Wanda and Ray following and weaving as they walked. Dale was singing San Antonio Rose, and Wanda was harmonizing in her coarse way on the few words she could remember. We walked across the parking lot: me in the lead, Dale and Wanda following arm in arm, and Ray bringing up the rear holding his left hand up to his eye in an attempt to keep the prosthesis in its place.

"Tommy, you still got my keys?" Dale asked.

"Yes, sir."

"Good. You take my truck and drive old Cassius Clay

here home. He needs to rest up that sore eye!" Wanda roared in exuberant laughter. Dale continued on with his orders. "You do the drivin'. Understand?" I unlocked the door to Dale's pickup and got in, and Ray obediently got in the passenger side while Dale and Wanda navigated themselves toward Wanda'a pickup which was parked a few feet away.

I drove west on Route 66 toward Chino Point, and then a couple miles out of town, I turned left on the county road that went toward Cow Creek. Ray was quiet for a good spell, holding his head and was obviously emotionally down more than he wanted anyone to know. I drove along with a full moon lighting up the countryside and marveled at the beauty of it. For a moment I forgot about Ray, and I began to think about Bevin and her red hair and green eyes. I thought about the difference between her and the loud and outrageous Wanda. Suddenly Ray lifted his head and brought me back to reality with a question that I couldn't answer. "What do you think, Peckerwood? What do you figure Pete got done today in Kingman?" Momentarily he paused and then he went on. "I'm going to give you some advice, kid. You keep your mouth shut and just make a hand and do what you're told, and me and Pete will make you a rich man." He looked at me with his meanest face, and then he grinned through his bloody lips. "You just keep your mouth shut, you understand!"

I drove on through the moonlight and said nothing but began to remember all the rumors I had heard about Ray in the past, and all the stuff I had now seen firsthand. He wasn't my idea of a man to trust or even to befriend. Ray had come from Riverton, Wyoming, a couple years before I showed up at the Cow Creek Ranch. He was about twenty-seven years old, which was ten years older than I was and stood probably six foot one and weighed a little over two hundred. He had a ruddy complexion and his hands and feet were big. His knuckles and fingers had bloody cracks and skinned places like a man who was used to grabbing things with brute force and hanging on at all costs, or perhaps a man who worked hard, or both. His lips were constantly chapped and bleeding and the freckles on his face had become permanently blurred from a continuously peeling sunburn. None of this bothered him or slowed him down. He was the personification of brutish forward motion.

Ray's most astonishing feature was his left eye, a prosthesis made out of glass, that was unhinged and seemed to roll around and look into places that were not supposed to be looked at. It was the result of a childhood accident, and occasionally it would fall out. He reveled in the oddity of this eye, daring anyone to comment on its queerness while simultaneously bragging about its uniqueness. Everything about him was a challenge: a challenge to any poor soul who might want to make something of the skinned knuckles, the chapped lips, or the roving eye that rolled uncontrollably in its socket.

Ray had drifted into Arizona claiming to be a top cowpuncher and upon arrival had landed a camp job on the Bogle outfit east of Wikieup. It was an isolated spot, and he stayed there for a year working for a famous old-timer named Hank Jenkins who had run that outfit for thirty years. Hank was a noted hard worker who, among other difficult ways of doing things, would tie every calf down by all four legs when the outfit branded. Ray received plenty of opportunities to skin his knuckles while helping to tie down twelve hundred calves in a year. He was content to stay there for a year, and then had landed a job working for Pete at Cow Creek.

Having been stuck in an isolated cow camp at Bogles, Ray had not made the rounds much before he went to work for Pete. But then he started making up for lost time.

He and Pete got on well because Pete was a man who knew how to use a man like Ray. They began frequenting the bars in Kingman and Prescott, with Pete's wife Mitzi always being present. They would drink, and Pete and Mitzi would dance if music was available. Ultimately they would manage to get a fight started with someone, and if Pete or Ray was getting the worst of it, Pete would manage to get himself over beside Mitzi who would open her purse where she always hid a small pistol.

Ray approached the opposite sex in the same manner he approached a horse or mule. With his bloody knuckles and chapped face, he would go at them like a bear tearing into a beehive or perhaps a garbage can. He would grin at them when he asked for a dance through the long hair of his rusty-colored mustache and mouthful of Copenhagen revealing the brown remnants of any number of dips of the powerful tobacco. And then if the damsel he was addressing hadn't escaped, he would turn the rolling eyeball loose as if he had pulled the lever of some ancient slot machine sending the numbers spinning but never stopping with three 7s landing side-by-side. Inevitably the girls would break and run when he turned his eyeball loose on them.

He was frustrated. But he hid his frustration behind a fabricated bluster complete with loud talk and wild gesticulations. He created an image of himself of being a great cowboy with few equals. With Pete's help he also built a reputation of being a tough guy. He began telling stories of being a Golden Gloves champion boxer in Wyoming. Pete had long been known as a rough customer in Northwest Arizona, and he and Ray began a reign of terror in Mohave and Yavapai Counties that lasted for several years, and Ray's inability to win a sweetheart was balanced out by his success at going to town and beating up someone. He was becoming famous.

In reality his cowboy skills were crude. He was a mediocre roper, and he had no feeling for a horse or cow. His cowboying was much like everything else he did, he just put his head down and pushed forward, knocking down all obstacles in his path. His one endearing quality was the fact that he rode for the brand and was loyal to whomever he followed. Pete recognized this and knew that he could use Ray's loyalty to his own advantage.

Chapter Four

I grew up around horses and cows. My dad and mom separated when I was six, and after that I stayed with my dad, except on a few occasions when he would ship me off to a relative somewhere to get rid of me for a while. But usually I was with my dad, and he made his living, for the most part, with horses. He was an exceptional horseman, and he was always breaking horses to ride for anyone who would haul one to him. I've heard lots of people say that he was the best man that ever lived to put the first thirty rides on a bronc. From the time I was half-grown, I was helping him ride the colts people brought him to break. Part of the reason he had me helping was the simple fact that he needed the help, but the other part of the reason was there was not always a woman around to look after me, so if I was there helping him, he could keep an eye on me. By the time I was fifteen, I was a seasoned horsebreaker and bronc rider, at least by old-time cowboy standards.

Dad's women, for whatever reason, came and went so our little ranch on the Hassayampa River was more like a bachelor's camp than a family ranch. Because of the lack of a constant mother figure in my life, I was ignorant about a lot of things and probably somewhat socially dysfunctional by modern standards. My school attendance was never any better than the bare minimum, and something like church attendance was nonexistent, but there were always horses to break. Sometimes we would go out and help different ranchers gather and work cattle, but it was mainly breaking horses to ride that put bread on the table.

~

On Sunday morning I got up at 5:30 and walked down to the horse corral to feed the wrangle horse that we had kept up in the corral. Then I went back to the bunkhouse and made coffee and fried myself some bacon and eggs while Ray slept off the hangover he had acquired in Seligman. I drank lots of black coffee and ate as much bacon as I wanted, not having to worry about eating any more than my share since no one was around spying on me. Then I washed my dishes and cleaned up the mess I had made. I sat at the kitchen table drinking coffee and wondering what I was going to do with myself all day and finally got up and started to walk through the large room where we all slept. I accidentally made some noise, and Ray woke up. He lifted his upper body out of his bedroll and the pillowcase was stuck to his face. The blood from his numerous wounds inflicted by the Winslow railroader's fists had dried to the dirty pillowcase wrapped around his pillow, and the pillow hung limply from his cheekbone. I started to laugh, and he gave me a threatening look so I quit laughing and walked outside and then started laughing again. "Hey, Peckerwood! Make me some coffee!" Ray yelled at me through the open bunkhouse door.

Make your own coffee, I thought to myself, and I walked to the barn and horse corral acting like I hadn't heard him.

That afternoon Pete and Mitzi drove in from their trip to Kingman where they had been since early the day before. Not long after they got back to the ranch, Wanda came driving her pickup into the yard with Dale leisurely riding shotgun and looking like a tourist. I was hanging out down at the barn where I had spent most of the day avoiding Ray who was in a very foul mood. Dale spied me at the horse corral so Wanda stopped the pickup and both doors flew open at the same time, and they got out. Wanda's new bellbottomed Wranglers were tighter than the ones she had worn the night before, and her shiny western blouse sparkled because of some special ingredient in the material that made it reflect the sunlight. It was silver colored, and the type that barrel racers and rodeo queens wore. It was also tight, and her breasts stuck out, but her stomach did also, and I was sure the stomach was bigger than she wanted. She had on a rodeo queen cowboy hat that was pink. Her big full lips, which were shaped like Patsy Clines', were painted fire engine red. I wanted to laugh because I thought she was ridiculous looking. They were both in a festive mood, acting like lovers after a weeklong honeymoon, Wanda in her rodeo queen costume and Dale in his cowboy clothes, his shirttail out and his hat on crooked, a half empty bottle of Jim Beam in his right hand and a tailor made cigarette in his left.

Dale sauntered on up to me, "Tommy, how's it goin'?"

"Doin' good, Dale. How are you? How are you, Wanda. You're looking good today." I wondered if lying because the truth was painful was considered a sin. And then I told myself that she really looked fine, it was just that spangled shirts, tight bellbottoms bursting at the seams, and pink cowboy hats just weren't my style.

"Ha ha ha ha! Tommy, how are ya? How's old Cyclops? Ha ha ha! Has his eye fell out again? Ha ha ha!" As Wanda laughed and talked, Dale offered me the bottle of Jim Beam.

"No thanks."

"Oh, take a drink! Anybody as good a hand as you deserves a drink!" I didn't want a drink, but I took one anyway. After all, that's what all good hands did—drink copious amounts of whiskey. "Where is ol' Ray anyway? Hidin' out?" Dale asked.

"He's in the bunkhouse. I don't think he feels very good. This morning when he got up, his pillow was glued to his head with blood." When I said that, Wanda started roaring with laughter, and she didn't stop for a while. Dale got a pretty good chuckle out of it himself.

"I was just fixin' on saddling that horse and wrangling the horses. It's about time, ain't it?"

"Yeah, Wanda and I will go over to the bunkhouse and see if Ray is alive. Wanda's gonna fry us some steak and taters. When the horses are in, holler, and we'll come out and help you catch horses for tomorrow." They got back in Wanda's pickup and drove over to the bunkhouse, and I saddled the horse that had been kept up. He was a colt in my string named, of all things, Whiskey. Whiskey was gentle, and in thirty minutes I had the remuda gathered, and before I could holler, Pete, Dale and Ray came walking to the corral. We caught horses for the next day and then fed them.

I had asked Pete to rope me one of the colts in my string, a sorrel horse named Cowboy who was probably the most talented horse among the half dozen I was riding. He was very quick footed and had lots of cow and was always alert. I planned on riding him for a few minutes before supper and do a little training on him. While I was saddling Cowboy, Pete, Dale and Ray walked back to the bunkhouse where Wanda was supposedly cooking some supper. Mitzi was probably helping her, at least I hoped so. I didn't figure Wanda was very domestic.

I saddled Cowboy and put a rawhide bosal on him instead of a snaffle bit, and then I stepped on him and rode around for a while. When I had him warmed up, I rode into a fence corner and loped some circles and then turned him back on the fence several times. I worked with him for a while, pulling slightly on my macate to one side and then the other until he started giving to the pressure of the rawhide bosal rubbing against his nose and chin. He was smart, and before long he would turn his head back toward my stirrup on both sides, willingly escaping the touch of the rawhide. Happy with my efforts and time spent on Cowboy's back, I rode back to the horse corral and unsaddled and turned him back out in the horse pasture because I had asked Pete to catch a different one for me to ride the next day.

I walked toward the bunkhouse and the wind was just right. I could smell beef and potatoes frying on the woodstove. I was hungry because I had eaten very little that day trying to escape any encounter with Ray. I stepped into the big room where all of our bedrolls were located, and I noticed the door to the kitchen was closed, but I could hear the men talking on the other side of it. I listened.

"Well, how many does he want?" It was Dale's voice talking.

Pete answered, "It doesn't matter to him; he will take a semi-load or five, whatever we can gather. The only hang-up is getting hauling papers on them. If it was just a couple bobtail loads we could sneak them across the Colorado River, but with this many cattle, we'll have to have some legal looking papers. But I've got that covered. I drove into Seligman this morning and talked to Jimmy Duncan, and he'll write me some papers. That self-important little jackass has a price like everyone else. The fact that he's a coward helps."

"What about the Double O cattle, are you figuring them in on the deal like you talked the other day?" This time it was Ray's voice talking.

"Yeah! It will be easy to get a load or two of those heifers gathered, but we'll have to not overload ourselves. If we get too many, we're going to have trouble keeping control of them as we come down that trail, and I also don't want to get them all or it will be obvious to the O R O boys that something's up. So we bring, say, a hundred down off of there, that will be more than a load. Then we slip out into that E L country of the Double O and gather 150 or 200 steers and bring them by Badger Flat, and the next day on into here. We'll shoot for three loads, maybe four if everything goes greasy smooth. That's somewhere between forty to fifty-five thousand dollars' worth of cattle, we'll say forty-five thousand. I get 40 percent or eighteen thousand, you guys split 40 percent, nine thousand apiece. Jimmy, the brand inspector, gets 10 percent, forty-five hundred. We'll split the other 10 percent between Ben and the kid."

"Do you trust them two, Pete?" It was Ray again.

"Hell yes! Ben's a damn coward, and the kid's just glad to be here. I've known that kid his whole life, and he'll do anything I say."

Suddenly there was a noise coming from the other end of the kitchen, and I realized it was Mitzi and Wanda coming in a door on the north end of the kitchen. That was why I hadn't heard them, because they had not been there. I used the interruption in the conversation I had just overheard to make my entrance. I opened the door and saw that Dale was at the stove stirring gravy. "Ya hungry, Tommy? I've been stirring this darn gravy while these two gals been over at Pete's looking at a catalog or something." Dale said

"We have been looking at the new couch Pete bought Mitzi, and some new cloths! Too bad you aren't man enough to buy a girl some cloths." Wanda said in a smart aleck voice.

"I'm man enough, sweetheart, I'm just too broke paying for all the beer you can drink and paying for the damage you do to every joint you go into."

Ray was behind on the count from the get go.

"Ha! I'm not the one who damaged anything last night." She looked at Ray whose head looked like his hands: cracked and bleeding. "What do you think, Ray? Should we hunt down that railroader and ask him to pay you damages? Ha ha ha! You should have seen him, Pete. I'll tell you what, he cleaned the place out!"

"Well, everyone has his day." Pete said obviously trying to change the subject so Ray wouldn't feel so self-conscious about his wounds.

"I think this is ready, don't you, Mitzi?"

"Yeah, Dale, it looks ready to me."

"Go ahead, Tommy, you be first." Pete ordered. I was still standing in the doorway between the kitchen and bedroom, so I stepped forward and got a plate and filled it with biscuits, potatoes, steak and gravy. I also got myself a cup of hot coffee and then sat down on the backside of the table. Everyone followed and filled their plates with food and chased the gravy down with Jim Beam or Old Crow. They were all in a merry temperament, except Ray who was somewhat sullen. His face was cut and bruised and his glass eye was almost hidden behind the purple and swollen skin that held it captive.

"I ran into ol' Don Kambitch down in the Beale Hotel last night, and we got to talkin', you know, telling old cowboy stories." Pete said. I didn't know who Don Kambitch was, but everyone else acted like they knew him. "Anyway, that old braggin', smooth-mouthed son of a buck started talking about his bronc riding days. Telling me what a great rider he was when he was young, and I guess he was, so old-timers say. And then he got to complaining about there was no good hands comin' on. Wasn't nobody around nowadays that could ride rank horses like there was when he was young. So we got to arguing, and I told him that I had a young kid working for me that could ride as good as anybody!" Pete looked at me and grinned. "So then ol' Don he says that he's got a five-year-old bronc that he's sure my kid," Pete grinned at me again, "can't ride. Well, we got to talking about it, and I bet the old fart two hundred dollars that you could ride him, Tommy!" Now everyone was looking at me. "He's gonna bring him up here on Wednesday for you to get on, Tommy—that is if you want to. I'll split the two hundred with you. A hundred apiece, all you have to do is get on his bronc, which I'm sure don't amount to nothing, and ride him, spur his guts out, and you got a hundred dollar bill in your pocket! What do you say, kid?"

I shrugged my shoulders and said sure. I didn't figure the horse would be much different than several I had been riding and punching cows on. I had got on several other horses in my short career as a result of a bet made by someone in a bar, and a hundred dollars sounded good, especially when I figured I only made two hundred a month in wages.

"I'm comin' out to watch! Does he want to place any more bets on the side?" Wanda asked.

"Sure! Don's got money, and he's convinced that Larry Mahan himself couldn't ride the horse. But I think Tommy will ride him easy. Later on that night I ran into Jimmy Pasco who neighbors ol' Don and asked him about the horse. Jimmy claims he's not that bad. Takes his head and puts it right down between his front feet. You can pull on him all you want and he won't get high in the front end or fight his head, just bucks straight. Don will show up with some money, and we'll offer him something to drink! He'll probably bet more than you want!"

Everyone was in a partying mood after Pete sprung the news about the old Mojave County rancher bringing the outlaw horse out for me to ride. Even Ray seemed to cheer up when he started drinking the beer that Wanda and Dale had hauled out from Seligman. After talking about the upcoming bronc ride in which I would be the star and drinking some whiskey and beer, someone came up with the idea of inviting some of the neighbors to come and watch. The idea grew into inviting some of them to bring their horses, and Pete would take advantage of the extra crew that would be around and he would have an extra big branding and get a lot of work done. I sat and listened and said little. I wasn't acquainted with the neighbors who were being talked about or the old-timer who was bringing the bucking horse.

When everyone was finished eating their fill of steak, potatoes and gravy, I sat and listened for a while and then got up and started doing the dishes. Wanda and Mitzi seemed to be as excited about the upcoming get-together as the men were, and by the time I finished cleaning up the kitchen, the idea had grown into a full scale event complete with barbecuing a steer and possibly a barn dance. Suddenly it occurred to me that the same people that we were going to be stealing cattle from would probably be invited to the party. I got a feeling that maybe my life was headed the wrong direction, but I pushed it to the back of my mind. I was having too much fun.

I said goodnight and went into the bedroom, leaving the crowd sitting at the table drinking and planning the big party. I had a horse in the corral named Toddy that I would have to get on the next morning. He was the only one of the colts in my string that had showed no improvement in his attitude. I knew he was going to buck and he was hard to handle. I didn't want to be hungover so I unrolled my bedroll onto the cement floor and crawled in. I thought of Bevin and drifted off to sleep.

The next morning I was up by four and slipped outside to relieve myself in the wide open spaces and then walked across to the barn and horse corral and threw our horses a little hay which was the usual procedure. By the time I got back to the house and washed, Dale was up and in the kitchen drinking coffee, and Mitzi was cooking breakfast. No one was saying much, and they looked like they needed lots of hot black coffee to nurse their hangovers. The meeting the night before to plan the upcoming barbecue and party had turned into a late night event, and everyone had consumed lots of alcohol.

I got some coffee and sat down at the table as Ray came walking into the kitchen. He looked horrible. His eyes, especially the left one, were puffy, almost to the point of being closed. The cuts on his face from Don the Rail's knuckles were red and looked infected. He was surly and sat down with his freshly poured coffee and said nothing.

Ben drove up in a pickup, having missed out on all the weekend doings, and came walking into the kitchen. "Good morning." he said to everyone in general.

"Mornin'," was all Pete said, not bothering to look at Ben but instead staring into the atmosphere through the smoke of his Camel cigarette.

"Good morning, Ben." Dale said, and Mitzi and I repeated the good morning.

Ben walked over to the cupboard, got a porcelain-covered cup, poured himself coffee, and then sat down with his back toward Mitzi and the stove and facing me and Ray on the opposite side of the table. Pete sat on the end to Ben's left, and Dale sat on the end to Ben's right, the same end as the door into the big bedroom. When he sat he looked directly at Ray, and he obviously couldn't help but stare at the whipped man's cuts and bruises. The lust for a good look was too powerful to overcome.

"What are you looking at, baby face?" Ray demanded.

"Nothin'! I mean, darn! You got bucked off and drug, or something?"

"He decided to clear out the Black Cat bar, and he got 'er done!" Dale said with a slight grin.

"Man! How many was there?"

"Last time Tommy and I seen 'em, they was all running out the front door too fast to count, and they didn't come back!" Dale said." There was a herd of 'em!"

"What did they look like, ah, I mean, were they in bad shape?"

"They were all scared as hell!"

"Breakfast is ready. You guys better eat, it's getting awful deep in here!" Mitzi observed as she sat down next to Pete who just smoked and drank coffee. Very little was said while we sat and ate. Ray got a big plateful of biscuits and gravy and sulked while he ate.

When we finished eating we walked to the horse corral, and like every other day, we threw our catch ropes to another man and formed a rope corral that surrounded the horses. There were only seven, one for each of the five of us, plus one for Luis and a mule that Luis might use to pack something during the day.

I had been on the outfit long enough now to know the drill by heart. When it was time to catch horses, we not only brought our own catch ropes that would be used as part of the makeshift corral but also a bridle or halter. Pete always did the roping and he was good at it. He led our horses up to us on the end of his rope, and expected a man to get his bridle or halter on fast and get his rope off of the horse's neck fast. I wasn't sure why this was so important, but if you wanted a butt chewin', dillydally around getting a bridle or halter on a horse. If you wanted to please Pete, slip the bridle or halter on your horse's head and remove his rope in one fluid motion.

Toddy, the colt I was going to ride that morning, was a muckledee dun or mouse-colored horse. He had no white on him anywhere. He was a bucker, actually the only horse in my string that didn't show a sign of giving it up. For the most part he was honest about it. He took his head and bucked pretty straight, but he bucked hard, his feet hitting the ground hard. I suppose part of it might have been he wasn't hitting the ground on all four feet at once, but from on top I couldn't tell for sure, I just knew he was hard to ride. A real bone crusher. Also in the remuda was a horse that Ray rode named Catclaw, and he was a mouse-colored horse also, the spitting image of Toddy. Toddy was probably a half inch shorter and twenty-five pounds lighter but very similar in appearance. Catclaw was old and gentle. I never rode him, but he looked like a clunker, but all Ray's horses looked like clunkers. He didn't bring out the best in a horse.

We got our ropes around the seven horses and Pete caught Toddy. He led him out of the ropes on the opposite side from me and Ray, and he started leading him to the right in my direction. Ray was holding the other end of my rope on my right side, and as Pete started to walk by Ray toward me, Ray took the ropes he was holding, the same ropes that formed our horse corral and tried to hand them to Pete, thinking that Pete was leading Catclaw. Pete almost walked past Ray leading Toddy and then realized Ray wanted him to hold the ropes so he could get his bridle on his horse. Pete hesitated and looked at Toddy, but Ray was already slipping his bridle over Toddy's ears and removing Pete's rope from off of Toddy's head.

I didn't know if Pete knew what was happening or if he wasn't sure which horse he had caught. It was still quite dark, but I could tell that Ray now had his bridle on my horse. I started to point out the mistake but decided to keep my mouth shut. Nobody could blame me for any wrongdoing, so I just went along not saying anything. When Pete caught Catclaw he led him around to me, and I quickly slipped my snaffle bit onto his head. Pete never let on if he knew I had the wrong horse. Toddy, for all his bronciness, was actually pretty gentle on the ground. He was easy to get on, just bucked after you did so.

Ray's outfit—his saddle, chaps, spurs, etc.—were all pretty basic Arizona stuff, crude by buckaroo standards with the exception of the Grijalva spade. Ray was very proud of the beautiful silver-mounted bit. He had about as much idea of the finer points of good bridle horses as I did of flying a spaceship, but he was proud of the Grijalva spade. Toddy acted to me like he had never had anything but a snaffle bit in his mouth, but Ray bridled him with the Eduardo Grijalva spade. The colt had never had that much copper and steel put into his mouth before, and as Ray was putting his saddle on him, the colt started slinging his head around and acting discontent. Ray had said almost nothing all morning, but when Toddy went to fighting his head, Ray jerked on the bridle reins and hollered, "What the hell is wrong with you, you old #$@%^&*(+!" No one seemed to pay attention. When saddled, we led our horses out the gate and got ready to get on. As usual Pete was on his horse before anyone else.

This was a morning of firsts. It was the first morning Ray had been the last one out of bed. It was the first time Ray had not said something smart aleck to me when I was about to get on a colt. It would also be the first time since I had gotten there that a horse bucked with someone besides me. I had thought that I might help Ray out of his predicament. I expected him to make a smart remark about me having to get on Toddy. I figured I would then reply with the words, "You're saddling Toddy, not me!" And then he would realize he had saddled the wrong horse. But he was still sulled up and in a sour temper, and he said nothing. I stepped on Catclaw about the same time Ray shoved his Champion Old-Timers into his left stirrup. Toddy was still slinging his head, and when Ray had his seat, Pete took off in a trot, but I noticed he was looking back over his shoulder.

Ray took his well-oiled reins and whipped Toddy good and hard across his fanny, and all the bedrocks of Hades started rumbling. Toddy went totally ballistic. He jumped low and fast the first jump and high and wide the second.

He fought his head and threw it side to side, and about the third jump, he started striking at his face with his paws in an attempt to free himself of the copper wire and steel spoon pressing against his pallet. Ray was behind on the count from the get-go and was leaning back of center with both hands pulling hard on the heavy harness-leather reins. In one of those moments of clarity that will occasionally come to a person for only a brief second, I thought what a conundrum it all was: a beautiful silver bit made by the master bit maker, Eduardo Grijalva, connected to a pair of crude harness-leather reins that a "Ray Lewis" was trying to ride a sure enough bucking horse with.

He never knew what hit him. Almost immediately Ray's head was snapping back and forth like a rubber ball out on the end of a rubber band being beat against a wooden paddle. His chin got higher every jump, and he rose higher out of the saddle. Somewhere around the fifth or sixth jump, Toddy set up hard and came up in the front end and then dropped. On the upswing, Ray's body was leaning back over the cantle, and he was looking up into the sky having lost control of his head, and when the horse dropped hard, the sheer force ripped Ray forward and his head and shoulders went over the fork of the saddle. The heavy piece of leather that held the two legs of Ray's chaps together hung up on his high saddle horn, and so with his upper body in front of the saddle going down and his feet coming up backwards out of his stirrups that were encased in bulldog tapaderos, Ray's chap string became an anchor, and his body spun one revolution above the saddle horn looking just like the rotor on a big helicopter. The next jump Toddy set up again and when he dropped, Ray went to the ground hard like the end of a whip. He landed on his back, and as Toddy passed by, he kicked him hard in the stomach. I didn't think I had ever heard a man groan in a more desperate way.

Toddy bucked down the country for several hundred feet fighting his head and striking at the silver-mounted spade bit. Finally he came to a stop and stood trembling in anger. The bridle was still on his head, but just barely, and the bit that Ray was so proud of had been destroyed. The horse had struck at it with his front feet and had also stepped on the heavy harness leather reins. The Santa Barbara cheeks were bent, especially on the right side, and some of the silver had been pawed off. The hinge that connected the loose-jawed mouth piece to the cheeks, having been forge welded when made, had been split and was barely connected, also on the right side, and Toddy's mouth was bleeding.

Pete told me to ride down and catch Toddy and lead him back to the corral. Ray had drug himself back up to a standing position and looked like he was going to shake off the pain and humiliation of being bucked down. "I think you got on the wrong horse." Pete said as he looked down at Ray from on top of his horse. Ray said nothing but took what was left of his prized bridle when I handed it to him and went to unsaddling Toddy, and I stepped off of Catclaw and pulled my saddle off of him, and then we put our saddles on the right horses. Nobody said anything but instead sat on their horses quietly watching. Ray had the look of a man who wanted to kill someone. I walked over to the picket fence where my small amount of plunder was stashed and got my hackamore and put it on Toddy because his mouth was in no shape to be tormented by any kind of bit. Ray had to go to where his gear was stashed and get another bridle because the Grijalva spade had been rendered useless. We finally got our correct horses saddled and were ready to go. It was now sunup and as Pete was wont to say, "Times a wastin'." We mounted up and rode off following Pete into another day of work. Toddy had bucked enough to suit himself for the time being and was also much happier since he didn't have a lot of iron in his mouth. As we rode off I could feel electrical currents drifting invisibly out of Ray's body. I had a distinct impression that he was figuring on getting even with somebody, and as we trotted along following Pete's horse, I noticed the man with the glass eye surrounded by bruised eye sockets looking at me from time to time. Ray had moved to take the horse from Pete as he went to walk by, so Pete had let him bridle the horse, and by the time we were all saddled, every man on the crew knew that he had saddled the wrong horse, everyone except him; and if anyone would have pointed out Ray's error, it would have made him mad, but that didn't matter, it was me he was staring at.

Chapter Five

That Monday morning, the morning that Toddy bucked Ray off, we made a drive in the high country west of the headquarters and gathered some cattle that had been running in an area watered principally by a very large dirt tank. That tank was going dry due to the extreme drought, and therefore we gathered the cattle and moved them farther west and a little lower in elevation toward the Black Creek Camp where Ben and his wife Sharon lived. We drove the cattle down a canyon and turned them loose on a creek that had a little live water running in it which was fed by several good springs in the area. There was no great amount of water but enough to keep a hundred to a hundred fifty head of cattle watered.

In the afternoon we loaded our beds and saddles into a pickup along with any other camp supplies we might need and moved to Black Creek where we were going to camp for about five days. Before we loaded up to leave, we ate lunch in the bunkhouse as usual, and Pete told everyone that the big party that was going to celebrate me riding Don Kambitch's bucking horse had been postponed until Saturday June twenty-first, which was about twelve days away. He explained that several of the neighbors he wanted to invite couldn't fit the event into their plans until that day. He also mentioned that at least one other rancher was going to bring a bucking outlaw for me to ride, which was going to give both Pete and me a chance to earn another hundred dollars apiece. It never occurred to Pete or me that I might get bucked off, and we would lose a hundred dollars.

After eating lunch and getting our camp loaded into the back of a pickup, Pete instructed Dale, Ben and me to gather the remuda and trail it down to Ben's Black Creek Camp, which was about twelve miles distance. While we were doing that, Pete and Ray would drive the pickup with all of our stuff and meet us there. So the three of us horse jinglers gathered the horse pasture and caught ourselves fresh mounts and then turned the remuda out a gate headed west, and we set out on the trail. Dale got out into the lead of the horses and led them toward Black Creek, with Ben and me bringing up the rear. There were about forty horses altogether, and we moved along at a brisk pace staying in a trot most of the way.

The Black Creek cow camp sat down in a shallow canyon with a spring fed creek in its bottom that during dry times, like the time we were living through, was only a small trickle of water. Up the creek from the camp about a quarter mile there was no surface water at all. Along the banks of the creek were a few very large sycamore trees with white bark that gave them a striking look. Up and out of the creek on the sides of the canyon walls, cedars and a few piñons grew. It was a very beautiful spot.

The old ranch house that Ben and Sharon lived in was a wooden frame structure with white paint on the outside and a large porch around the south and west sides. There was nothing fancy about it but was kept up in a decent way, and Ben and Sharon had kept the area around the camp clean. On the same side of the creek, located about a hundred yards from the house, there was the usual small saddle house with a couple of cedar picket corrals connected to it. One of the corrals was a big round one, and the other, rectangular and big enough to hold our small remuda. There was nothing but a small lean-to off of one side of the saddle house where a man could store some hay, but it would not hold over thirty bales at a time.

When Dale, Ben and I arrived with the horses, we drove them into the picket corral next to the saddle house and commenced to catching horses for the next morning's circle. When we accomplished that, we turned the rest of the remuda out a gate into the horse pasture that ran up the canyon wall to the northwest.

There was no bunkhouse or outbuildings around with the exception of the saddle house, and so I wondered where we were going to roll our beds out and sleep. I decided without asking anyone that I would use up some of the limited space on the saddle house floor, but about the time I made that decision, Pete backed his pickup up to the saddle house, and we went to throwing our beds and gear out on the ground. Ray immediately packed his bed through the saddle house door, and Pete and Dale soon followed suit. Upon inspection it was obvious that all of the available space was taken up, and so I figured I would roll my bed out somewhere outside. My lack of seniority having limited me from joining that fraternity. I packed my bedroll off toward the creek and found a clean spot under a large sycamore tree.

Before long it was suppertime, and we went into the house where Ben and Sharon lived and found her back in the kitchen preparing the evening meal. I had not met Sharon before, or seen her. Actually, very little had been said about her by anyone. She was an attractive kind of gal in a country sort of way, long black hair, average size, and no makeup. She was friendly but not overly talkative and appeared to be all business as she put the finishing touches on our supper. I got the impression she was not intimidated by having a bunch of cowboys in her kitchen and that she knew how to act around them. I later learned that she had grown up on a cow outfit west of Prescott, and she was used to similar circumstances.

Whereas she was at ease, or so it seemed to me, her husband, Ben, was on edge. He had never seemed to me to be confident in his ability as a cowboy, but his demeanor went beyond that. He was obviously intimidated by Pete and Ray, and now that we were moved in for a several day stay at his camp and eating food that his wife was cooking for us in her kitchen, he acted like he was sitting on a cholla cactus.

Sharon hollered, "It's ready!" like a girl who knew how to summon cowboys to the table. Unlike eating in the bunkhouse kitchen at the Cow Creek headquarters where the prepared food had always been left on the stove and each man walked by with a plate in his hand serving himself buffet style, Sharon set all the food on the table and a place complete with a plate and silverware for each man. There was also a place for her, and she sat and ate with us. She sat between Ray and her husband. The food was probably the best tasting I had ever eaten, or at least the best in a long time.

We sat and passed the food around, roast beef and gravy, real garden salad, homemade light bread baked golden brown in the form of buns, applesauce with just a touch of cinnamon and obviously homemade. On the kitchen counter was a hot peach cobbler. I hadn't tasted anything this good in a long time. Everyone ate and seemed to be enjoying it, but very little was said. Finally Dale broke the silence. "Boy, Sharon, you done 'er again! This is really good! I mean, really good!"

"Thank you! Please eat some more."

Yes, Sharon, very good." Pete said.

I was too busy eating to say anything, but I wondered at the lack of conversation. Ben ate fast and got up to make some coffee. "Anyone want some coffee," he asked?

"No thanks, I believe I'll eat a little cobbler and go off to bed." Pete answered.

"No, I think I'll be headin' out to the saddle house myself." Ray replied and that was the first thing he had said since entering the house.

Dale and I both said thank you and yes, we would like some coffee, and about then Pete and Ray got up and excused themselves and walked outside. I noticed as I looked through the door as the two men exited that it was dusk and only minutes before it would be dark.

When Pete and Ray were gone, Ben seemed to relax and the atmosphere grew more pleasant. Where are you from, Tom?" Sharon asked.

"Wickenburg, ma'am."

"Is that what you go by—Tom?"

"No. Actually, most people call me Tommy."

"Did you know some people up the road from Wickenburg at Congress named Reeves?" Sharon went on. "Charlie Reeves, the father of the bunch, is the pastor of a church there. He and my dad are good friends, and I've been there quite a few times, to Congress I mean, and Charlie Reeves' church.

"Well, no ma'am, I guess I don't know them."

Ben looked at me and said, "Sharon's a church-goer! She knows all the church people from here to Tucson." He acted like he was letting me in on some confidential news. Bad news. Like perhaps his wife was carrying an infectious disease.

She looked at her husband and rolled her eyes. "He's ashamed that his wife attends church occasionally."

"Oh bologna, Sharon, I'm just lettin' the boy know what to expect." She held her ground and sat with her hand on her coffee cup and looked at her husband calmly. He squirmed in his seat.

"Well, I can tell him what to expect, and that's some

darn good cookin'! Church or no church!" Dale said in an obvious attempt to lighten the conversation. He went on, "Tommy here might be goin' to church himself! He's took a likin' to the green-eyed, red head at the service station. She's a church friend of yours, isn't she, Sharon?"

"You know Bevin Magennis?" Sharon was looking at me when she asked the question.

I wondered if I should lie and act like I was well acquainted with Bevin. *Hmm, so her last name was Magennis.* I decided to be truthful. "Well, not exactly, we sorta met. But I'm hoping to see her again this weekend at a street dance in town.

Sharon started to tell me about Bevin then suddenly a baby started crying from the opposite side of a half closed door that led into an adjacent room. Through the crack in the door I could tell that the room was dark. Sharon rose up out of her chair and went into the darkened room and reappeared with a small child in her arms that appeared to be about a year old. The baby was grinning and was obviously happy to be held. Sharon was grinning and obviously happy to be holding. She sat down and began to interact with the child. "How old is the baby?" I asked.

"Next month she'll be fifteen months." Sharon said as she held the little girl up into the air and then gently dropped her a few inches and caught her again. Sharon was completely different acting than she had been during dinner. She was animate and beaming with excitement. I couldn't help but notice that she was much more attractive than I had first thought. Her face looked like a chiseled marble bust of an Italian beauty that had been sculpted by Michelangelo. Her smooth olive-colored skin stretched over bone structure that was striking. Her black hair was smooth and long and shone like it was reflecting off of the sun. I realized that I was staring at her and looked away hoping my gawking hadn't been noticed by her husband.

I looked at him and thought I should say something about his child but noticed he was staring blankly off into another room. I held my tongue.

"Sharon! Ben! Thank you, I think I'll head toward the saddle house. What do ya think, hotshot? You comin'?"

"Well, actually I was going to offer to do the dishes." I said it like a question and looked at Sharon who was rising out of her chair.

"No, I'll get them, but thanks."

"Really, I don't mind, I do them all the time and don't mind at all!"

"Well, okay, that would be nice if you really don't mind. I need to go change this kid. Are you sure you don't care?" I expressed my desire to stay and do them. "Ben, would you mind helping Tommy clean this table off and show him where the dish soap and stuff is? I need to take Cheyenne to the bathroom."

"I'll help clean off the table myself." Dale said, having not completed his exit out of the room. We began stacking dirty dishes on the counter to the left of a big sink with old-fashioned spigots coming out of the wall just above it. I turned on the hot water and got some running after inserting a rubber plug into the drain. Ben had not given me help finding soap or a dish cloth, and so I looked around and found what I was looking for under the sink. I found a tray and drain board also and placed them to the right of the sink. I wasn't sure just how Sharon might have done it, but I began washing, and when I had a dish scrubbed clean, I rinsed it with hot water that was trickling out of the faucet that I had left cracked open. There were still several serving dishes on the table with uneaten food on them, like leftover roast beef and applesauce and several pieces of homemade bread. Ben had sat down again and was sipping on another cup of coffee. Dale had left the house. I figured that Sharon would soon return and tend to the leftover food. I glanced at Ben and read by his body language that he wasn't into conversation at the moment, so I washed on.

Directly Sharon returned with a clean looking Cheyenne whom she handed to an inanimate Ben. She got out a small bowl and put some applesauce in it and retrieved a spoon out of a drawer in the kitchen counter and handed all of it to Ben. "Would you mind feeding your child?" I thought I detected a slight bit of sarcasm in the voice of this newly discovered Italian goddess.

"Okay, I'll try." Ben said taking the baby into his arms nonchalantly.

Sharon busied herself with putting the leftovers in the Serval propane refrigerator and cleaning the remaining dishes off the table and putting them in their various proper places "So you're kinda sweet on Bevin? Or did I hear you wrong?" she asked. Her tone of voice wasn't flippant or giggly nor did it have the sound of someone looking for gossip. It was matter of fact.

"Yeah, well, you know, I just met her once on Saturday night so I can't claim to even know her. But, yeah, I guess you could say I was impressed, or you know...

"You liked what you saw."

"Yeah! Thanks, I guess that's a good way to put it. I liked what I saw. She said there was going to be a street dance on Saturday night, and I'm hoping I can make it in there to see her again."

We worked on for several minutes, me doing dishes and Sharon stacking clean plates into cupboards, putting silverware away and wiping the table off with a clean cloth. Ben fed the baby but said nothing. Sharon began to tell me what little she knew about Bevin. Her family was from Abilene, Texas, and they had only been in Arizona for three or four years. Her father owned the service station and also owned a dump truck and backhoe and did a little dirt work around the area. Her family all attended a Foursquare Gospel church where Sharon had been three or four times. She didn't know them well but knew by reputation that they were good upstanding people. She talked and I listened. She acted like she was happy to talk to me. I was enjoying talking to her, or mainly listening. I found myself staring at her and thinking how beautiful she was. In my mind I compared her to Wanda and even Mitzi and couldn't help but think how they couldn't hold a candle to her.

The dishes were finished, and I forced myself to look somewhere besides at Sharon. I was embarrassed and feeling awkward. I looked at Ben hoping that he had not noticed me staring at his wife. He seemed unaware of his surroundings. I thought I ought to say something to him. "How's feeding the kid going?"

"Oh, fine I guess. Not too much complicated about feeding applesauce to a little baby."

"You two must have been married quite a while, huh?" I asked feeling like I should keep a conversation going.

"No, we've only been married for a year and a half." Ben said and he handed Sharon the child. She walked out of the room. He stared at me. I thought something was amiss, but my mind was temporarily scrambled.

"Well, I guess I better go to bed. See you in the morning."

"Yeah, see you in the morning," he answered and he continued sitting there while I walked out the door.

I woke up early the next morning to a very faint glow in the eastern sky. The glow was nothing more than a slight paleness presenting itself to the starry sky. My bed under the huge sycamore tree was probably the best of any of us who were outside the confines of the house. There was a soft cool breeze, and I could smell the water from the shallow creek a few feet away. By a light in the house, I knew that Sharon was up cooking. There would be coffee. I shook my bed tarp making sure there wasn't a rattlesnake resting on top of me and shook my clothes as I put them on. I then went down to the creek and washed myself. The cool water felt good, and I reminded myself that it would be hot before our work was through at the end of the day.

Before heading to the house, I walked over to the picket horse corral and saw that someone had already thrown the horses a flake of hay. When I walked inside Dale and Pete where sitting with Ben at the table drinking coffee and talking about where most of the cattle might be running. Before long Ray walked in and we ate breakfast, sourdough hotcakes and homemade syrup with bacon and eggs. I hadn't eaten good hot cakes in a long time. I had never eaten homemade syrup before. I figured that, for sure, Sharon must be the best cook in the entire world.

Before we finished eating Cheyenne had started making noise in the other room, and Sharon went and got her and returned to the kitchen and her work. As she cooked more hot cakes and eggs and filled coffee cups, she carried the baby on her hip and had no trouble doing any of it. She was confident. Like the night before, I found it hard not to watch her.

When breakfast was over we ventured forward to catch and saddle our horses. I had overheard Pete give Ben and Sharon orders for Sharon to bring us a lunch at eleven o'clock to someplace called the Hole in the Wall. I was riding Cowboy, my favorite horse, that day and was looking forward to what lay ahead.

We rode down the creek from the house, and almost immediately after going out of the corral gate, Pete split the crew up. He left me in the bottom of the canyon and took Ben out to the northwest side or to my right and told Ray to take Dale and climb out the other side. The canyon walls got steeper as we went downstream, and I had been told to go slow and allow the men on both sides of me to get out ahead where they could throw cattle down into the canyon in front of me. Soon cattle from both sides started drifting down and lined out traveling downstream. That particular drive was one of the easiest we made all spring, and within an hour we had come to a place where the canyon made an abrupt turn to the right at a ninety degree angle. There was also another short canyon coming in from directly in front of the direction I had been traveling. This canyon was nothing more than a small cul-de-sac several hundred yards long and very steep. There was a definite rim rock above on all sides of this little canyon, and there were no breaks in it and therefore no trail out of it. On the bottom of this short canyon was a couple acres of soft dirt, but very steep on three sides, and the whole thing made sort of a three-sided corral or holding place. I learned that this indentation in the course of the main canyon was what was called the Hole in the Wall. It was a perfect and naturally made roundup ground.

On the southeast side and a little upstream from the roundup ground was a round steel water trough that was fed by a live spring a couple hundred yards above it on the slope of the canyon wall. The water was carried downhill to the trough by an inch and a quarter steel pipe. Fifty yards away and in between the trough and the roundup ground was a small and rather dilapidated barbed wire and picket corral about the size that a hundred cows would fill completely up.

I was following a considerable bunch of cattle down the bottom of the canyon when I saw, about a quarter mile ahead, a bunch of cattle come running downhill from my left and above the water trough. From where I was it looked like about a dozen head, and when the leaders reached the trough they were runnin' wide open. A man came down on the opposite side of the leaders and a little behind, and he also was traveling fast and obviously trying to be in position to stop the cattle from going on down the canyon. I could tell the man I was seeing was Ray, and I also could tell he was not going to make it in time to stop the cattle, instead he pushed them and the leaders from my bunch downstream at a high rate of speed.

When we had split up only an hour earlier, Pete had told everyone that he would move along fast and make sure he reached the canyon bottom downstream and a ways past the trough and would be there to hold the cattle up. He had also given me specific instructions to stay behind any cattle I followed down to the trough and roundup ground, and I was supposed to wait above the roundup ground in case cattle got turned around and started running back upstream, the way we had come from. From my position several hundred yards away, it looked to me like Ray should have stopped uphill and to the left of the roundup ground and depended on Pete to stop the cattle that tried to go downstream. But instead he raced downhill and began chasing the leaders of everything that had been gathered, trying to get in front of them. I could hear him cursing loudly as he disappeared around the bend of the canyon whipping his horse with his bridle reins and traveling as fast as he could. Cattle continued to trot downstream and out of sight following Ray, and it looked like a wreck to me, but there was nothing I could do but keep my position. I told myself that after a while I might be glad I had done so.

After about fifteen minutes, Dale appeared on the ridge at the same place Ray had emerged from, and Dale was following about thirty head of cattle. And then almost simultaneously, Ben appeared on the opposite side of the canyon from Dale, or to my right, and he was following a dozen or so head of cattle. And the cattle came trotting upstream from below the roundup ground and soon all the cattle were coming my direction.

Several big old Brahma cross cows that had come upstream from Ray and Pete's direction blew through the herd and came loping toward me. I could tell that they were stirred up, the result from having a bad experience with a man somewhere in the canyon bottom below the roundup ground. And when they got close, I saw that one of them was wearing a nylon rope that was dragging for sixty feet behind her. I knew it had to be Ray's because Pete never packed more than thirty-five feet.

The cow was on the fight but she also had most of the wind knocked out of her. She came to me and wouldn't stop, and I could tell by the red in her eyes that there would be no reasoning with her until she had cooled off. She never slowed down, and when she got a few feet from me, she charged me with her horns drooped. I simply sidestepped Cowboy off to the side and let the cow keep trotting upstream, but as she passed I took two swings with a loop that I had ready and waiting and roped the mad cow by two hind legs. She fell to the ground. Ben had spurred his horse and rode high and up out of the creek bed and had reached me in time to stop the rest of the cattle.

I jumped down off of Cowboy with my horse holding my rope tight while I took a nylon piggin' string and tied the cow's two hind legs together. Ben had the cattle stopped and was sitting on his horse sixty feet away. Ben was usually quiet, but he was agitated and wanted to tell me something. "Pete's madder than hell! Ray run that whole darn bunch right over the top of him down the creek a ways. He was chasin' that darn cow that was draggin' his rope!"

"He didn't rope her down there?"

"No! I was up on top trying to keep control of the cattle I brought in, and I saw him come crashin' down country trying to lean over in the saddle and grab his draggin' rope, and he run right smack into Pete's cattle and scattered 'em to hell and back. Pete's horse kinda went lame back on top, but he hurried on makin' sure he got down there to hold everything up, and then Ray scattered the whole mess. Now Pete's horse is really limpin', and he's pissed—I mean really pissed. I heard him tell Ray he was gonna kill him!"

"So he actually roped her up this other side somewhere, and she was draggin' his rope when he came off the hill. That's why he didn't hold up where he shoulda!"

Ben went on again. He was excited. "Yeah, shoulda! That's the key word here, shoulda. Now we're all gonna suffer because of his stupidity! You ain't never seen Pete mad before, but I have. It ain't fun. I'm tellin' ya, it ain't fun!"

I took Ray's rope off of the Brahma's neck and coiled it up and then looked down the creek to surmise the situation. The cow needed a few minutes to cool off, and I thought that a few minutes of timeout might cool things off on the other side of the herd. Ray had ridden off a hundred yards from Pete and unsaddled his horse to let his back cool off. Pete was afoot and holding his horse in the bottom of the creek, and his horse was also unsaddled so I decided to just sit tight for a moment and let everyone cool down. I made the decision on my own because I had worked with Ben long enough to know that he didn't like to make decisions.

After five minutes I saw Pete saddling his horse and then Ray did the same, so I got on Cowboy and dallied my rope which was still on the cow's hind legs and pulled her around where her head was pointed downstream toward all the other cattle. I stepped off and got my piggin' string off of her hind legs. "Do me a favor, Ben, and go down there and see if you can push a few of those cows up here close. I'll hold this old thing down while you bring me some paddin'." I stepped on Cowboy and dallied up tight holding the cow down but backed Cowboy up letting my dallies run while I did so. I was soon out on the end of thirty-five feet of rope. Ben drove a few cows up to the downed cow, and then I let go of my rope and turned her loose letting my rope fall to the ground. I still had Ray's rope so I had something to use in case another wreck started. I built myself a loop in Ray's rope and waited, but Ben and I gave the cow plenty of room, and after half a minute or so the mad cow got up and shook her head at us a couple times, but then she gave up and the whole bunch started walking downstream toward the roundup ground. As I passed by I stepped off of Cowboy and picked my rope up. I chuckled to myself thinking I was having a great time even though no one else was.

From three hundred yards away, Ben and I could see Pete motion to us to push the cattle toward him and the Hole in the Wall. Everyone got in place to do just that, and in several minutes we had the cattle sitting in the soft dirt at the mouth of the Hole in the Wall and held in place on three sides by the steep canyon wall and rim rock, and on the fourth side, which was north, the five of us on the crew held them in place. There was no way for the herd to escape except to come out in the direction of the men on horseback. To my left was Dale and on the right was Ben, Pete and then Ray, who was still ropeless because I was still in possession of the rope he had applied to the big brindle cow and then lost. Pete rode around behind Ben and approached me on his horse that was dragging a hind leg. "Tommy, my horse is lame, and beings you are riding the best horse, I need you to sort on these cows for me." He looked at me as if the statement was more of a question than an order.

"Sure!"

"I want all those yearlings out of there, plus a few of those old cull cows. There's probably only four or five of those, like that red cow over there with the drooped horns." He pointed to a cow to our right standing in front of Ray. "And that old yeller cow over there on the backside, she looks like hell, you see her?" Again he pointed.

Cowboy cuts the Red Bull.

"Yeah, I think I know what you're talking about."

"Okay! Get after it but be smooth and don't get 'em stirred up or we won't be able to hold them. My horse is lame, and one of us is going to have to hold the cut so act like you got a brain in your head and make a hand." Having said that he rode to the right and ordered Ben to go out a couple hundred yards and be ready to hold any cattle that we separated from the herd.

I rode Cowboy into the herd, and Pete hollered at me, "Cut a couple of those old cows first for some padding for those yearlings!" I rode straight to the backside of the herd and got behind the old yellow cow that he had mentioned and pushed her out to the edge, and Dale and Pete made a wide hole, and the cow passed through it. In the middle of the herd was an old Hereford bull that was obviously pretty shelley and needed sold. Pete had said nothing about bulls, but I decided to cut him anyway, trusting my own judgment. If he didn't want him cut, he would say so. The bull walked past him and Dale and nothing was said. So far, so good. As I passed Ray, I handed him his rope.

Next I got the red cow in front of Ray and cut her and about five others, so I now had eight head of gentle old cattle out in front of the herd with Ben holding them. It was time to start on the yearlings. I zeroed in on a brindle heifer weighing about six hundred pounds. I pushed her toward the outside and the space between Pete and Ray. She went toward the edge and then hesitated and turned and looked at me, and we stared at each other for five seconds, and then she ducked to my right. Without much coaxing, Cowboy moved her direction, and she took a run but we stayed alongside, and Pete moved his crippled horse to my left toward Ray which created a bigger hole between him and Dale, and the heifer saw the hole and ran out to the cattle that Ben was holding.

I kept cutting and some of the yearlings went out without much trouble while others required several turns and a run or two, but things were going smoothly. With each critter I cut, Cowboy seemed more into what we were supposed to accomplish. After I had twenty or so yearlings cut out, I went after a red bull that weighed five hundred and was unbranded. He went toward the edge acting completely gentle, but when we were at the point of no return, he whirled around and tried to run past me. Cowboy jumped in front and blocked him, and he went to the left and Cowboy laid his ears plumb back against his neck and blocked him again. The bull didn't move fast but was persistent at trying to go back into the herd, and we cut several di dos back and forth. Then the bull stopped and faced me for a second. Cowboy dropped his chin low toward the ground and laid his ears down against his neck, and we faced each other. Cowboy couldn't stand the anticipation, or that was what it felt like to me, and he pushed his body backwards which caused his front feet to be stretched out underneath his chin. My feet were only a foot off the ground when the bull ducked left, and Cowboy pounced on him like a lion so he whirled the other way, and Cowboy beat him to the punch. The bull bellowed in frustration at the horse that wouldn't give up. As all this was going on, Dale let out a war whoop or two in admiration of the show Cowboy and I were putting on. I even saw Pete smile one time, and it felt like earlier days when the crew was enjoying themselves instead of being mad all the time, which was what it had felt like ever since Toddy had bucked Ray down and humiliated him.

After an hour or so, I had forty-five head of cattle cut out into the separate herd that Ben held. I rode out and told Pete that I couldn't see anything else to cut, expecting him to point something out that I had missed, but he acted like he was satisfied. "You and Dale and Ben and I will pen the cut into that corral over there," he told me. "Come on, Dale!" And then he hollered at Ray, "Hold 'em while we pen the cut!"

We rode toward the cut, and Pete motioned with his hand toward Ben letting him know that we were going to drive the cut into the corral. Dale took his rope down and built himself a loop to be ready should some yearling try to escape. I did the same, and we moved the cattle toward the open corral gate. As the leaders passed through the opening into the corral, one big six hundred pound steer whirled around and escaped between Dale and Pete. Had Pete's horse been completely sound, it no doubt wouldn't have happened, but that wasn't the case, and the yearling escaped. Everyone stayed in place and let the yearling go until everything else was securely inside the corral. "Go get him boys, I'm afoot." Pete said.

The steer had trotted back toward the herd and stopped, and Ray was ready to run him off and keep him from reentering the roundup. Dale went high around the uphill side on the left, and Ben and I circled around in the creek bottom to the steer's right. We slowly cut him off where he had no chance of reentering the roundup, and then Dale pressured him and he ran downhill and close in front of me. I leaned forward and squeezed Cowboy, and we built to him like a rocket, and I took three swings with my loop and laced it around the steer's neck and dallied and stopped the sorrel horse. The steer bucked and bawled, and I turned uphill toward the corral fifty yards away where Pete sat on his crippled horse watching the gate and not letting anything escape. When we got him through the gate, Dale heeled him and I took my rope off.

At the same time I had finished cutting, Sharon had showed up driving Pete's company pickup and had parked off on the opposite side of the wire and picket pen where we had just put the cut. She had taken some wood out of the pickup bed and built a fire to make coffee and warm up whatever kind of lunch she had brought. Pete said to Ben and me, "Dale and I will hold the herd and I'll send Ray on in. You three guys eat first, and when you're done you can trade with us." He rode off toward the roundup ground and the herd, and Ben and I rode toward the pickup truck.

Sharon had her fire built near a lone cedar tree just where the canyon wall started rising on the northwest side. We hobbled our horses twenty yards away so we wouldn't stir up any dust that might reach her portable kitchen that surrounded the fire, and then we walked up and said hello. Sharon had let the tailgate of the pickup down and had a box with porcelain-covered coffee cups and plates, and silverware resting on it. There was also a pan of homemade sourdough bread made into dinner rolls. Alongside the pan of rolls was another pan of sourdough cinnamon rolls, and you could tell both pans of sourdough had been taken out of the oven just minutes before she left to bring them to us. She had made a good fire that had already burned down to coals. She had found some flat looking rocks and stacked them next to the fire, and a pot of coffee was sitting on the flat rocks and a big metal pan and was sitting there also filled with round steak that had been rolled in flour and then fried. The coffee and steak were close enough to the fire to be nicely heated. That was lunch: round steak, sourdough bread, and cinnamon rolls, and all the coffee you could drink.

Ben and I got ourselves a plate and coffee cup and a bunch of steak and bread and sat down in the shade of the cedar tree on the uphill side of the fire and about fifteen feet away. Cheyenne, the baby, played while crawling around in the dirt between the pickup and the fire. The meat was cooked just right with crispy chunks of fried flour and lots of salt and pepper on the outside. Life was good.

Ray rode up and parked and hobbled his horse next to Ben's and walked up to the crude kitchen in the sunshine, and he managed to say hello to Sharon, and she said hello back. Ray retrieved a plate and cup and walked up to the fire and squatted down on his haunches. After setting his metal plate on the ground, he poured himself a cup of coffee and then put the coffee cup down and stabbed three pieces of steak with a fork and put them in his plate. With this all done, he began to stand up while holding the coffee cup in one hand and his plate in the other. He hadn't seen Cheyenne crawl up behind him, but she was still four or five feet away from his feet. Sharon was watching the baby and was acting like she didn't think Cheyenne was in harm's way. Ray stood up and turned and looked down at the child, and it startled him. By reflex he quickly turned back around to escape, but in the process either his long-shanked spurs or his heavy chap legs hit the coffee pot and pan of meat and dumped the whole affair upside down and into the flames, coals and dirt, ruining the meat and dampening the fire and tranquility.

Ray screamed in a fit of anger and threw his plate and coffee cup as far as he could throw them up the hillside. Without looking at any of us, he stomped off down to his horse cursing and muttering. "This is a hell of a damned outfit! #$%^&*@()! Women and little kids crawling around like a bunch of #$%^&*@() varmints! Dirty no good..."

"Jiminy Christmas, Sharon, why'd you have to set the meat and coffee that close to the fire!" Ben shouted at her but didn't get up to help.

Sharon jumped into action picking up the baby and the coffee pot, and in a low voice she lit into Ben. "Don't tell me how to set up a camp and feed a bunch of cowboys, Benjamin! I was cooking for men and making a hand before you ever learned how to saddle a horse!" Her voice got louder. "Why don't you get off your butt and put some wood on the fire or do something, but don't tell me how to cook for a bunch of men!" Now she was talking pretty loud. "And don't you dare blame me for that clumsy gunsul hoodlum stomping around camp like an ox!"

I had gotten up and was trying to revive the fire that had been drenched by coffee. Sharon was in full attack mode while pouring water into the coffee pot and dumping some fresh grounds into it. Ben stood up like he was going to fight. "Well, you don't have to scream at me!" he yelled.

Ray had loped back to the herd without eating or drinking, and Pete headed our way on his limping horse. With the fire rebuilt I walked over and got myself a couple of cinnamon rolls. Sharon had sat Cheyenne down in the back of the truck and was trying to restore order in camp. Ben had sat back down and was staring off into the distance. Cheyenne started crawling toward the pan of cinnamon rolls while her mother had her back turned, so I put an extra one on my plate and picked up the kid and went back over to my spot and sat down holding her and feeding us both cinnamon rolls. Sharon looked at me, and for a moment I thought she was going to chew me out, but she turned and walked away. Cheyenne liked cinnamon rolls and so did I. Everyone else was mad.

Pete rode up on his crippled horse and stepped off and hobbled him. As he walked over to the fire, Ben got real busy and dropped his dirty plate and coffee cup into the roundup pan in the back of the pickup bed and started walking toward his horse. He seemed to be in an awful big hurry to relieve Dale at the herd's edge. I decided to sit tight and eat my cinnamon roll and hold the baby. We weren't going to be able to start branding or doing anything until everyone had eaten, and Dale hadn't even gotten there yet.

Pete walked up and got a cup and a plate and Sharon spoke up, "I'm sorry but the steak got knocked into the fire and ruined. All I've got is bread and cinnamon rolls, but there is a new pot of coffee."

Pete looked at her and then looked at the fire. "That's all right. I'll eat bread and cinnamon rolls, sure better than nothin'." He took three rolls out of the pan and poured some coffee and sat down. He seemed to be in a better mood than I expected. I got up and put my plate into the roundup pan, sat Cheyenne back in the bed of the pickup, and started to leave, but Pete stopped me. "Have another cup of coffee, kid. There ain't nothin' to do 'til we're all through eatin' anyhow, so relax. Ray and Ben can hold the herd."

I sat down and relaxed and Dale came walking up. He got a cup and walked over to the fire and poured some coffee and grabbed a couple pieces of bread in his hand and sat down. No one mentioned the wreck concerning the meat and probably thought that Ben had warned him about the lack of available protein. He acted content to have the bread and coffee and a chance to sit down. Sharon had taken Cheyenne out of the pickup and walked up the slope to pick up the metal plate and cup that Ray had thrown during his tantrum.

"I'm going to unsaddle that crippled horse and turn him loose and throw my saddle in the pickup and go back to camp with the cook. I can't get anything done on a crippled horse. It won't take me too long to catch me another horse to ride and lope back down here. In the meantime, you guys start branding." Pete directed his orders to Dale as he spoke. "Put Tommy to neckin' those calves and draggin' 'em out of there, you and Ben can take turns heeling them and holding the herd. Ray can do the groundwork by himself. I'll be back before long but there is no sense in waiting. It's going to be a long day, so get after it."

Sharon had returned with the plate and cup and put them in the roundup pan. "Sharon, I'm going to catch a ride with you back to camp. I've got a crippled horse, and I need to go back and catch me a new one."

"Alright with me."

Pete stood up and walked over and put his plate and cup where all the other dirty ones had been placed and said, "Well, I hate to break up the party but we better get goin'. Time's a wastin'!"

Dale who hadn't been sitting down more than a couple minutes stood up and gulped his coffee. He stuffed another piece of bread into a big pocket on his left chap leg and grabbed a cinnamon roll as he walked toward his horse. Time's a wastin' and get going meant, now, so we walked down to our horses and headed to the herd.

"Dale, come back and get the Blackleg!" Pete hollered as we rode off. So Dale rode back to the pickup, and Pete handed him a bottle of Blackleg vaccine and a syringe and some needles. Dale rode up to me at the edge of the herd and ordered me to start dragging wood up for a branding fire and told me where to put it. He rode over to the wire pen where our cut was penned and brought back four branding irons that were lying on the ground by the edge of the corral. The wood, which was plentiful, was dry and there was no humidity, and in short order we had a raging fire that wouldn't take long to create some good coals that would make the branding irons hot.

It seemed odd to hold the herd of cows and calves that we were branding outside and the cut inside a corral, but after thinking about it, I realized that under the circumstances it was our only option. The corral was almost too small to hold the herd of cows and calves anyway, but the cut fit nicely inside. The cut of skittish yearlings would have been hard to hold with a small crew like we had, whereas the cows and their calves were settled down and trapped on three sides by the hill and rim rock. With confidence we could ignore the yearlings and give all of our attention on the herd of cows and calves and doing the branding.

Dale had motioned Ray to come in and hobble his horse and had relayed to him what Pete's instructions were. Having said that, Dale got back on his horse and said they were ready, which meant that I should start roping calves around the neck and pulling them out of the herd toward the fire. "Don't get too wild, Tommy, and scatter 'em all over hell and back!" I didn't answer him, considering myself to be a top hand who didn't need to be instructed how to rope calves out of a roundup without causing a wreck.

I rode into the herd and hoolihanded a big juicy crossbred heifer around her neck and then dallied on twelve foot of rope and pulled her in a straight line toward the branding fire. Dale rode up behind her and roped her by two hind feet. Ray took my rope off of her neck and put it on her front legs, and Dale and I held her with tight ropes while Ray branded, vaccinated and earmarked her. I roped the second without missing a loop or running my horse in the herd, and Ben rode up behind her after I got her out near the fire, and he roped her by two feet. And so it went. Things went smoothly and after an hour and a half, Pete came loping up on a fresh horse which he hobbled off to the side, and he started helping Ray on the ground. I roped a couple more and asked Pete if he wanted me to trade with either him or Ray, but he replied, "No, keep roping." And so I did.

We ended up branding a total of fifty calves, and by the time we were finished, it was midafternoon. It was hot, and we rode off leaving the herd where they sat and rode over to the steel-rimmed water trough and took turns drinking out of the pipe that hung over the edge of the trough and allowed spring water to empty into the trough. We watered our horses out and lingered for a minute or two and then headed to the corral. Pete instructed Ben to open the gate and go inside and push the cattle out. The rest of us took our places outside and prepared to keep them in a bunch and going north toward camp that was several miles distance. Making the cattle go was no problem but, instead, keeping them from running off was the challenge. They came to us fast and we rode hard to keep them bunched. We then pointed them upstream, and by chance or forethought, I wasn't sure, I ended up on the right point opposite of Dale who was on the left, with Pete out in front holding off the leaders. At first it was fast, in a trot or lope, but with maneuvering and hollering and whistling and the slapping of chaps and other things to get their attention, we kept them bunched. Before long they were hot and more than one had their tongues hanging out and were panting. We slowed down and walked up the canyon where no air was moving, and it became a slow trail. By the time we reached camp and turned our cut into a holding pasture and wrangled and caught horses for the next day's circle, it was late. I went to the creek near the sycamore tree where my bed was, and I washed in the small stream of clear water that was there. As I walked up to the front door of the house to eat supper, I could smell beefsteak and gravy cooking on the stove. The sun was going down and I was glad to be going inside.

Chapter Six

After working in the country around the Black Creek Camp for four days, we had branded a total of 250 calves. We had also gathered and separated right at two hundred yearlings which we deposited into the holding trap at the Black Creek Camp. Early on Saturday morning about a half hour before sunup, we gathered those two hundred yearlings and set out for another holding pasture on the west side of the headquarters. We reached the backside of the pasture and put the yearlings through the gate about ten in the morning and then turned back around and hit a high trot back to Black Creek and were there in time to eat a nice lunch that Sharon had prepared for us. As soon as we got finished with lunch, we broke camp, loaded our beds and other plunder into the pickup, and Pete and Dale took off toward headquarters leaving Ray and me to gather the remuda and trail it to headquarters. We left Ben, Sharon and Cheyenne behind. Ben had disappeared into the house, but Sharon and Cheyenne were standing on the porch of their home waving at me as I rode off from the barn driving the remuda west toward headquarters with Ray way out in front leading them on. She was the best cook I had ever had the pleasure of eating after, or maybe I was admiring of her for other reasons, but I put those thoughts behind and thought about Bevin. It was Saturday, June fourteenth, and I planned on driving into Seligman and searching for her at the street dance.

The trail from Black Creek back east to the headquarters seemed to go on forever. It was very hot and dusty, and by the time we turned the remuda into the horse pasture at the headquarters, Ray was caked in dust and sweat. His whole countenance shone like a neon sign because of the dust on his face reflecting off of the afternoon sun, and I figured I looked the same or worse. We caught a wrangle horse, unsaddled our mounts, and headed into the bunkhouse. It was five thirty.

Mitzi was in the kitchen cooking some supper, and I approached with caution and asked if I could be excused from eating because I wanted to drive into Seligman to the street dance, and I was sort of in a hurry. I knew enough about cowboy manners to know a cook might be mad if no one showed up to eat the meal they had slaved over to fix. She smiled at me and said, "You're excused." I realized that it was the first time I had seen her smile.

Pete was nowhere to be seen, and Ray and Dale were lounging and doing nothing in the big room so I grabbed some clean clothes and took possession of the bathroom and showered and shaved. I was beginning to need to. I polished my Tony Lama boots and put on my nicest white shirt and newest Resistol hat and started toward the door. "Where are you going, Bronco Billy?" Dale asked.

I didn't even slow down as I walked past but did turn and look at him and Ray, and I grinned. After I had cleared the doorway and was outside in the afternoon sun, I could hear Ray hollering at me, "Lay a big one on her for me! Fact is, tell 'er I might be in there later and do it myself!" That was the first remotely friendly thing Ray had said to me in a week or more if, in fact, you could describe his crude statement as something friendly.

I had an old '63 Ford pickup. It was somewhat beat up, and the little six-cylinder engine smoked because of piston rings that were worn out, and when I shifted the three-speed gear shift that was on the steering column, it would backfire. I got it fired up and backed out into the gravel in front of the bunkhouse and turned eastward toward Seligman forty miles away. Dale had stepped out of the bunkhouse door, and as I let out the clutch and started moving forward, I could hear him hollering at me, "See you later, kid!" He was grinning at me.

I roared down the dirt road as fast as my worn-out pickup would go. I passed Cross Mountain and then Black Tub and drove on toward Markham Well. I wondered if Bevin would be there. I wondered if she would be with a boyfriend that I didn't know about. I wondered if she would remember me. I wondered if she liked to dance. It occurred to me that her religion or her parents might forbid dancing. But she had mentioned the street dance and had made me think she would be there. Me and the tan Ford truck roared on lost in an unlimited supply of conundrums and unaware of the reality of the passing countryside. Somewhere near Twin Buttes I entered a curve in the dirt road going downhill and lost control of the short wheelbase pickup, and it swerved to the outside of the corner. I pushed hard on the brake pedal and overcorrected the steering wheel, and the truck came off the ground on the left side and started to roll. I pressed even harder on the brakes and it settled back down on all four legs, and then I brought it to a halt sliding sideways with the passenger side being downhill. A great cloud of dust enveloped me, and since there was no wind it took a good while for the dust to subside. I wasn't scared but was immediately overcome with a feeling of shame as if I had committed some gross social blunder. When the dust finally settled, I looked in all directions and was put at peace because I could find no one watching.

I chuckled to myself and decided that I needed to slow down. I envisioned myself driving a brand-new three-quarter ton Ford pickup bought with the money I would be paid for helping Pete steal several hundred head of cattle.

I wanted the money but didn't want to think about how I was going to get it. I drove on into town at a reasonable rate of speed.

I drove through town on Route 66 and passed the Black Cat and the Copper Cart and then the Red Ram Saloon. I could see a crowd gathering north of the Black Cat and wondered if that was where the street dance would be, but I drove on to the Conoco service station. I pulled in and stopped at a gas pump and proceeded to pump gas into my pickup. Inside the small office building I could see a man standing behind the cash register. When I had filled my truck up with gas, I walked in to pay for it and handed the man, whom I had never seen before, a five dollar bill.

"You don't know where Bevin is, do you?" I inquired.

The man counted out a dollar and fifteen cents in change and handed it to me. "You a friend of Bevin's, are you?"

"Yeah, I am."

"Well, you ought to know where she is then, shouldn't you?" He stared at me. I stared back.

"You her uncle or something?"

"No, just a secret admirer."

I looked at him. He was about thirty years old and needed to shave. The T-shirt that he wore wasn't exactly clean. He resembled a high-classed street person. I couldn't imagine Bevin having anything to do with him unless maybe he was a family member. I could tell he wasn't going to give me any information. "Well, thanks for the help! There's nothing secret about my admiration of her."

I fired up Old Dirty, which was what I called my pickup, drove back toward the center of town, and pulled into the Black Cat parking lot, found an empty spot and parked. I got out and walked north toward the crowd that was obviously growing larger. The sun was just sinking below the horizon out toward Chino Point, and I hurried forth into the mass of people hoping to see her.

In the distance I could hear music playing, and I finally got close enough to see a band, which was no more than a guitar player, a fiddle player, and a man with a standup bass. The guitar player stood behind a microphone and was singing "I'm Walking the Floor Over You." The band was located at the end of the street in the very entrance to the Seligman schoolyard and was facing south toward the Black Cat and Copper Cart three blocks away. People were dancing in the street south of where the band was playing. I walked and mingled through the people, none of whom I knew.

I saw her from a distance on the west side of the street one hundred feet or so south of the band. She was standing with a couple of other girls and a boy or two. The other girls were dressed up in Western attire, bell-bottomed Western jeans and Western blouses. They had on buck stitched cowboy belts with cheap nickel silver trophy buckles. Bevin had on a turquoise-colored dress. It was one piece, like the skirt and the part above her waist were connected, sewed together but cut very neatly making her waist seem small. She wore a narrow black leather belt with a small brass buckle, and the color of the dress and the way it was shaped made her look like a million dollars. Her hair was pulled back on the left side and held in place above her ear by a silver hair comb that was made in the style of Navajo silversmiths. I took it all in as I walked toward her. She saw me coming. I noticed her shoes. They were very neatly made black leather shoes that were laced up in front with fine black laces. They had high heels, not spike heels but heels resembling boots, but very feminine. They had square toes. They were out of date, more like a shoe worn by a lady in the 1940s, or so I thought. She was different but she was confident. I approached her. "How

How about dancing with me?

about dancing with me?" The band had started playing "Fräulein." She held out her hand, and I took it and led her out into the street.

> *Far across the deep blue waters*
> *Lives an old German's daughter*
> *By the banks of the old river Rhine*
> *Where I loved her and left her*
> *But I can't forget her*
> *Cause I miss my pretty fräulein*

Fräulein, Fräulein
Look up toward the heavens each night
When the stars seem to shine
By the same stars above you
I swear that I love you
You are my pretty fräulein

We danced across the rough pavement, which isn't conducive to good dancing, but it didn't matter. If we had been gliding across a hardwood floor, it wouldn't have been better. I said nothing. She said nothing. But she smiled. That was enough.

Fraulein ended and the band went immediately into:

Came in last night half past ten
That baby of mine wouldn't let me in
So move it on over (move it on over)
Move over little dog because the big dog's moving in
She changed the lock on my front door
Now my door key don't work no more
So get it on over (move it on over)
Scoot it on over (move it on over)
Move over skinny dog because the fat dog's moving in

I pushed her out to my arm's length, and she bounced back and twirled under my right arm and came around my backside and twirled under my left arm. I thought I could jitterbug, but within four chord changes, I was hurrying to keep up. I realized she was leading me instead of me leading her. She grinned and when she was on the out swing at arms' length, she had a way of pointing the toes of those old black shoes that resembled the moves of some famous dancer like Ginger Rogers. Her ankles were like solid gold jewelry fashioned by some famous artist, and the turquoise dress moved across her skin like silk covering a moonbeam. She laughed at me trying to look like I knew how to dance. I had thought I did, but now was aware that I didn't. It didn't matter, I would learn.

"Move It On Over" stopped and "Faded Love" began.

> *As I look at the letters that you wrote to me*
> *It's you that I am thinking of*
> *As I read the lines that to me were so sweet*
> *I remember our faded love*
> *I miss you darlin' more and more every day*
> *As heaven would miss the stars above*
> *With every heartbeat I still think of you*
> *And remember our faded love*

The guy who played the fiddle was really good, and he backed up the guitar-playing singer well, but when he played a break in between each verse he sounded like Bob Wills himself. We danced along, and I forgot about Ray and Pete and Toddy and the Cow Creek Ranch. We danced to six songs in a row without taking a break, and then she wanted to walk off to the side and sit one out. But she didn't act like she was trying to escape, which I feared. Bevin introduced me to several of her friends from town. We saw a young girl, who looked several years younger, and Bevin waved at her to come over to where we stood and introduced her to me. She was a younger sister named Ailene. Ailene shook my hand and smiled and then ran off with several friends and disappeared into the crowd.

Bevin liked to dance, and I liked Bevin, so we danced to almost every tune the band played. We mingled in the crowd a little, and numerous people said hello to her. She introduced me to some including a couple boys who seemed to be her age, or our age. I wasn't sure how old she was but thought she was close in age to me. I figured I needed to find out, and thought I would do so soon. We kept dancing, and she seemed content to be with me, but I kept looking for some other young man to try and butt in. No one did.

Around ten o'clock I asked her if she was hungry. To my surprise she said yes, so I suggested we walk down to the Copper Cart and get something to eat, and she agreed. We had danced to many a tune but had not really talked that much. Just danced, and danced some more.

"So where did you get your shoes?" I asked.

"You like them?"

"Ahh... Yeah, I do. They are very well made, they ah... are stylish! I haven't seen any like them though, you know what I mean. Well, other girls don't wear shoes like that... well, not that I've seen... do they?"

"Should I wear what other girls wear?"

"No! That's not what I meant, it's just that you're the only girl that's got a pair, but I like them very much. And the dress... you were the only girl there in a dress, but it's the most beautiful dress I've ever seen, and ah... I like it." Nothing was said for a moment, and as we walked along I wondered if I had offended her. Finally she spoke.

"The shoes were my grandmother's. She gave them to me before she died about a year ago. For some reason they always fascinated me, and I would wear them when I was a kid. But now I'm grown and they fit me perfectly. They are very comfortable so I decided to wear them. I thought they might raise some eyebrows because they were out of style before I was born. Aileen calls them my old lady shoes, but I love them and don't care what other people think! As for the dress, I like dresses and this one is my favorite."

Yeah, mine too, I thought to myself, but I kept my mouth shut for a moment afraid that I would say something wrong. We crossed the street from the corner by the Black Cat across Route 66 to the Copper Cart. The place was full, but just as we walked in four people got out of a booth in a back corner against the big plateglass window looking out onto the sidewalk. We made our way to it and sat down before the waitress was finished cleaning away the dirty dishes.

"Tommy, you are a very good dancer, but you're kind of slow on talking." She looked at me and grinned. "Girls like to be talked to as well as danced with."

I looked at her and thought about saying, You're the most beautiful girl I've ever seen—bar none! But thought against it. "What do you want to talk about?"

"Well... let's talk about you. Where are you from? What are your plans? What do you do? Ride horses all day? Do they actually pay you to do that? That kind of stuff."

I looked at her and thought, Tommy, you better get your butt in gear and start talking or she is going to get up and walk out. "Well, I'm from Wickenburg, south of here 120 miles. I grew up on a place out of town a ways and my dad broke and trained horses for a living and did some cowboying around on ranches, but mostly we rode colts for people. I've been doing that since I was little. I graduated from high school a couple weeks ago and came up here to work for Pete out on the Cow Creek outfit. My dad knew him going back before I was born, and he sent word to my dad to send me up here to work because he has a bunch of colts that need rode. So here I am, working for Pete punching cows and riding colts. And yes, I get paid to ride horses all day, that's what I do. I'm a cowboy, I guess that's the best way to put it."

A lady who looked tired and overworked walked up and said, "Hi, Bevin. You kids know what you want or do you need to see a menu?" She stood looking at us chewing gum and holding a notepad and a pencil.

"I want a hamburger and french fries!" I said.

"Me too, Vivian, please! And a chocolate milkshake,

lots of chocolate!" Vivian wrote on the notepad and then looked sideways at me. "What about you, cowhand, you drink chocolate milkshakes, too? Or maybe just black coffee?"

"No, ah... I mean yes, I want a milkshake, just like hers!" Vivian turned and walked away.

"What about you? It's your turn."

"Well, I just graduated, too, just like you. My dad owns that Conoco station, and I work for him sometimes and will probably work for him a lot more this summer. I'm thinking about going to college this fall in Prescott. I like to dance, I like to sing, I like to go to church. I like boys who like to do the same things I do."

"Are there a lot of those around here?"

"No! There's none! Zero. I was hoping you would be different." She looked at me and grinned. She was in control and we both knew it. "You are a good dancer. But your conversation skills need some work." I determined to work on my conversation skills.

A bunch of local kids about our age came in looking for a place to sit. All the booths were occupied so they strolled our way and started talking to Bevin who introduced me to everyone. We could have easily fit a couple of them in with us, but there were six of them, and I didn't want to share Bevin with any of them, so I didn't offer. She didn't either and they finally drifted away, and then Vivian brought us our hamburgers and milkshakes. I began preparing my hamburger to eat which meant applying copious amounts of salt, not only to the fries but to the meat as well.

"Wow! You like salt, I take it."

Conversation skills I told myself, concentrate on your conversation skills. "Yeah! I'm salty!" She bugged her eyes at me while taking a bite of her hamburger. "Well, you know, that's a pun, sort of a cowboy term. If a horse is a rank bucker you might say he's salty! Or if a man is a good bronc rider, he might be known as a salty hand; you know, that sort of thing. So I put lots of salt on my food so I can say, I'm salty.

"So are you a salty bronc rider?"

"Well, I'm probably not the best around, but I ain't the worst either. I guess I'm pretty fair."

"Not, ain't isn't a word. You're not the worst around."

"Not, right, I knew that. I'm not the worst around."

She laughed and took a drink of her chocolate milkshake. I laughed and took a drink of mine. I stared at her. She stared back. Conversation skills, work on your conversation skills, Tommy! I was talking to myself. Talk to her you idiot.

"So speaking of bronc riding, there's going to be sort of a bronc riding next weekend out at the ranch. You think you could come out? There's going to be some kind of party I think, maybe some neighbors coming over and a barbecue. You know, that sort of thing."

"So what's the bronc riding? You mean a rodeo?"

"Well, you see the fellow that I work for, Pete, ran into some old cowboy down in Kingman a week ago. And this old fella claimed he had a horse that nobody could ride because he's a rank buckin' son of a gun. And Pete, he bets the old guy that I can ride him. Bets him two hundred dollars! So the old man, he's bringing his bronc out, and I'm going to ride him. And I guess some other neighbors, I think it's the people from the Double O's, they're going to bring one out, too. Pete bet them two hundred dollars also. If I ride them, I get to split the two hundred with Pete. So if I ride both of them, I'll make two hundred dollars!"

"So, can you ride them? I mean are you actually able to do that kind of thing? Aren't you scared?" She convinced me that she was actually interested.

"Well, you never know for sure if you can ride a bucker or not, but yes I think I can ride them, and no I'm not scared. I've been around that sort of thing all my life!" She looked at me and grinned. She was beautiful! Right then was when I decided she was the prettiest girl I had ever seen. Her hair was the color of shiny copper and her emerald eyes were out of this world. I noticed how perfect her eyebrows were.

Bevin sipped her chocolate milkshake through a straw and teased me. "You've been doing that sort of thing all your life? Wow! I mean that must be a whole seventeen or eighteen years? Wow!" She laughed at me. "You never have told me how old you are. My father wouldn't approve of me going out with an older man!"

"I'm seventeen. My birthday is in a couple weeks. The second of July I'll be eighteen."

"Yes. If you're seventeen and your birthday is in a couple weeks, you will be eighteen." She laughed and drank the last of her chocolate milkshake.

"How old are you?" I thought I would try to match her sarcasm. "My boss wouldn't want me to hang out with a girl that was too young."

"Your boss? Does your boss tell you who your friends can be?" Now she really laughed.

"No! What I meant was, well, I was trying to be funny. No, nobody tells me who I can choose to like or not like. And I like you!" I tried to say it like a man.

"Well, you're safe. I'm eighteen. Turned eighteen three weeks ago. And I like you, too, enough, that is, that I'm going to let you walk me home. I'm ready to go now." She got up; she was going somewhere with or without me, so I got up and followed her down through the crowded café. She waited while I paid, and then we stepped out onto the sidewalk.

The dance was over but a large crowd was still roaming the streets from the corner by the Black Cat Bar going north toward the Seligman school and the area where the dance had been. Several car loads of kids were hollering at each other and racing their engines. There was lots of noise and rowdiness. Several boys in a hot rod car hollered at Bevin and whistled. I could tell they had been drinking.

"Hey, Bevin, you good looking angel, come over and take a ride with us! Leave that goofy looking cowpoke alone and get over here!" I took her hand and she let me. She directed me to walk west on Route 66 and away from the crowd. "Bevin! Baby, I need you! Please, Bevin!" The voice hollered after us. I started to turn around and say something, but she pulled me on down the street.

"Don't pay any attention to those idiots! That's Donnie Pendergast and Butch Smith, they're a couple of Seligman dropouts. Total losers! If you went over there, they would gang up on you, and you could still whip them. I know you could. But I don't want you to. I want you to walk me home. This way."

I was holding onto her hand and feeling protective, but the truth was, she was leading the way. I would have followed her anywhere, so we walked on. A block west of the Black Cat Saloon, we turned right, or north. The street was more deserted, and it became dark because of the absence of streetlights. "So, do you think you can come out to the ranch next Saturday, to the party I was talking about?"

"Can you come in and get me?"

"Well, that's the problem. I think Pete has this thing planned where some neighbors are coming over, and we'll be getting up really early and gathering a bunch of cows and branding some calves. Then after that we'll have this bronc riding, and then they're talking about a barbecue. So I don't know how I could get away to come and get you."

"So where's it going to be? How would I get there? I mean, you'll have to tell me how to get there, because I don't think I've ever been out there."

I started to answer her question, but I heard a car coming around the corner behind us with screeching tires and the sound of loose gravel and a racing engine. The Seligman dropouts Bevin had mentioned had their heads out the windows of the hot rod and were hollering. "Bevin, where are you going? Take me with you, baby!" They slowed down as they pulled up alongside of us. "Whewie, Look at those legs. Baby, I'm telling you, you've got the best looking legs in Seligman, Arizona! Even if they do have freckles on them! Whew! Baby!" We walked on and I sized them up. There were three of them in the car. I figured they were eighteen to twenty years old, and they were in some stage of being drunk. But I didn't know how drunk. We were now two blocks north of the main drag, and I had no idea how far it was to Bevin's house.

"Hey, cowboy!" I tried to look straight ahead. "Yeah, you cowboy, I'm talking to you! You know who you're walking with? Well now, that is the nicest little Christian girl in Yavapai County. Ain't that right, Bevin, sweetie?" They raced their engines and gawked at us as we walked along. I whispered to Bevin, "How far to your house?"

"Two more blocks."

I looked on the ground trying to spy a big stick or some kind of club to defend us with in case they decided to get out of the car. I wanted to pick up a big rock and throw it through the window, but I feared that Bevin would get caught in the middle if a fight broke out. "If something happens, you run like hell, you hear me?"

She squeezed my hand signaling that she understood. We walked on and then about a block from her house, the idiot driving the car gunned the engine and sped off and then spun a brody and came straight toward us. "Go to the right!" I pushed her toward a power pole on the side of the street, and she ducked behind it as the car came left toward me. I saw a rock about the size of a baseball and picked it and reared back and threw it straight at the driver. The car swerved to my left, and the rock flew past it, missing it by a few inches. Bevin ran on to her house, and the car sped off south toward 66 with the occupants leaning out the windows laughing at me. They no doubt knew that they were dangerously close to Bevin's home and there might be reinforcements inside.

She was now at her yard gate, and I was still a block south standing in the street watching our antagonists drive off. "Tommy, are you all right?"

"Yeah, I'm fine. You?"

"I'm fine. Come on in and sit down for a minute." I walked up to her yard gate where she waited, and she held it open for me to walk in. I followed her up on the front porch and we sat down on a swing. She sat close to me and took my hand, but said nothing. I could feel her heart beating.

"Are you shook up?"

"Yeah, I guess so, a little anyway!"

I sat there wishing I would have beat them up or threw a rock through their window or something heroic. "I should have stomped them!"

She raised up and looked at me. "Really? What good would that have done? You pushed me out of the way and let me run away while standing there letting them come straight at you. Isn't that enough? Besides, there were three of them! You did enough." She sat back and took my hand again and stared straight ahead.

"So, have you had trouble with those guys before?"

"No, not me, but last summer they raped a local girl, at least the two guys in the front of the car did. I don't know who was riding in back. Anyway, they took this girl down and, well you know what goes on. Her name was Linda Ortiz. I went to school with her. She turned them in, but the local cattle inspector, a guy named Jim Duncan, stood up for them and said they were innocent. I don't even know what a cattle inspector is, but there is no sheriff or police here in town and a cattle inspector is some kind of law I guess. Anyway, he is the one who investigated, and he is friends with that one boy's dad, Lee Pendergast. Lee Pendergast works out here at the big Boquillas Ranch, and he and Jimmy Duncan are cronies. At least that's what my dad says. So, because of that, Donnie Pendergast and Butch Smith raped Linda Ortiz and got away with it. She had the baby about a month ago. They did leave town for a while though, to let things cool down. My dad says Jim Duncan probably advised them to and tonight is the first time I've seen them since then. They are real thugs and cowards and otherwise wicked, evil human beings. You are a cowboy, what in the world is a cattle inspector anyway?"

My head was spinning thinking of the connection I was about to have with Jimmy Duncan. "Well, usually they are called brand inspectors. When a rancher ships cattle to market they are supposed to have a brand inspector like Jimmy Duncan look at the cattle before they are shipped to make sure that the cattle being sold and loaded onto a truck are what they are supposed to be. It keeps people from shipping the neighbors' cattle."

"You mean it keeps people from stealing them?"

"Yeah, that's what I mean." We sat on the swing staring straight ahead for a few minutes, then I brought up the big event planned for the next weekend, and we discussed how I could get her out there. Finally we decided that I would leave with the phone number to the gas station where she would be working until eight in the evening. I would call her when I acquired more details about exactly when and where the excitement would all happen. "Well, I guess I better go." I stood up and she did the same, and we faced each other.

"Thanks for walking me home."

"Thanks for dancing with me."

"Thanks for the hamburger and milkshake." I looked at her and said nothing. I was speechless. "You need to go or my dad is going to come out here and cut your throat!" She smiled and stood on her tiptoes and started to give me a kiss on the check. I put my arms around her and pulled her close and kissed her. It was short but enough to convince me I wanted more.

Chapter Seven

Most of my childhood I had lived with Dad with the exception of a couple of periods when he sent me to live with other relatives. There were really only two times that I could remember. Once when my dad was going through a particularly rough spell and was drinking a lot, he sent me to live with his folks for several months, and that was when I was about eight. Another time, when I was twelve, my dad brought home a woman to live with us. Her name was Thelma, and my dad decided he really liked her and was trying real hard to make her a permanent fixture.

Thelma took an immediate dislike to me. She said I was too dirty, too messy, too much trouble to cook for, and she didn't want me hanging around the house. She didn't want to help me get ready for school, and she sure didn't want to help me with any homework. She suggested to my father that perhaps it would be a good idea if he could send me to live with relatives or friends for a while, maybe just for the summer, so she and he could get better acquainted. She talked to my dad about it for several days, and he finally relented.

My dad had an uncle named Harry who lived in Northern Nevada where he ran a great big ranch. Harry Lee was probably fifteen years older than Dad and was a legendary old codger, a heck of a cowboy and cowman but famous for being eccentric. The ranch that he ran had a big crew. There were always several cowboys on the payroll plus half a dozen farm hands that were called rosinjaws. At that ranch there was a large bunkhouse with a big kitchen and dining area for the single men. Uncle Harry always had a man cook on the payroll. He always instructed the various cooks to set the big table in the bunkhouse dining area with plates, knives, forks, etc. When the crew was called in to eat, the table was already set. It was customary for the plates to be turned upside down, and so when a man sat down he would immediately turn his plate over. It was an odd practice, but Uncle Harry did a lot of odd things.

When Uncle Harry would get mad and decide to fire someone on the crew, which was quite often, he would put the man's final paycheck under his plate on the dining room table. When the man turned his plate over and found a paycheck underneath, he knew his employment had been terminated. This had happened many times and everyone knew about it.

So the summer I turned twelve, Thelma talked my dad into sending me to Nevada. Uncle Harry for the most part ignored me, and I kept myself busy following various people on the crew around. Some days I helped the cowboy crew, and some days I tried to help the farmers who were putting up hay that would be fed to the cattle through the winter. But there was never any talk of me being on the payroll. I was just there.

A pack of wild dogs showed up on the ranch and began to molest cattle. They would gang up on a cow or calf and chew them up, and most of the time, the livestock they abused were ruined. Their usual tactic was to gang up on a cow and bite the hamstrings on a hind leg and chew on them until the cow was completely crippled. The dogs were around for several weeks and had destroyed about fifteen head of cattle, and there were always lots of dog tracks and other evidence so there was no doubt in anyone's mind what was happening. Uncle Harry was getting madder and madder and told the crew the minute anyone saw the dogs they were to report to him immediately.

One evening about half an hour before sundown, I was in the bunkhouse dining room with Uncle Harry. He was sitting at the dining table drinking a cup of coffee and visiting with the cook. All of a sudden the door flew open, and a rosinjaw yelled at Uncle Harry. "Those dogs are down in the meadow, and they're right by the road!" Uncle Harry jumped up and raced out the door toward his pickup. I jumped up and followed him and grabbed an old double-barreled 12gauge shotgun that was leaned up in a corner of the room.

When I reached Uncle Harry's Chevy pickup it was already moving, and I barely managed to jump into the back as he sped off toward the hay meadow which was a couple miles away. I had thrown the shotgun in the pickup bed before I jumped, and as we flew down the dirt road, I broke the shotgun down and made sure it was loaded. It was. All I had to do was pull the hammers back and squeeze the trigger.

Uncle Harry was driving so fast and the road so bumpy that I had to stay sat down in the pickup bed as we hurried on. Even then I was tossed about and knocked flat on my back several times. Because of the speed we traveled, we were smack dab in the middle of the meadow in several minutes, and, sure enough, the dogs were still there. There were seven of them and none of them looked alike. The smallest looked like a terrier cross about twelve inches high with curly white hair. The biggest was a heavy-jawed hound cross of some kind, probably a Catahoula or something similar. There was something for everyone, but they were definitely outlaws.

I spied them before Uncle Harry got stopped, and I managed to stand up and was leaning over the cab of the old truck. Harry slid to a stop, and as he stuck his .30 .30 Winchester out the driver's door window, I heard him let out a string of descriptive profanity pointed at the dogs who stood panting some forty feet away. My uncle Harry didn't know it, but I was there to help destroy the cow molesters, and before he pulled the trigger on his Winchester, I discharged both loads of double O buckshot from the shotgun I had acquired in the corner of the bunkhouse dining room. Ka Boom! Ka Boom! The double blast from the piece I had aimed at the dogs almost knocked me out of the truck backwards. But both my shots missed. Not one ball of double O buckshot hit a dog, and they were all running like greyhounds when Uncle Henry fired his Winchester.

Uncle Harry threw the pickup door open and looked up at me where I stood in the pickup bed, and I cannot describe the flow of curse words that came out of his mouth. After cursing me for quite a spell, he began walking in a circle stomping the ground and shaking his head. Finally he took the Winchester, and with both fists wrapped around the front sites out on the end of the barrel, he threw the rifle like a Frisbee, sending it fifty yards out into the middle of the hayfield. Without further adieu he got back in the Chevy truck and drove back to the ranch. When he parked the truck, he marched off to his house which was a hundred yards distance from the bunkhouse where I was staying. The next morning when I turned my plate over at the breakfast table, I found a Greyhound bus ticket to Wickenburg, Arizona, hiding underneath it. I never saw Uncle Harry again. I was deposited by the cook at the Greyhound bus station in Yerington, Nevada, and as the bus rolled down across the desert expanses of Nevada, I stared out the window and wondered where I belonged.

~~~

On Sunday, the day after the street dance, we took it easy in the morning. The three of us in the bunkhouse, Dale,

Ray and I, cooked breakfast for ourselves. In the middle of the day, Pete and Mitzi showed up, and she cooked us all a lunch and then we rolled up our beds and gathered up enough plunder to last us until Friday. We loaded our stuff, which included a kitchen outfit and groceries, into Pete's pickup and prepared to move our camp to Badger Flat where we would work for five days. Ray rode out into the horse pasture and wrangled the remuda and brought it into the corral, and a horse was caught for me to ride and help trail the remuda west to Badger Flat. We left behind a gentle horse and mule for Luis, plus a couple of horses that were lame, and then Ray and I set out with the horses with Ray in the lead and headed east. I felt good. Pete had been treating me like I was a sure-enough good hand, Dale was his usual friendly self, and Ray had raised himself up and out of the pit of depression and vitriol he had sunken into for a spell. Ben showed up soon after lunch, and he and Dale were accompanying Pete driving and hauling our camp stuff in Pete's pickup.

Ray and I drove the remuda into a barb wire corral at Badger Flat at four thirty in the afternoon. When the horses had all watered out, we made our temporary rope corral, as was the custom, and Pete roped the horses that we were all wanting to ride the next morning. I called for Toddy, whom I had not ridden in a week. The incident between Toddy and Ray had not been mentioned by anyone since it had happened.

When the horses had been caught and fed, we retired to the little camp house at Badger Flat and Pete and Dale got busy cooking supper. They made simple cowboy groceries, which was what we were accustomed to: fried steak, biscuits and gravy. But it was good. After supper I washed the dishes while Ray and Ben retired to a shade tree outside and told stories with Dale and Pete.

Early in the morning it was the same, Dale and Pete cooked and I did the dishes. Ben got an old broom and swept the floor, and Ray reminded me to be fast with the dishwashing so I wouldn't be holding up the day's work.

We caught horses when it was about half light and getting brighter by the minute in the eastern sky. I stepped on Toddy and was prepared to go for a bronc ride, but he surprised me and everyone else and took off in a trot following Pete northward toward the morning's drive. After we had trotted about a quarter mile, Dale said quite loudly, "Boy, ole Toddy acted quite a bit gentler this morning than the last time I saw someone get on him!"

"Yeah, it's the result of the soft hands I'm getting from doing lots of dishes!" I remarked. I looked at Dale and he grinned, but nothing more was said.

We went north for several miles riding in a country of draws and ridges with lots of black malpai rock and thick cedar trees. Pete dropped Dale off first and explained that we were making a drive into a dirt tank several miles to the east. Dale would have to make it into the tank first to hold the cattle up and keep them from going on to somewhere else. But Pete said the rest of us would have to flank hard to the man on our left because cattle running in this piece of country always wanted to run on east and into the country we would work the next day. He called it a flanking drive and stressed the importance of keeping track of each other as much as possible. He also said that there were a half dozen grown steers that had gotten away on several roundups, and he sure wanted to get them so we needed to be on our toes as much as possible.

After going over a ridge and trotting about a third of a mile, Pete dropped Ben off and pointed him down a draw but emphasized the need to throw any cattle he got to Dale if possible and then flank toward me when he could. "Throw your cattle toward the south," he said as we rode off and over another ridge bearing northeast.

After going another half mile or so, he dropped me

off and made the same speech to me, telling me to throw any cattle I found toward Ben or in a general southerly direction and, when possible, to flank toward Ray, who would be to my left, and try and relieve him of any cattle he could give me. He mentioned to me that the draw I was in when he dropped me off would run into the same draw Ben was in, a mile or so to the south.

Things went smoothly for a while, and I found several head of cattle and was able to find Ben and hand them over to him. And then I flanked to my left, or the northeast, and ran into Ray and took some cattle that he had gathered, which in turn allowed him to flank on to his left to assist Pete. And so it went for about an hour, and we repeated this process several times and everything seemed to be going correctly.

I had thrown Ben a half dozen head of cattle and connected with him for about the third time and was headed back over a malpai ridge toward where I thought Ray should be when I jumped about a dozen head of cattle that took to running and continuing at a high trot and lope. The place where I found them was on top of a ridge and covered with very thick cedar trees. Almost immediately I got hung up in a thicket that slowed me down to a slow trot and even a walk. I could see the cattle moving out in front of me and gaining ground, going northeast, which was the wrong direction. I whipped and spurred and was having a hard time keeping up. Toddy and I crashed into a low hanging cedar limb, and my hat got knocked off my head, and I had to stop and get off and get it. I got back on and whipped Toddy through the thicket, a great deal of the time with my head down low against the saddle horn and crashing through the cedar trees. As I moved along, trying to keep up with the running cattle, I could see lots of green manure splattered on the ground amidst deep cow tracks.

Finally we broke out into a clear spot, and I got a good look at the cattle that I had been following for about a quarter mile. There were seven cows and at least five sucking calves and five big steers weighing about a thousand pounds. I figured the steers to be some that Pete had mentioned, saying he hoped we could gather them. I had my bearings and knew that me and the cattle were going east by northeast when we needed to be bearing south/southeast, or straight south, I wasn't sure. I whipped Toddy into a run and tried to turn the cattle to my right, or south, but they only picked up steam and at a great rate of speed crashed headlong into a new thicket. I was hoping that I would run into Ray, and he would help me get them turned, but we raced on in the wrong direction.

After a quarter mile we came to another spot that was open for several hundred yards, and I found that I had picked up another cow and calf, plus another thousand pound steer. The country had become slightly higher in elevation and flatter, but also rockier and thicker with trees. As I loped across my newfound clearing in an attempt to keep abreast of the running cattle, I noticed horse tracks going at a right angle and off to my right, to the south, and I figured they were Ray's, which meant that he had already gone by this spot; and me and the wild bunch were traveling farther out of the drive and in the wrong direction. I had managed to bend the cattle slightly to the south but not enough to put them into the flow of things. So now I needed to make a decision, should I continue on trying to gather this bunch that was going astray or should I drop them and return to my place between Ray and Ben and try and connect with the drive that was now out of sync because of me following this wild bunch going cross-grained to the battle plan. Pete had purposely mentioned the importance of gathering the wild steers, six of which I had been following. But he had also mentioned the importance of staying in formation and connecting as much as possible with the men on both sides. I wasn't sure what to do. I figured I was damned if I did and damned if I didn't. I decided to stay with the cattle, hoping that a fence or canyon or something would finally stop or turn them. Maybe I would get lucky and be spotted by Pete or Ray. I rode on trying to turn the cattle south.

I finally came out into a draw that was going southeast, and the wild bunch had become winded and, therefore, more manageable. I thought I could probably turn them to the right and down the draw, and then I looked up and saw a half dozen more straight ahead about a quarter mile. Should I let my cattle go on and try and gather them, too, or should I force the wild bunch down the draw. I wasn't sure. The cattle wanted to go on toward the cattle in the distance, so I let them and then those cattle saw me and started running. It was going from bad to worse! I told myself that I was ruining the whole day's work. I realized that perhaps I was now in the next day's drive and was probably really messing things up.

I whipped Toddy into a run for another time in an attempt to get around and handle the newest addition to my little herd, and I raced over a ridge and soon entered yet another shallow canyon, but there, running parallel to it on its eastern edge, was a barb wire fence. I got there in time to keep the leaders of all the cattle I now had from turning left, or to the north. I momentarily got the leaders stopped, and the drags from the bunch I had been following caught up. I now had a dozen cows seven or eight sucking calves, a branded herd bull, eight big steers, and a long yearling bull that was not branded. I wasn't lost, but I had no idea where I was. The dirt tank and corral where we were supposed to have driven into and congregated at was somewhere off to the southwest, but I really had no idea where or how far. I figured five or six miles. I also figured I was probably several miles further east of where I was supposed to be. But I had eight big wild steers and a maverick bull held up. Had I done right? I didn't know.

The cattle weren't going to stay put so I let them go to the southeast along the fence line that I had now found myself on. I did not know where it would lead me, but I didn't think I could control the cattle if I tried to turn them

Shutting the gate with Toddy.

off of it and head them to the southwest, which was the direction I thought we should go. We drifted down the fence, and after what I figured was two miles, we came to a wire corral that was connected to the fence and was no doubt something that had been built to brand calves in. There was a dry dirt tank a short distance away.

I raced around the herd and got in front of them and opened the wire gate leading into the corral, but while I did that, some of the cattle pulled out going west while the others stayed on the fence. I ran Toddy around the westbound cattle and turned them back toward the fence and then some of the others turned and headed north, or the direction we had come from.

For ten minutes I ran Toddy one direction and then the other trying to keep the cattle bunched. I felt like a gunsel who could accomplish nothing. My horse was sweating profusely because the sun was now high in the morning sky, and it was hot. The cattle refused to cooperate. When I was about to give up and say to heck with it, the old herd bull walked through the gate I had opened and into the wire corral, and then as if by magic, all the rest followed him. I was almost in tears, and I had said more than one cuss word as I raced about trying to keep the cattle bunched.

I rode up and dismounted and shut the wire gate. Toddy's sides were heaving, and sweat was running off of him just like I had turned a garden hose on him. I uncinched my saddle and pulled it off of Toddy's back and threw it on its side on the ground. There was no need to hobble the horse because he was not wanting to escape, but only stand there and pant. I sat down on the ground with my back leaned up against the saddle and contemplated my predicament. I was obviously in the wrong spot. I wasn't sure I had done the right thing. I figured there was at least a 50-50 chance I had done the wrong thing. What should

I do now? Thoughts raced through my head as I sat there. Should I leave the cattle here in the corral or should I try and drive them somewhere else? Would I get a royal butt chewing for ruining everyone's life because of my stupidity and inability to make a hand?

It took at least fifteen minutes for Toddy to cool off, so I sat there and for a few moments I shut my eyes and weighed my options. Finally I rose and threw my saddle on the dun horse and cinched him up. Since I didn't know where I was or what direction I was supposed to go, I decided to leave the cattle trapped in the wire corral. I hoped that the fact I had some big steers and a long-eared bull penned might excuse some of the gross sin I had committed. I stepped on Toddy and pointed him west and rode in a trot hoping to find a cow trail with some tracks of a horse that would lead me to where the crew was. We traveled for several miles and over a couple ridges and then down and across several draws. I started running into some sign, and I kept going until I found a shod horse track going down the bottom of a draw that was running to the southwest. I kicked Toddy into a lope and rode what I thought was a couple more miles, and the trail I was on went up and over a ridge to my right. The country I was now in had opened up and was not so thick with cedars. When I topped that ridge, I looked down and in the bottom of the next draw and a mile to the southwest was the crew. I could see a large water lot and branding pen and what appeared to be a very large dirt tank. It was obvious that the herd had already been put into the branding corral, and the men were busy branding calves.

I rode up close to the corral and dismounted and hobbled my horse. I then opened the wire gate going into the corral and approached the crew. Dale and Ray were roping while Ben and Pete were doing all the groundwork. "What happened, Peckerwood, you dumb ass? You get lost?" Ray shouted from on top of his horse. Pete looked at me and said nothing for a minute while Dale and Ray got another calf headed and heeled. I went right to the calf and helped Ben tail him down. We put Dale's rope on the calf's front legs. Pete was running the knife and Ben was branding so I found a vaccine gun and gave the calf a shot of Blackleg.

"So what happened, Tommy? You get confused?" Pete said as the two men roped another calf.

"No. I knew I was going wrong, but I jumped a bunch of cattle in a thicket, and they ran the wrong way, to the east. I couldn't turn them and then I ran into some more. Things sorta went from bad to worse. But I knew I had some big steers in them so I stayed with them. Then I crossed horse tracks going south, and I knew I was messed up, but I didn't want to drop the big steers. So I kept going, trying to keep them bunched, and then I ran into some more. Finally I ran into a fence way over there, and I got 'em all stopped for a minute and I turned 'em south. And then after a long time, I came to a corral on the fence. There is a dirt tank nearby that's dry. And finally I got them locked up in the corral. There's twenty or more cattle in the bunch including eight big steers and a big yearling bull that weighs about eight hundred, and he's unbranded. I decided I couldn't do anything better than leave them there since I was lost anyway. And then I rode 'til I found you guys here."

"You've got eight big steers penned?"

"Yes sir, I'd say they weigh about a thousand pounds. They are over that way maybe four or five miles." I pointed toward the corral where I had left the cattle penned.

"Good job, kid! Good job!" Pete said as Ray came loping toward us with a big calf jumping out on the end of his rope. Dale heeled the calf and I went to help Ben get him down on his side.

"Where the hell was you this morning when the rest of us was working our butts off trying to gather all these cattle?" Ray looked at me with disgust.

"Shut up, Ray! He's got eight big steers and a maverick bull penned over there at East Gate, so that's what he's been doin'!"

Chapter Eight

We worked at Badger Flat for four days gathering a piece of country every day, branding the calves, and weaning a few yearlings that had been left on a cow the fall before. The country in that part of the ranch was not as rough as the bottom of Cow Creek or the canyons and ridges at Black Creek, where Ben and Sharon lived, and because of that our drives were bigger, and we could gather more cattle each day. Because of the drought conditions there was also less water, and so the cattle were bunched up more than some years; and according to what Pete said, we were missing very few cattle on drive, which meant, bottom line, we were doing a good job. Pete was in a good mood, and after four days we had branded about three hundred calves and gathered 120 yearlings that could be put with all the others we had been accumulating all spring. We also gathered a total of fifteen big steers, which included the ones I had gathered that first morning we were camped there, plus a half dozen unbranded yearlings.

On Friday morning, the fifth day we were there at Badger Flat, we gathered those yearlings and big steers, along with a few old cows and bulls that needed to be sold, and trailed that herd west to a holding pasture near the headquarters. That took up most of the morning, and when we had shut the holding pasture gate, we struck a trot and headed back to Badger Flat. We ate a quick lunch, rolled up our camp, loaded it into Pete's ranch pickup and set about moving back to headquarters.

Pete was in a good mood and after four days we had branded about three hundred calves and gathered 120 yearlings that could be put with all the others we had been accumulating all spring

To my surprise Pete told me to ride with him and Dale in the truck and gave Ray and Ben orders to trail the horse herd back to headquarters. I didn't know it, but Dale had been talking to Pete, telling him of my prospective romance with Bevin and how I was trying to figure out a way of getting her out to the ranch the next day to witness the bronc riding and be a part of the day's events. So Dale had worked out the details with Pete to give the two of us the afternoon off so we could go into Seligman. Dale suggested we take both of our pickups into town. I could offer to leave mine with Bevin so she could drive it out to the ranch the next day, and then I could ride back out to the ranch with Dale after, that is, he had a visit with Wanda.

Wanda was going to come out and help Mitzi prepare for the big barbecue, and Dale needed to give her some last-minute instructions concerning that situation. So as Pete, Dale and I drove along in the pickup toward the ranch, I learned all of this and jumped at the chance to go and see Bevin and work out the details. I had left her on Saturday night saying I would phone her with some kind of plan, but I had failed to phone her because there was no phone at Badger Flat, so Dale really saved my bacon, so to speak.

When we got to the headquarters Dale and I got cleaned up and ready to go to town, and while we were doing that he gave me a rundown about the next day's events, most of which I knew, but Dale said that Pete had invited the Doubled O crew to come over and help gather a big piece of country and help us brand and work the cattle. Ole Don Kambitch was also coming and bringing a cowboy with him so there was going to be at least six extra cowboys, and possibly seven. Because of the extra men, Pete was going to gather and work a bigger piece of country than usual, meaning the equivalent of two or three days work would get done. After we got all the branding done and the yearlings turned out into a holding pasture, we would have the showdown between me and the outlaw horses that Don Kambitch and the Double O crew were bringing. Pete wanted to do all that before we ate lunch, thinking I would ride better on an empty stomach. I was happy with that idea. After the bronc riding a big party was going to take place.

Mitzi and Wanda had been working on getting food prepared for a day or two. Word had been sent to the wives of the Double O crew to come and bring food, and Mitzi had driven down to Black Creek to ask Sharon if she would be willing to help. There would undoubtedly be plenty of beer and whiskey to drink. Dale said that word had gotten around, and there was no telling who might show up. When folks heard there was free food somewhere, he figured they would come running.

Dale was going to drive into Seligman and help Wanda with some food preparation, and Pete had given him enough money to buy several cases of beer. I was going in to see if I could find Bevin and leave her my truck so she could drive out in the morning, that is, if I could talk her into it. I really wasn't sure if she could or would, but I was anxious to find out. Dale and I left at about the same time, he in his nice Chevy truck and me in Old Dirty. We had agreed to meet at the Black Cat at nine o'clock to ride back together in his truck. It was four in the afternoon when we left the ranch and started into town forty miles away.

It was about five when I reached town, and I drove straight down to the Conoco station. The man with the dirty shirt, whom I had seen six days earlier, was working, and I asked of Bevin's whereabouts. He claimed he knew nothing and was not going to budge on that lack of information, so I turned around and drove back downtown and turned on First Street, and after a couple blocks I stopped in front of Bevin's house. I walked into the yard gate and then up to the front door and knocked. The door opened and there stood her father. "Hello, Tommy, how are you today?"

"Doing well, sir, how about you?"

"I bet you're here to see Bevin?" I nodded. "Well, come on inside." I stepped into the house. The first thing I noticed was that it was clean and didn't smell like cigarettes, but, instead, it smelled like cinnamon and apples. He led me from the living room through a large doorway into the kitchen. Bevin and her mother were cooking dinner. Bevin looked at me and smiled.

"Hi! I wondered if you would come! This is my mom, Katie. Mom this is Tommy."

Katie wiped her right hand on the apron she wore and held it out so I could shake it. I managed to remember to take my cowboy hat off. She smiled, almost laughing. "Tommy, nice to meet you! You're all I've heard about for the last four or five days." She looked at Bevin and grinned.

"Oh, Mom, really! Don't be a liar." Bevin was blushing!

"Oh, Tommy this, Tommy that, Tommy can really dance! Tommy bought me a hamburger and milk shake. Tommy killed seventeen dragons with his bare hands while he walked me home." Katie turned and looked at me and laughed. "So nice to meet you, Tommy Dragonslayer. I'm glad you've come, and it's nice to see that you're actually human!"

"You better sit down, Tommy, or you'll faint from all this nonsense," her dad said. "How about something to drink, some coffee or iced tea?"

Bevin came toward the chair where I had sat down. Like her mother she had on an apron that covered her white blouse. She was wearing Levis and sandals, and her copper-colored hair was pulled back on both sides. "Let me get you something to drink. We have coffee, tea, water, and we might have a soda. What will it be?"

"Coffee." It sounded more grown up than the other choices.

"You are just in time! We've almost got dinner ready and you can stay and eat with us." Bevin looked at me questioningly, "Right?"

"Yeah... sure!"

She went back to the cookstove where a pot of coffee was resting on a burner that was turned down low, and she poured some into a cup and returned to the dining room table where her father and I sat. The table set in one end of a large room that served as dining room on one end and kitchen on the other, so we were all where we could see each other and visit. Bevin and her mom put the finishing touches on the evening meal, and her father and I sat drinking coffee. Her mom and dad asked me questions about the ranch and what exactly it was that I did on the ranch. They asked about my family. I noticed that they treated Bevin like she was an adult, and she treated them like they were her friends. They were happy and comfortable with each other.

Bevin set plates and silverware around the table, and she and her mother started bringing the food. I noticed that she only set the table for four people, and I inquired about her sister whom I had met at the dance. She explained that her sister was staying at a friend's house for the night.

Finally everything was on the table, and we were obviously ready to eat. Bevin's father sat at the end of the table to my right and her mother sat on the other end to my left, and Bevin was across from me on the other side of the table. When everyone was sitting down, Bevin's father said, "Let's return thanks." When he was saying that, the three of them stretched out their arms and hands toward the person on either side and held hands. Her father and mother reached out on both sides and offered to take my hands, one on the left and one on the right. I took Bevin's father's hand in my right and Katie's hand in my left. They bowed their heads and her father began to pray. I sat there with my head bowed and thought to myself, I came to town to see this girl that I've got the hots for, and I'm sitting at a table holding her mother's hand! This is a little different!

The food was outstanding, spaghetti with meatballs, homemade bread, and a salad. I hadn't eaten a salad in a month of Sundays. And apple pie for dessert. They ate slowly and visited with each other, and I tried to act intelligent and join in the conversation. They were happy people! That made the biggest impression on me, the fact that they were happy.

When we were finally finished eating, Bevin and Katie started clearing the table, and I jumped up and offered to help with the dishes. Before Bevin could say anything, Katie said that would be a good idea, and she and Bevin's father went outside to the front porch and sat down and left Bevin and me to ourselves to do all the work cleaning up the kitchen.

We did the dishes and made small talk. I washed and she dried. She poked me with a fork and I stabbed her with a butter knife, and she laughed. I loved to hear her laugh. She had the most beautiful smile, and those eyebrows above those emerald eyes were made in heaven; I was convinced they were. It was then while we washed the dishes, that I realized it was as if she was the first girl I had ever seen, and I didn't care to see another. "Can you come out to the ranch tomorrow?"

"Yes! I thought you had forgotten, or you weren't going to ask me. Thought maybe you had found someone to replace me down at the Black Cat Saloon or at the Red Ram." She poked me again, this time with a spoon.

"If I had replaced you, I wouldn't be here washing the dishes and letting you poke me."

"That's a fact, you wouldn't be. But I don't know how I'm going to get there. I don't have a car and my folks are busy tomorrow, so we have a problem!"

"Well now, let me tell you, I am a seventeen- almost eighteen-year-old genius! I've got it all figured out! I'm going to leave you Old Dirty, my Ford pickup, and you can drive yourself out there. I'm supposed to meet Dale at nine o'clock, and I'm going to ride back out to the ranch with him. And then tomorrow night I'll bring you back into town. How's that?"

"Okay! Great! What time should I be there? And how long will it take me to get there?"

"It will take you about an hour because it's almost all dirt road and about forty miles. But the county keeps it graded, and you won't have any trouble. Your folks are alright with you coming out there? I mean, I'm not talking you into something that will get you into trouble, am I?"

She laughed at that question and answered, "My parents trust me to make my own decisions, and I believe in the principles they taught me growing up, so there's no problem. At least I don't think so. Is there a problem? Would you lead me into something bad?" She smiled at me and raised her eyebrows.

"No, I would never hurt you."

She kissed me on the cheek, and I was scared to death her dad would see us and throw me out of their house. She sensed the tension and laughed, "You scared?" I lied to her and said that I wasn't.

It was almost eight, and I was wondering what we would do for another hour when her father unexpectedly walked into the kitchen and asked if I played dominoes.

"You mean 42," I asked?

"Yeah. You know about 42?"

"Yes, sir, I do."

"How about it, Bevin? Your mom and I will challenge you and Tommy to a game or two of 42. What do you say?"

Absolutely! It will give me a chance to check out this bronco buster's IQ, see if he's smart enough to keep up with me playing dominoes. He can barely keep up with me dancing!" She laughed.

"It was the shoes you wore. They mesmerized me!" Katie walked in, and she and everyone else roared with laughter at my answer.

"That's why I wore them, to mesmerize you. Now I'm going to mesmerize you with my skills as a domino player. After all, we are from Texas, and everyone in Texas plays dominoes, especially Irish Texans!"

Her dad admonished her in a joking way and said Texans were sure-enough domino players, but the Irish weren't famous for anything but drinking and playing the fiddle. Again we all laughed.

We sat down at the dinner table with Bevin sitting across the table and her mother on my left and her father on my right. Bevin and I were partners and we annihilated them. We played eight games, and we won six of them. We kept getting the best hands, and we laughed and laughed. It was one of the most enjoyable hours I could remember.

At a quarter to nine, I announced that it was time for me to leave because I was supposed to meet Dale promptly at the top of the hour. I got up to go, and Bevin started walking to the door with me. Suddenly her father spoke, "I want to thank you, Tommy, for walking Bevin home from the dance last weekend. I understand there was a little trouble, and I'm grateful that you did what you did."

"Oh, well, I didn't do much actually, but thanks for saying something."

"Well, you probably did more than you think! Those are very selfish misguided young men, and because of that, they are dangerous. It was good you were there."

"Yes, sir!" I replied, but I thought to myself that selfish and misguided weren't the words I would use to describe them. They were the same as drunken thieves and thugs who knew darn good and well what they were doing. They were trying to get their hands on my redheaded girlfriend. But I kept those thoughts to myself.

Bevin and I walked outside and stood by the driver's door of Old Dirty. I told her in detail how to get out to the ranch. I told her that I would return in a few minutes and leave my pickup in front of her house with the keys in the ignition and ready for her to use in the morning. I put my hands around her slim waist, and she came closer. I kissed her and she kissed me like she meant it. "See you tomorrow."

"See you tomorrow." She turned and walked back to her house, and me an ole Dirty took off for the Black Cat Saloon.

When I got to the parking lot, Dale and Wanda were waiting for me and sitting in the cab of Dale's Chevy pickup. "Change of plans, Tommy! Wanda's pickup is broke down so I need to leave her mine, and we will have to go back to the ranch in yours!"

"But what about Bevin," I asked?

"Your little sweetheart can ride out to the ranch with me, honey. I'll get her there in one piece, I promise. Ha! Ha!" Everything was funny to Wanda.

"Well, follow me back over there so I can tell her what's going on before they all go to bed." I fired Dirty up and headed back to Bevin's house without waiting for them to answer. As I took off down the street, I could see in my rearview mirror that they were following. I drove up to the house and jumped out and ran to the door and knocked. With great relief I sighed when Bevin opened the door; I didn't want to have to explain everything to her folks.

"Tommy, what's going on? You all right?" She stepped out onto the porch. When she saw I was not limping or something, she said, "Couldn't live without me?"

Right then Dale and Wanda pulled up. "Dale's girlfriend's truck is broke down, so Dale needs to leave his truck in town for her to drive to the ranch tomorrow. Dale and I have to take mine back to the ranch tonight. You can ride out with Wanda in the morning and then I'll bring you home tomorrow night. Is that all right?" I was thinking, "Please say it's all right."

"Okay, sure, I guess."

"Come on, I will introduce you to Wanda." We walked down the steps of the porch and over to Dale's truck. When we got to the driver's door, I saw that Wanda was driving. "Wanda, this is Bevin."

"Hi, honey, how are you? I've heard so much about you!

You are all this little-movie-star boyfriend of yours talks about! Ha ha ha ha ha! Truth is, honey, this wore out old fart of a boyfriend I've got talks about you, too! Ha ha ha ha ha! I will say that you are just as pretty as I heard you was!"

"Well, thanks, I didn't know people were talking about me."

"Ha Ha ha ha ha! You ain't foolin' me none, honey. Any girl as pretty as you knows that boys are talking about you! Ha ha ha ha!" She slapped Dale on the leg when she said that and then laughed at her own intelligence.

I saw Bevin raising her eyebrows. I thought, Oh, please don't back out on me. I wished that Wanda would shut up.

Dale was obviously drunk, but he tried hard to rise to the occasion and put Bevin at ease. "Wanda will take care of you, Bevin, I promise, and you would be doing me a favor if you would keep her company as she drives out to the ranch. I would really appreciate it."

Wanda affirmed what Dale had already said, "Sure, I will! You bet I'll take good care of you, sweetheart! Any friend of Tommy's is a friend of mine!"

"What time are you leaving?" Bevin inquired.

"I'll come by and get you at seven o'clock on the dot! How's that?"

Bevin looked at me with her head tilted slightly and a questioning expression. I nodded reassuringly. "Okay, I'll be ready at seven." I took her hand and pulled her toward the house, and looking back over my shoulder, I told Dale, "We better get going."

Bevin and I walked to the house and I wasn't sure what to say. I was afraid she was going to say she wasn't going to come, but instead she said, "Well, if she isn't a little soberer in the morning, I'm going to do the driving. She is a doozy! Ha ha ha ha!" she said, mimicking Wanda's laugh. I squeezed her hand and grinned at her but walked away before she could change her mind."

I got Dale transferred from his pickup to Old Dirty, and we took off toward Cow Creek with me behind the wheel. Dale was in a jovial mood, the alcohol in his bloodstream being at that perfect place, trapped somewhere between tipsy and falling down, and leaving its host in a state of whimsical bliss.

Deep within my heart
Lies a melody
A song of old San Antonio

As I drove, Dale crooned and sang numerous Bob Wills and Merle Haggard tunes. He had a quart of Wild Turkey, which I figured was pretty high-classed whiskey, but I made him keep it corked until we turned off of Route 66 and onto the Cow Creek road. When we were driving on dirt, he took the top off and began to celebrate in earnest. "Tommy, I want you to have a drink with your old friend, Dale!" He handed me the Wild Turkey. I turned the bottle up but didn't swallow much. "Listen, kid, you're one of my favoriteist people on this whole planet! You are without a doubt the best young hand I've been around in a long time! No! That ain't right, I should have said—ever! I want you to know that, you hear?" He handed me the bottle, and I turned it up and faked a big swallow.

The warden led a prisoner down the hallway to his doom
I stood up to say goodbye like all the rest
And I heard him tell the warden just before he reached my cell
Let my guitar playin' friend do my request

Sing me back home with a song I like to hear
Make my old memories come alive
Take me away and turn back the years
Sing me back home before I die

I drove on and was amazed at how good he sang. He was drunk, and his talking voice was on the verge of being slurred, but the singing was crisp and on perfect pitch.

"Tommy, listen to me, kid, I'm gonna tell you something! This little cow deal we're going to do here in a couple weeks ain't none a'your affair! You understand?" He handed me the bottle, and I faked another big swallow thinking to myself that if I drank as much as he wanted I wouldn't get out of bed in the morning let alone ride some bucking horses! "What I mean is, you ain't plannin' this little illegal cow roundup that's gonna take place, you're just doin' what you're told, you hear me, son?" He looked at me. I looked back and nodded. He went on, "A kid like you just follows orders, and that's what you're doing, just following orders. Take it from an old son that's been to Nevada and back, as well as to Korea and a few other hellholes, it ain't gonna hurt nothing to take advantage of a little good luck that comes your way, and that's what this safe crackin' job we're going to do is, a little good luck! Are you listening? It ain't your idea, so just take your share of the money and tell yourself you was just following orders from older men!"

> *I got a mansion just over the hilltop*
> *In that bright land where we'll never grow old*
> *And someday yonder we will never more wander*
> *But walk on streets that are purest gold*

"My wife used to sing that." There was a long pause, "And then she ran off with her best friend's husband. Took my kids, too."

> *I'm satisfied with just a cottage below*

"Ha! Tommy, I ain't satisfied with no cottage. I don't care what that old song says, I'm gonna get what I got comin'!" He handed me the Wild Turkey as we drove past the big windmill at Markham Well. "Tommy, you are a darn good driver and a better friend!" He was starting to weave in his seat. "Listen to me, kid, you stay away from that Ray. I mean don't get into no agreements or deals with him. And watch him! You'll be alright cause you're smart, and that big meathead is as dumb as a cedar fence post. I'm just telling you to keep him out where you can watch him. You understand, son?" He looked at me and for the first time he demanded an answer.

"Yes, sir, I'll watch him. Actually, I already am. I mean, I think he's a fine guy, but I don't want to be best friends with him or anything."

"You've got the idea right! Just watch him. The worst part about our old friend Ray is, he ain't very damned smart, and he'd dissect his own grandmother for a few laughs and a free rib steak!"

In an Arizona town one day
Billy Venero heard them say
That a band of Apache Indians
Were on the trail that way

Heard them tell of murder done
Three men killed at Rocky Run
They're in danger at the cow ranch
Said Venero under his breath

Nearly forty miles away
Was a little place that lay
In a deep and shady valley
In the mighty wilderness

Half a score of homes were there
And in one a maiden fair

Held the heart of Bill Venero
Bill Venero's little Bess

So no wonder he grew pale
When he heard the cowboy's tale
Of the men that he'd seen murdered
There at Rocky Run

"Sure as there's a God above
I will save the girl I love
By that love I hold for Bessie
I will see that somethin's done!"

Not one minute he delayed
When this brave resolve he'd made
"But man," his comrades told him
When they hears his daring plan

"You are riding straight to death!"
But he answered, "Save your breath,
I may never reach the cow ranch
But I'll do the best I can."

As he crossed the alkali
All his thoughts flew on ahead
To the little band at the cow ranch
Thinking not a danger near

With his quirt's unceasing whirl
And the jingle of his spurs
Little Chapo bore the cowboy
O'er the far away frontier

Sharp and dear a rifle shot
Woke the echoes of the spot

"I am wounded," cried Venero
As he swayed from side to side

"While there is life there is always hope
Slowly onward I will lope
If I fail to reach the cow ranch
Bessie Lee will know I tried."

There at dusk a horse of brown
Wet with sweat came panting down
The little lane at the cow ranch
Stopped in front of Bessie's door.

But the cowboy was asleep
And his slumber was so deep
Little Bess could never wake him
Though she tried forevermore.

You have heard this story told
By the young and by the old
How the Indians killed Venero
On his way to Rocky Run.

Many years have passed away
And the maiden's hair is gray
But she still places roses
On Bill Venero's grave

He sang the Marty Robbins' ballad plumb to the end. It reminded me of my dad because he used to sing it. Dale fell silent, and as the gate going into the headquarters showed in the headlights, I became sentimental. I hadn't thought about my dad in three or four weeks.

"That's a damn fine woman you've got, Tommy!" Dale woke me out of my memories as I pulled Old Dirty up in front of the bunkhouse and shut the engine off. "She ain't the kind that will run off with another man! She'll stick with you, kid! I can tell!" He handed me the bottle of Wild Turkey. "Thanks for being my friend, kid! Let's have one more drink!" I turned the bottle up and this time I took some. I handed the bottle back to him. "Here's to that redhead of yours!" When he was done with the drink and the toast, the Wild Turkey was gone.

Chapter Nine

Pete was originally from Texas where, according to legend, he had killed a man in a barroom fistfight. For that misdeed he had been encouraged to leave and never come back. It had been determined that it was done in self-defense, mainly because several of his brothers were present, and they testified on his behalf. He was never arrested, but his survival in those parts was a condition impossible to maintain.

As a young man with extraordinary cowboy skills and a very large chip on his shoulder, Pete drifted west. He landed a job on the big Babbitt Ranch north of Flagstaff working for Frank Banks, the wagon boss. There he was very well liked. He could ride a bucking horse and Babbitts had lots of them. He liked to drink whiskey and didn't mind working very hard while doing it, traits that suited Frank; and he got on very well for a time. But then, almost simultaneously, he pulled two stunts that destroyed his relationship with the outfit. He tried to walk out of a local grocery store with a carton of Camel cigarettes hidden inside his denim shirt and was caught red-handed. At the same time he and another Babbitt cowboy were caught trying to steal a band of wild Indian horses that were always plentiful on the Babbitt Ranch winter range along the Little Colorado River. Babbitts and Frank Banks were perpetually annoyed at the presence of the horses but did not want men on the ranch payroll stealing them. Frank Banks had to let Pete go, and he was 86ed off of the outfit for eternity.

Pete eventually moved to Southern California and worked for several large cow outfits around Bakersfield, Coalinga, and Visalia. He made a big name for himself there in the ten years he lived in that area. He was a horseman, a roper, and stood out in a crowd. He also made a few lifelong connections with men who would trade in stolen goods. There were stories told about him that involved bloodshed, not only from hard knuckles, but from knives and guns as well. He had lots of personality and could talk to anyone on any social level. He knew when to be quiet, and he knew how to apply pressure with his words.

On the surface Pete seemed to be fearless, but at the same time, he was feared. He was an enigma. He did things his way and was a master at making his way work. One of the first things I noticed about his way of doing things that was different was the way we usually branded calves on the Cow Creek outfit. We always roped the calves by the head and heels, California style. Every other outfit in Northern Arizona that I had ever heard stories about branded calves in the spring with a man heeling the calves and dragging them by the heels to the fire where two men would flank them (get them down on their side) and after the rope was removed would hold the calf while someone else did the branding, castrating, etc. Up until the morning of the big barbeque and bronc riding, every calf we branded had been roped around the neck and then heeled.

∼

At 3:30 Saturday morning, Pete and Mitzi were in the kitchen rattling pots and pans, making coffee and doing anything they could think of to make noise. I sat up in my bedroll and dressed, and then I washed my face and hands and went out to the horse corral to throw our horses some hay. The morning was warm with a slight wind blowing out of the west. Officially it was the first day of summer and the longest day of the year. Even in the wee hours of the morning, I could tell it was going to be hot by midday.

When I got back to the bunkhouse, Ray and Dale were getting up, and Ben, who had gone to Black Creek the night before, was driving up and parking his ranch pickup in front of the bunkhouse. We all congregated in the kitchen and consumed cups of coffee, and everyone but me smoked cigarettes.

"Did Wanda say what time she would be out, Dale?" Mitzi asked.

"She ought to be here about eight o'clock, and she's bringing Tommy's girlfriend, Bevin, with her."

"Can your girl cook, Tommy?" Mitzi asked, looking at me with real interest.

"Yeah, she can. I ate some of her cooking last night as a matter of fact. I'd say she comes from a family of cookers!" I replied.

"What else can she do, Peckerwood? Huh? Huh? Huh?" Ray said in a vulgar tone of voice.

"Oh shut up, Ray! Nobody's talkin' to you!" Mitzi snapped at him and then looked at me and went on. "No, really, do you suppose she would be willing to help me get this food put together?"

"Sure, I bet she would! If you ask her, I'll bet money she would love to help you."

"Okay, good! Believe you me, I might need some help feeding this many people so I will definitely ask her."

Mitzi and Pete rustled up a quick breakfast, steak, biscuits, no gravy; and we could tell by Pete's actions and mood he wanted us to eat and get out to the horse corral to catch horses. He did not want Don Kambitch and the Double O crew to show up and find him and his crew still sitting in the house, and so by 4:45 we were walking to the corral. It was a good thing because off in the distance we saw headlights coming, and the sound of approaching trucks drifted across the morning air. Pete roped our horses without missing a loop, and we saddled them in snappy fashion and were ready to ride when Don Kambitch came pulling into the ranch in an old 1951 Ford bobtail truck with a stock rack on it and two horses loaded. The Double O crew pulled in several minutes later in a newer and bigger truck, and I could see at least six horses loaded on their truck.

For ten or fifteen minutes there was a considerable amount of confusion and rustling around as the men in both trucks got their horses and gear unloaded, and the two outlaw bucking horses were put in a corral and fed hay. Then everyone was introduced around. Pete, Ray, Dale and Ben all seemed to know the Double O crew, and they all shook hands, and I was introduced. I was told they were Ken, Leroy, Dallas, Charlie, and the boss's name was Howard. Howard King was a big man wearing khaki pants and a shirt of the same type that old-timers called Booger Reds. He wore glasses and smoked a pipe and resembled a banker or bookkeeper more than a cowboy. He shook my hand with great solemnity and exclaimed he was pleased to meet "the young bronc rider of such great acclaim!" The rest of the Double O crew remained quiet with the exception of saying hello or good morning to everyone.

Don Kambitch was another story. He walked up to everyone, all of whom were ready to mount up and ride away, and hollered a big, "Mornin' boys!" Behind him came a Mexican cowboy riding a gray horse. He was sitting in a Sonoran form-fitter saddle with a brass horn. The saddle horn had grooves worn in it from dallied rope spinning around it at a high rate of speed. Everything about his outfit was puro Mexicano, Sonoran to be specific.

Don introduced him as Vidal Garcia Pizarro. Vidal rode around shaking hands with everyone saying, "Buenos dias." He was a handsome man who bore himself with good posture and had a well-groomed appearance. He did not seem to me to be intimidated by any or all of us gringos. He packed at least seventy feet of new maguey rope on a string hung from the fork of his saddle. The bridle bit in the gray horse's mouth was a long, straight-shanked Mexican bit that was silver-mounted and had long split rawhide braided reins attached to it. Hung on the heels of his pointed-toed cowboy boots was a set of beautiful Chihuahua spurs mounted with silver. Vidal Garcia Pizarro had style and rode the gray horse while he sat as straight as an arrow in the saddle.

And then there was Don Kambitch who was the polar opposite to the impeccable Vidal. He stood about five foot six inches and had a twenty-nine inch waist on his Levis, but his measurement at the naval, three inches above the waistline of his pants, was no less than forty-eight inches. The top button on his Levis was undone, and a very wide set of suspenders held his pants up. His shirttail to the left side was hanging out but was tucked in on the right. His cowboy hat looked like he had slept in it. The bottom of his pant leg on the left side was sorta tucked into his boot top, but the right leg hung over the boot top and fell to his Chihuahua spur. He had spurs on but evidently had no intention of riding for he did not bring a saddled horse. The spit soaked remnants of a cigar protruded out of the left side of his mouth. "What in hell is going on, Pedro, you old scoundrel!? You gonna gather the whole damn country? I never seen so many cowpunchers?"

Pete answered, "Don Juan the Kambitch, don't be callin' me a scoundrel! You are the tightest old miser and cow thief in Mojave County, Arizona! Where's your horse, viejo?"

"I don't need no horse except the one that's going to throw your cowboy off! Where is he? I want to take a look at him! Or maybe you got scared and run him off! Ha, ha!" He started walking around and shaking everyone's hand acting like he was Santa Claus or at least a long lost friend. He came to me last, and Pete indicated that I was the aforementioned bronc stomper. "Yeah, well, I'll have to admit that you are a fine lookin' boy! Yes sir, I like you, and I ain't never met ya 'til now!" He shook my hand. "Have you written your poor old mother and told her goodbye?" He said it just right, and everyone began to laugh including me. There was no animosity in his voice.

Behind him came riding a Mexican Cowboy, riding a gray horse.

"Well, if you're not going to ride with us, we are all going to gather some cows. Go on over to the bunkhouse and Mitzi will feed you some coffee and maybe a biscuit." Pete told him.

"Yeah, go ahead. That's what I came up here for, to visit with the good lookin' women and take your money. Gambling pays a lot better than wearing out saddle leather!"

"For a man whose braggin' about being a rich gambler, you sure drive a wore out lookin' old truck!" Ray said and everyone started to laugh.

"Yeah! You don't worry about my truck! I might have an old truck, but I've got money in my pocket. My Mexican, Vidal, will represent me when you're roundin' up, and I'm expecting you to treat him right, so take off boys, the girls are waiting for me in yonder casa!"

With that salutation from Mr. Kambitch giving us the green light to take our leave, Pete whipped his horse down the hind leg and took off into the dawn in a lope. I was riding Cowboy, my favorite horse, and as we loped away, I rode off to the side and took in all the riders. Pete slowed down to a high trot and continued on toward the northeast, and we ate up the miles.

The Double O crew did not seem to be of any one particular style. One of them had a cheap factory roping saddle and tight shotgun chaps with zippers that closed the legs tight. That individual rode as if the continuous trotting was causing him pain, and I occasionally saw him press the palm of his hand to his gut and massage it as if it was hurting. Twice he stopped momentarily to catch his breath only to struggle harder to catch up. He was obviously in great misery from the pace. Another man rode in a saddle which was a flower-carved form fitter. He had a Will James looking hat with a very high crown and wide brim that was rolled up. He rode straight up and his high-heeled boots were resting in leather covered oxbow stirrups. I suspected that he was from Montana, but in reality I had no idea where he came from. Howard King, the Double O manager, had no chaps, but instead rode with the Booger Red pants exposed. I noticed he had on a very nice pair of what looked like handmade cowboy boots. The balls of his feet rested on the flat part of Visalia stirrups about two inches wide. The pipe protruded out of his lips, and I saw a puff of smoke rolling out of his mouth on occasion, but I never saw him replenish the supply of tobacco or strike a match. As we trotted along Mr. King leaned his upper body way out forward and over the fork of his saddle and steadied himself with his right hand leaned on the fork to the right of the saddle horn. He had no rope, no chaps, and no spurs. To me he did not look like a cowboy, but he seemed to be completely comfortable as we continued to trot along.

The Mexican, Vidal Garcia Pizarro, rode off to the side. He rode as straight as a pin. While everyone else trotted, he rode in a slow lope, and I saw him prick his gray horse with a Chihuahua spur if he started to slow down to a trot. If the horse gained speed, he gathered up the rawhide reins with a swift jerk keeping the gray collected. He had on a white shirt and his hat was a true straw sombrero shaped in the traditional Mexican fashion. The vaquero held his chin high and looked straight ahead. He was proud. He was handsome. He had style!

We trotted on for at least six miles. The man from the Double O crew with the cheap roping saddle and zippered up chaps was in misery, but everyone else seemed to be fine. I rode along observing these new acquaintances and trying to formulate scenarios about their backgrounds and their abilities as cowboys. The Mexican rode the same stride for stride and looked as if he could go on forever.

Finally Pete pulled up on a malpai knoll that rose up off of the country we had just passed through. It was now light enough to see. Several of the men dismounted and proceeded to relieve themselves of their morning's allotment of coffee. And of course it was time for a cigarette. I finally caught a glimpse of Howard King cleaning his pipe and refilling it with tobacco.

"Dale, I want you to take Ben, Howard and Leroy here and go off to the west side here. We'll drive back into the big water lot there at the headquarters." Pete had taken to giving Dale most of the orders and using him as his second-in-command since the day Ray roped the cow down in the canyon from Black Creek and caused the wreck. Nothing was ever said, but I surmised that it was a comedown to Ray.

"Sorry to bother you, sir, but are we going much farther? I'm just about played out!" The man with the zippered-up chaps broke in and interrupted Pete's giving of orders. His right chap leg had crawled up his leg taking his Levis with it as it went upstream. There was a considerable amount of his naked calf exposed, and it was rubbed raw and bloody. He was grimacing with torment, either from the rough trotting horse he had been riding or the exposure to the elements.

"My nephew, Leroy, is new to the cowboy life and sometimes must be helped just a little." Howard King looked at Pete as he said these words, but they were said matter-of-factly and with no urgency. He continued but turned his address toward his nephew. "Now buck up, Leroy, we've not much longer to go, I'm sure, and remember we came to help these men, not make ourselves a handicap to them. Mount up on your cow pony and get prepared to make the best of it."

Pete answered the gunsel in a rather condescending way, "Just another thirty miles, pilgrim, and I'll turn you loose!" The words, and the attitude they were said with, were over the head of the man they were intended for.

Leroy had remounted his horse but was leaning over in the saddle and trying to pull his right chap leg and pant leg down to cover the blistered flesh on his shinbone. Pete's comment was missed.

"Tommy," Pete went on. "I'm leaving you and Pancho Villa here. You boys give us a few minutes to get ahead of you and then go straight back toward headquarters. Tie both sides of the drive together because we'll be throwing cattle your direction. The rest of you come with me." With that said he took off in a high trot heading east. The Mexican waited for a moment before he spoke. I had believed that he spoke no English, but he evidently understood Pete's words because he acted like he knew everything that was going on.

"Su patron es muy bravo!" Vidal Gracia Pizarro looked at me intently.

"Si. Muy bravo esta hombre." I answered back thinking that my knowledge of Spanish would soon be exhausted.

"Soy libre! Caballero! Vaquaro de Sonora! Esta Pancho Villo es un chivo!" He spat on the ground. "Cabron! Posible esta Pedro cabron tombien!?"

He looked at me with fire in his eyes, and I surmised that he was angry, and I understood enough Mexican talk to know his anger was directed toward Pete but not at me. I tried to answer his question. "Si, maybe." I figured that the cowboy from Sonora didn't like being called Pancho Villa. I wondered if the famous Mexican revolutionary had stolen his family's ranch or perhaps he had raped his grandmother or murdered his grandfather. It was time that we got started because enough time had passed that Pete and his half of the crew and Dale and his part would be driving back toward headquarters. I mounted Cowboy and wondered how much I should say to the proud Mexican who had been insulted by Pete's remarks.

"Sabe que nosotros por aya, por el rancho?" I pointed off toward the south and the Cow Creek headquarters that was six miles away.

"Se sabe! Vamos para rodear las vacas! Yo voy por esta lado." He pointed off to the west, the direction that Dale and his crew had ridden. "Vd puede ir al otro lado!" He pointed east the direction Pete had gone. He was now giving me orders, or perhaps we were working together. I wasn't sure but it made no difference. Left or right we would all end up back at the headquarters, and soon enough. He rode off to the west and I went east, and before long there were cattle traveling in front of us, and the momentum of the morning's drive carried us along. I decided to let the vaquero from Sonora settle his own differences with Pete. Cabron! Chivo! I wondered if Vidal Garcia Pizarro would use those select adjectives when he addressed Pete later in the day.

The drive flowed south, and whether it was because of the lay of the land, sheer luck, or Pete's masterful leadership, things progressed smoothly. We had never had such a large crew, nor had we attempted to gather as large a piece of country in one big drive, and the herd was the biggest that had been thrown together since I had been there at Cow Creek. I supposed we had over 300 cows, perhaps 350. When we got them penned in a large corral, Pete instructed all the neighbors who were there helping to go outside the corral and wait and watch while he cut the yearlings and cull cows out of the herd and into an adjacent corral. He and Dale did the cutting, and Ben and I turned back for them and watched the gate. Ray had been sent off to gather up the branding irons and other stuff such as Blackleg vaccine.

The cutting went smoothly, all of us being mounted on our best horses and wanting to show off. Bevin, Wanda and several of the Double O cowboys' wives came out to watch and perched themselves on the top rail of a fence far enough away that their presence did not interfere with our work. I could see her sitting there with her carrot-colored hair pulled back on the sides of her head and wearing a white short-sleeved blouse and blue jeans. I squeezed Cowboy with my legs and used the tail of my rope like a quirt to get a little extra forward motion out of him and relied on his knowledge of a cow's presence to slow him down. Between my nudging and his ability, we put on a show of sliding hooves, figure-eleven marks in the deep dirt, and half turns that were as quick as lightning. I felt for sure that she was the most beautiful woman on earth and surely I was the best cowboy and horseman.

The cutting did not last as long as I would have liked, and then we set up the branding fire at the west end of the corral and proceeded to brand. Pete instructed Dale and Howard King to do the roping, and they were told to heel the calves and drag them to the fire. He put me to flanking on one side of the fire with the Double O cowboy named Dallas. On the other side of the fire, he instructed Vidal Garcia Pizarro to flank with Howard King's nephew, Leroy. Don Kambitch showed up, and Pete told him to vaccinate, and everyone else had a job such as castrating, branding or running the dope bucket. We had never had a dope bucket at any branding all spring, but now, today, we were smearing motor oil on the steer calves' wounded scrotums. I supposed Pete was trying to impress the neighbors.

The branding commenced at Pete's nod of the head with Howard King dragging to me and Dallas's side of the fire and Dale dragging to Vidal and Leroy's. Mr. King was tied hard and fast to the saddle horn with a rope that he had to borrow from one of his cowboys. It was tied short, probably twenty-one or twenty-two feet long, and to me he looked like a gunsel in his Booger Reds and pipe, but the son of a gun could drag calves, and me and Dallas would barely let one up when he would bring another to us. Dale was a dally man but could rope as good as anyone, and he brought 'em all out by two feet to Vidal and Leroy. Leroy didn't have the slightest idea what he was doing because the Double O Ranch was mostly a yearling outfit, and he had never helped at a branding. When Dale drug one up, the Mexican pulled on the tail expected Leroy to pull on the rope the other direction, but the man was clueless. Pete sent Ray over to give him instructions, and Ray helped the Mexican cowboy get several on the ground to illustrate the correct technique and then told Leroy to get back to trying.

It was ugly, and usually Vidal got the calf down on its side without Leroy's help. Then Leroy inevitably had trouble taking the rope off the calf's hind feet and then holding the calf's legs himself. The calf would kick loose and almost get up. On several occasions Vidal got kicked hard by flailing hind legs that had been turned loose because of the gunsel's incompetence. Vidal was getting the worst of it. Everyone else in the corral was able to work and accomplish the task at hand because of their counterparts working with them, but Vidal and Leroy became a spectacle of incongruousness. Vidal was getting madder by the minute, and I wondered if he might pull a sharp knife and cut the gunsel's throat. His steely black eyes looked dangerous to me. As I watched the situation, I could see Pete glancing toward the Mexican and the gunsel with little or no concern.

We branded about a hundred calves and it didn't take long, an hour at the most, and everything was going just right except with Vidal and Leroy. Don Kambitch had been watching his cowboy having to work with the gunsel who was showing no sign of improvement. Finally a rather large calf got away from the gunsel, and even though Vidal moved his head quickly, the calf clipped him in the jaw; and the calf's hooves cut him on the point of his chin. The Mexican cursed profusely in Spanish and Don Kambitch spoke up loud enough for all of us to hear, "By golly, Pedro, I didn't bring my hired man up here to get him killed! How about lettin' one of these other boys take a turn workin' with that tenderfoot? I think my boy's had about all he deserves!"

"Yeah, sure, Don Juan! Maybe we ought to do a little tradin' around anyway. Might be time to let somebody else rope," Pete replied.

"Yeah! Good idea! Why don't you and my Mexican cowboy rope? I've got another hundred says you can't out-rope him!" Don Kambitch took the deteriorating remnants of a cigar out of his mouth and grinned at Pete. The grin on his face was the same kind a pool shark would have on his face when he was about to fleece a local boy of all his change.

Pete stared back at Mr. Kambitch and then glanced at the Mexican who stood wiping blood off of his face. "Nah, I don't want to have all of the fun roping when there's other boys here who would like to rope."

"Hell! They don't care!" Everyone was now tuned into the conversation taking place between Pete and the conniving old-timer from Kingman. "You boys wanna see a real roping contest? Somethin' you might want to talk about on the Fourth of July, maybe tell your grandkids? I'll bet you a hundred dollars that that Mexican can rope more calves and miss fewer loops than you. I came up here to take your money; that was our agreement. We were going to do a little wagerin'!"

It was now silent. Mitzi, Wanda, Bevin and Sharon as well as some women folk from the Double O's had climbed up and were sitting on the top rail of the two by twelve board fence, and for a split second everyone stared at Pete.

As if frozen in time, he faltered. It was the only time I ever saw him hesitate, but he was trapped. Don Kambitch had jerked a barbed hook into his gill and was reeling him in. But Pete got his wits about him, composed himself and began acting like the whole affair was his idea all along.

Don Kambitch was in his element. "Well now! We're gonna need an unbiased score keeper." He looked around. "Who's that good lookin' redhead over there? She related to you, Pedro?"

"No, that's Tommy's girlfriend. She's from Seligman."

"Well? She suit ya?"

"Sure, I don't care. I'm gonna get your hundred dollars anyway. Do it however you want to."

Don Kambitch walked over to where the girls sat on the fence. He looked up at Bevin and took the soggy cigar out of his mouth. "Okay, gal, you willin' to help us out here?"

"Sure! What do you want me to do?" Bevin looked down at the potbellied old cowboy.

"Okay!" Don Kambitch said as he retrieved a piece of paper and a pen out of his shirt pocket. "All you have to do is keep track of how many loops each of these two men misses when they're tryin' to catch these calves. Pete over there," he pointed at Pete, "and Vidal over here." This time he pointed at the Mexican. "Don't keep track of nothin' else! Just the number of times one of them throws a loop that comes up empty. Real simple! Ya understand?"

"Sure!" She looked at him and grinned, "Real simple, I can do that."

"I like you! You're as pretty as a red knob on a slot machine with three 7s lined up in a row!" With that said, he turned around and walked toward the branding fire. "Well, what are you waitin' for? I got that redhead all lined out with a pen and paper so we're ready to get started with the first event!"

The old cowboy from Kingman had taken over, and there wasn't anything Pete could do but go along with the show. The crew from the Double O was watching, there were women on the fence watching, Pete's own crew was watching, and Don Kambitch knew he had him between a rock and a hard place. Pete wasn't going to be able to fight or shoot his way out of this predicament, he was going to have to rope his way out. He was, at least, going to take back control over his crew and the work even if he couldn't get out of being forced into a wager against the Mexican. He told me to continue flanking with the same partner and put two other Double O men flanking on the other side of the fire. He asked Howard King to help Ben run the branding irons and Don Kambitch to run the vaccine gun. Dale and Ray were going to castrate and earmark. Leroy had been leaning against a fence post on the edge of the corral licking his wounds. His knuckles and elbows as well as his chin were bruised and cut from the calves that had gotten away from him and kicked him profusely. He acted and looked like a man that was beaten down lower than whale manure. Pete told the gunsel to run the dope bucket.

Everything was ready. Pete stepped on his horse, a sorrel named Pistol that was his favorite. He looked across the corral at Vidal Garcia Pizarro who set straight in the saddle on the gray. "Listo?"

"Si! Listo." The two men stared at each other for a second. I never saw two men take such a disliking to one another with so few words, and only having met several hours earlier.

They rode into the herd and the roping started. It was a contrast of two styles. Pete was very methodical and waited patiently and set up each shot that he took. He swung his rope very little and rode his horse to the perfect place and took a swing or two and then threw a perfectly placed trap in front of a calf's hind legs. He took his time and worked at obtaining position, but he never missed and because of that he was fast. The calves came to the fire like clockwork, smooth and steady. The Mexican was different, he used a bigger loop, and he was not stingy with the swinging of it. He stayed farther away from his desired victim than Pete and threw from a variety of angles, but the maguey lasso was like magic in his hands, it was a serpent, a demon; and like Pete, he didn't miss.

When Pete first rode into the herd, he rode close and got the perfect lay at an unsuspecting bull calf and dallied, and came to the fire. Vidal watched and then rode to the edge of the herd, and when a wild heifer came around behind him and circled around coming from his right to his left in a lope, the Mexican began swinging clockwise, which is the common way, but when the heifer passed in front of him fifteen feet away, coming right to the left, he launched a loop that sailed through the air, and he roped two feet in midair in a most uncommon fashion. He dallied and brought her to the fire, and Don Kambitch squalled, "Aye! Madre de Dios! Hasta la cuchara es de oro hombre!" The loop was so fantastic that the women on the fence clapped, including Bevin who was obviously enjoying herself.

And so it went for an hour and ten minutes. Pete with his cool precision, his smaller loop, his patient quest for position; and Vidal with his fantastic artistry with a piece of maguey, twice as long as Pete's nylon, but appearing to have radar that could track its prey from long distances. Every once in a while, Don Kambitch would let out a loud Mexican exclamation in the vernacular, the meaning of which was unknown to everyone but him and Vidal. Pete intentionally ignored them, which caused Don to enjoy the situation even more. Finally they got down to the last calf, a big red heifer that had stayed hid out in the back of the corral. There were no marks on the piece of paper that Bevin held.

Vidal Garcia Pizarro cut her off and he turned her to his left.

The two men spied the red heifer at the same time as they rode through the cows and calves looking for something that had not been branded and marked. Pete came at her from the left side toward her hind end, and Vidal came forward facing her. Pete naturally had the best lay at her, and Vidal nodded at his opponent as if to say, "Go ahead." So Pete pressed in toward her, but he did not get a good shot. It was very crowded in the back of the corral, and so Pete followed her out toward the other end in the direction of the fire and the men standing and waiting. The heifer was wild and kept fading away, always a stride or two too far away for Pete to throw. Vidal rode toward the edge of the herd also, but on the other side of the corral and out of Pete's way. Finally she reached the edge, and Pete moved in closer and followed her around the edge of the herd and toward Vidal's side of the corral. Pete pressed for position, and when she reached the fence she turned back toward the outside and to Pete's right. At the perfect time, when she was at a forty-five degree angle from Pistol's right shoulder and eight feet away, Pete took two quick swings and threw a perfect loop—and missed. I saw Bevin put a mark on her piece of paper.

Vidal Garcia Pizarro had been sitting quietly on his horse thirty feet away, and now he spurred the gray horse into action and pursued the red heifer toward the other side of the corral. When the heifer reached the fence, Vidal cut her off and turned her to his left. She whirled and ran back under his left stirrup. He swung his loop from his right stirrup and up over his head and turned the gray horse to the left all in one fluid motion, and then he sent the rope flying like a rocket. The Mexican's loop passed over the wild heifer's head, and Vidal held his slack high and let her run through it until everything but her hips passed through, and then he slid his gray horse to a stop, and when the maguey became tight in his hand, he went to the brass horn and dallied. There were two hind feet in his loop. The Mexican loped to the fire dragging the red heifer, and Don Kambitch went to chewing on his soggy cigar. Several of the Double O women let out a loud cheer for the Mexican's roping exhibition, but Mitzi crawled off of the backside of the corral fence and walked toward the bunkhouse where the big feast was being prepared. I could tell even from a distance that she didn't want to deal with the emotions of Pete being bested by a Mexican.

"Well, Pedro, mighty fine roping, even if you did lose a hundred dollar bet! Yes sir, you boys sure put on a show. Shall we settle up now or are you going to let that hundred ride until this boy here gets bucked off and then you'll owe me three hundred?" Don Kambitch had taken the cigar out of his mouth, and he was grinning from ear to ear.

"No, we'll just let it ride, Don, because this boy here isn't going to get bucked off, and you're still going to owe me money!"

"Okay! Okay now, no hard feelings! You and I are old pards, and this is just a little friendly wager! Don't be forgettin' that now!" Don Kambitch suddenly became diplomatic.

"Let's get these cattle turned out of the corral, and we'll get this bronc riding started!" Pete said. "Why don't you and Pancho go over to that corral and lead your outlaw over here, and we'll do the bronc riding right here just as soon as we get the cows out of the way."

We gathered up the branding outfit, the irons, vaccination syringe, and everything else, and put it all outside the corral and out of the way; and then Pete ordered me and Ben to push the herd out of the corral gate as soon as he and all the other cowboys got outside and ready to hold the cattle up for a moment or two to let them mother up. While Pete and the others rode out, I rode over to say hello to Bevin who was still sitting on the fence. I was filthy dirty, covered in dust mixed with sweat caked all over my face and clothes. She was beautiful, and so was Sharon who sat there with her. It was Sharon who spoke first, "You two are dirtier than any two men I've ever seen!"

Ben had ridden up alongside of me, and he answered her, "Yeah, and you still love us, don't you?"

"Yeah, we do." Sharon said. It was the first sign of affection I had witnessed between the two of them.

I looked at Bevin and she smiled at me. "You're irresistible! From a distance!" We all laughed and then Pete hollered at us saying they were ready, so Ben and I left the girls sitting on the fence and rode off to put the cowherd out the gate.

They held the cows and calves for about five minutes, and then Pete motioned for everyone to ride off and turn the cattle loose, and they all rode back to the corral. Pete became animated and started giving orders. He asked me if

I was feeling good, and I said I was. "Unsaddle your horse here and then lead him over to the horse corral and bring back your stake hackamore. You can wash up in the horse trough while you're there. You are a little dirty looking for a champion!" It wasn't a suggestion but an order. He rode over and told Sharon and Bevin to go round up everyone who was over at the bunkhouse and tell them the bronc riding was about to happen. He then told Howard King that he should send one of his men over to the corral to lead back the Double O outlaw. Then he ordered everyone out of the corral except Dale and himself. They would remain in the corral to act as pickup men or snubbers or whatever was needed. About that time Jimmy Duncan and his wife drove up and parked and walked up to the fence and crawled up and sat on the top rail. The women who had been in the bunkhouse kitchen all showed up, and so all of a sudden there was a crowd watching, about thirty people.

I had walked over to the horse corral and bathed myself in the water trough and swatted my pants with the palms of my hands trying to knock the dust out of them. I even took my shirt off and shook a pint full of dust out of it. When I got back to the big corral where we had branded, everyone was waiting, including Don Kambitch who was standing in the middle of the corral holding the lead rope connected to a halter buckled on a big buckskin horse's head. The buckskin stood about 15.2 and probably weighed twelve hundred. I guessed that his head alone weighed two hundred. It was large and ugly. His feet were not long because he had been running in the rocks, but they were big. He held his head high and looked around and snorted.

I walked up to Don Kambitch and observed the halter that his outlaw was already wearing, and it looked good to me. The lead rope was a piece of cotton rope that had been unraveled and braided like a bronc rein. It was about

He continued to jump high and he was stout.

the right length. The halter looked stout. "I'll just use your halter if you don't care?"

"No, that's fine. I braided that lead rope especially for you. It's all good stuff, ain't gonna break!" I reached out and took the lead rope from his hand, and he gave it to me.

"Has he ever been hobbled?"

"Oh, sure! Hell, he's been saddled and rode! Just not very far! But sure, he knows all about hobbles."

I took a piggin' string from my chaps and went to hobbling the bronc. He picked his head up and cocked it sideways and peered down at me. He snorted and rolled his nose, but he stood there. I stayed off to the side and in front of his shoulder in an attempt to keep from getting kicked, but he did nothing wrong except make a sound like a thousand rolling dice coming out of his nostrils. As Don walked off I hollered at him, "What's his name?"

"Vidal calls him Diablo!" He stopped and turned and looked at me, "You never answered me, button. Did you call your mother and tell her goodbye?"

The cowboys on the fence all roared with laughter when they heard that. I got my saddle and threw it up on Diablo's back and reached underneath and grabbed the front cinch and sucked it up tight and buckled it. Then I did the same with the flank cinch.

"What do you think, Tommy? Do you want us to run a rope through the halter and snub him so you can get on?" Pete asked.

"No, I bet that he's all right to get on. Maybe just ride up here by his head until I get mounted. I can get on him."

Pete rode up to the right side of the buckskin's neck and head. Dale pressed his horse's rump into the right side of the buckskin's hind end. I pulled my front cinch up another hole and then reached down and untied the piggin' string that tied the horse's front feet together. I left the string draped around the buckskin's legs so he could feel it, but he was completely untied. "When I get on give me plenty of room!" The two men nodded. I stood by the horse's shoulder with the cotton lead rope tight in my left hand along with a bunch of mane hair. I got ahold of the saddle horn with my right hand and put my left toe in the stirrup and was on so fast the buckskin didn't even know it. Pete and Dale rode off and away, and for a second old Diablo just stood there, and then I lifted my right foot out and stabbed him in the belly with a spur rowel.

He farted and squealed and took a high dive but came down on all four feet at the same time. He continued to jump high, and he was stout, and he was long winded, but he also put his big jug-head right down between his front legs, and I could have pulled on his head with a winch and not budged it. Because of that I just had to keep myself pulled up against my swells and keep spurring. He bucked for a long time, maybe twenty jumps, I didn't know; but about halfway through he got weaker, and I took my hat off and went to fanning him. I even saw Bevin cheering as we bucked past her. As far as great buckers go on a scale from one being very easy to a ten being very hard to ride, I gave him about a six. Toddy was far and away a ranker horse than old Diablo. When he got done bucking, he broke and ran around the big corral, and I could tell that he was completely unbroke. I took my rope down, as I had left it on my saddle, and built a loop and went to swinging it. Diablo blew up and went to bucking again because of the rope, but soon quit, and we made several circles with my rope whistling over his ears. The crowd loved it.

There was plenty of cheering and clapping that died down to talking, but it was all done in good humor, and everyone was wanting to have a good time. Someone hollered, "Let's ride another one!" and everyone clapped. I loped the horse around the corral several more laps and then got the outlaw stopped and bailed off of him making sure I landed in front of his shoulder so he couldn't kick me. I unsaddled him and led the bronc over to Don Kambitch and handed him the cotton lead rope. "Nice ride, kid! I guess they haven't all died after all." He stuck out his hand and handed me a hundred dollar bill. "I believe this is supposed to be yours," he said. I thanked him and put the hundred dollars in my pocket. It was the first hundred dollar bill that I personally had ever possessed.

Pete had been busy instructing the Double O crew to lead their outlaw into the corral. Dallas, the fellow I had flanked calves with, led him to me. "So what's the deal with this one? What's he gonna do?"

"He's trashy. If he sees you're going to ride him, he'll probably stampede and crash into the fence or fall over backwards. He'll try to hurt you if he can, and he will be dishonest about it. I'm going to bet that you'll ride him though. He's just a piece of junk." Dallas said all this in a friendly and matter-of-fact way, so I figured the description was accurate, but I still didn't know what to expect. I took the halter he had on off and put my stake hackamore on him, which had a short lead rope. Then I led him up to my saddle and hobbled him and saddled him up and pulled the cinches tight. Like before Pete and Dale rode their horses up close on the offside, and I unhobbled him and gathered him up and went to put my toe in the left stirrup, but he managed to squirm and move forward, and then he faced me. I had been standing to the side of his left shoulder, and then, all of a sudden, I was in front of him. When I tried to step to the side, he whirled his butt away and faced me, and I would be in front of him again. He had obviously been using this move with someone else, because he was good at it, and quick. "You want me to snub him up, Tommy?" Pete said.

"No, I'd like to get on him without doing that if I can. Let's get him over against the fence, and we'll mash him up against it."

I led him over to the fence and pushed his body up tight against it. Dale pressed his horse's shoulder against the bronc's rump in an attempt to keep him pushed up against the fence. Pete had his horse pressed against the bronc's shoulder and head and pushing him against the fence. But now the bronc was so tight against the fence, I was going to have a hard time getting my right leg between him and the fence once I got on. I also had very little room to get up to his shoulder because Pete's horse was in the way. I decided to try it, but my body was back by my flank cinch, and when I went to put my foot in the stirrup, he jumped and kicked at me, and barely missed.

"Lead that sorry ^*&%$#@* out here in the middle of the corral!" Pete ordered. "You're gettin' paid to ride him, not be nice to him." We got to the middle of the corral, and Pete had me put his rope around the bronc's front legs and told me to act like I was going to get on. When I did the bronc lunged forward, and Pete jerked him down on his head. He jerked him hard and it rang the bronc's bell pretty good. "Now, maybe he'll let you get on. Try it." Pete still had the bronc's front legs in his loop, and he was dallied and the rope was tight. All of this time the crowd had been watching but saying nothing.

Pete had a lot of tension on his rope that was connected to the horse's front legs as I eased up and got the lead rope in my hand and slipped my left toe in the stirrup and got on, and Pete turned him loose. The bronc took off like a flash and ran all out for about three strides and then bogged his head and jumped and then reared up high in the front end and lunged forward and slapped the ground with his front feet out in front of him, and then set up and did it again. I was still on, so next he tried to throw me off by jumping sideways to the right and then went into a nasty spin, and after about two revolutions he threw himself down on his side. My right leg was under him, but I wasn't hurt so I just hung on to all my holds, and he jumped up with me still in the saddle, and he went to bucking off in a straight line. He wasn't a big horse, weighing about 950 pounds, and he wasn't stout or powerful, just nasty. The bucking didn't last long and soon he was running around the corral, so I took my rope down and built me a loop and went to swinging it. At first he stampeded a little faster but then slowed down, and I rode him four or five revolutions around the corral. He was smooth and quick, and I figured that he probably had the makings of a nice horse. He had just got used to buffaloing everyone or someone in particular. Who, I didn't know, but I was willing to bet with a few lessons like he just had he would get gentle.

The crowd had seemed to be quite entertained when I rode Diablo, and there had been a lot of noise associated with a party atmosphere, but while I was riding the Double O outlaw, the excitement had died down. The most exciting thing about the Double O horse was the fact that he had to be fore-footed and jerked down before I could get on, but after the first three or four jumps, his bucking had not been much more than a wild horse fit and was not that impressive. After we had made a couple laps around the corral most of the women folks and Jimmy Duncan, the brand inspector, got down off the fence and headed toward the kitchen. But Bevin stayed, and I jumped off the horse and landed right next to where she was perched on the fence. I climbed up and sat down beside her holding onto the lead rope of my stake hackamore. "So what do you think?" I asked her.

"Well, I am afraid to tell you because you might get the big head!"

"Oh, come on! Surely you can say something. Are you having a good time?"

"Yes, I'm having a great day. Lots of fun and I loved watching you ride. I didn't know you were so famous."

"Famous? I'm not famous."

"That isn't what I hear. All the women say you are the best young cowboy and rider there is!"

All the cowboys were still around, and they walked over to where Bevin and I sat. Dallas asked if he could take the Double O outlaw back over to the corral and turn him loose. I said sure and jumped down and took my saddle off of his back.

"Nice riding, Tommy."

"Gee, thanks."

"Good show!"

"Yeah, it was fun!" Everyone complimented me and bragged on my bronc riding skills. Vidal Garcia Pizarro walked up and shook my hand. "Muy buen, vaquero!"

"Gracias! Tu tambien."

Pete and Dale were riding over to the saddle house to unsaddle their horses so nobody was around except the Double O crew, Don Kambitch and Vidal, plus Bevin and me. "Tommy, I was visiting with Pete and Mr. Kambitch, and we all think that you should consider entering the amateur saddle bronc riding at the Prescott Frontier Days during the Fourth of July rodeo. You're quite a bronc rider and that might be somewhere to win a little hard cash. They are putting up five hundred in added money plus all the entry fees. Last year first place paid over four hundred." It was Howard King talking, and he was acting genuinely friendly.

"Gee, I hadn't thought about that. But you've got to use an Association saddle, and I don't have one."

"I've got one and I'll loan it to you!" It was Ken talking, the Double O cowboy with the form-fitter saddle and the Will James looking hat. "I've rode lots of saddle broncs, at least in my younger days I did, and I've still got my saddle. It's an old Hamley. I could loan it to you, help you get your stirrups set right, the whole deal, and I'd be glad to."

"Young man, you have exceptional skills, absolutely exceptional." Howard King said. "I have connections down there in Prescott. I was on the Frontier Days' rodeo committee for several years, and I know all those folks down there. I can make sure you get entered if you want to do it. I would love to help you. Ken's got the equipment. All you have to do is say you're interested and you're in. I will even pay your entry fees!"

I had never ridden a bucking horse in an Association saddle. All of my experience was strictly ranch cowboy-style bronc riding. Do-whatever-it-takes-to-stay-on type bronc riding: grab the saddle horn, tie a nightlatch through the fork of your saddle, or wrap your arms around the bronc's neck. My bronc riding was survival bronc riding, stay on no matter what it takes to do so. I knew nothing about riding in a rodeo competition. But I had just ridden two outlaws in front of a crowd. I had made two hundred dollars doing it, and now a bunch of cowboys were bragging on me and my beautiful red-headed girlfriend was beaming with admiration. "Sure, I'd like to enter. What day is it?"

"They always run the amateur bronc riding during the Fourth of July performance of the Frontier Days. This year that will be a Friday." Howard King said.

"Okay! I'll be there."

Everyone else had drifted over to the bunkhouse where the women had been busy preparing the feed, and so the Double O cowboys and I headed that direction. Bevin hurried on ahead of us after telling me that she should be there to help Mitzi in the kitchen.

Even though I had washed in the horse trough earlier, I was a filthy mess and wanted to make myself more acceptable for close company, especially to Bevin, and even though the bunkhouse was full of visitors, I got some clean clothes and barricaded myself in the bathroom and got cleaned up. When I reappeared I was a new man. Clean body, clean white shirt and Levis, and my Tony Lama boots were freshly polished.

I went looking for Bevin and found her in the kitchen helping serve steak, potato salad and freshly baked bread, and talking to the gunsel, Leroy, who was bruised and bloody from head to toe because of his inability to ride a horse or flank a calf. He was intently telling her of an institution of higher learning known as the Moody Bible Institution in Chicago, a school which he had attended. She was listening and talking and looking interested—and smiling. I got myself a plate and positioned myself in front of Leroy where she could load me up with a steak and some salad. "Have you got time to come and sit with me?" I asked. "Want me to get you a plate?" I added.

"I'll get myself one. You're about the last one to need served so I think they'll let me sit down for a minute." I turned my back on Leroy, and when Bevin had filled herself a plate, I led her into the big room where most everyone was sitting. Pete, Mitzi, Dale, Wanda, Don Kambitch, Howard King, Jimmy Duncan and his wife were all sitting together, and Pete motioned for us to join them. Bevin and I sat down with them and joined in the conversation. Everyone was pleasant, perhaps even jovial. They were all washing down the steak with Coors beer.

Pete appeared to be very happy. He and Don Kambitch seemed to have patched up any bad feelings resulting from the roping contest. He also was acting extra friendly toward the Double O manager. "So have you got the Double O well stocked this year, Howard, or did the droughty conditions make you cut back?"

"We are down on our numbers compared to most years; we have about four thousand steers turned out, whereas some years we've had as many as seven thousand at this time of year. I'm guessing it will go to raining in July, and we will probably get some more if it does."

Well, I noticed what looked like a lot of cattle in that E L country, at least it seemed that way lookin' over the fence when we were camped at Badger Flat." Pete commented.

"Yes, by golly, we have probably five hundred turned out in that area."

"Who have you got camped at the H's taking care of that country?" Pete went on.

"My nephew, Leroy, is going to be staying there for the next several weeks. Ken, who usually stays there, is going to Montana for a couple days, and I have to make a trip to New Mexico for a few days at the end of next week and won't be back until around the first of July. Leroy is going to hold the fort down, so to speak, while Ken and I are gone."

"So Leroy will be the only man on this end of the outfit next weekend?" Pete inquired nonchalantly.

"By golly, Pedro, you sound like you're casing the joint! I never heard a guy ask his neighbor so many questions!" Don Kambitch said as if he was joking.

"Ha, ha, ha! Pete wouldn't ever do anything to his neighbors!" It was Wanda talking.

"The heck he wouldn't!" Don Kambitch was really enjoying himself now.

Pete and Dale both took a big long drink of Coors, Mitzi lit herself a cigarette and stared off into the distance, Jimmy Duncan choked as if he had drunk some gasoline, and Wanda continued to laugh like a braying mule.

"No, by george! That's one thing I've always liked about this part of the country." Howard King said. "I have wonderful neighbors!"

Chapter Ten

Bevin and I stayed out at the ranch party until about eight in the evening when everyone else who was still there was starting to get obviously intoxicated. When Ben and Sharon left, going back to Black Creek for the night, Bevin said she was getting tired and wanted to go home. She and Sharon had visited and had a great time, but staying longer, sober among a crowd of drunks, didn't interest her, so we left heading back into Seligman. On the way Bevin asked me about ranch life and all about a cowboy's work. She said she had enjoyed the day and seemed very interested in the lifestyle, which she knew nothing about.

I had overheard Pete tell Ben that he planned on working steady until the next Friday, which would be June twenty-seventh, a day he planned on giving everyone off. And from June twenty-eighth until July second, we would be very busy, then we were going to take several days off and go to the big Prescott rodeo. Bevin and I agreed that if all of that worked out on the next Friday I would pick her up, and we would drive down to Prescott together and spend the day. She said she knew of a good Mexican restaurant, and I was happy to agree to that. Then we could go to a movie.

We pulled up in front of Bevin's house at a quarter to nine, and her folks were sitting on the front porch. They asked us to come in and play dominoes, and so we did. This time the old folks beat us bad, but we all laughed and had a great time. Bevin told them how I had ridden the two outlaw horses, and she described in great detail how they bucked and then bragged about me fanning them with my hat and then roping on them. I had to explain that swinging a rope while on a horse's back and actually catching something while mounted on that horse were two entirely different things. They treated me like I was surely one of the world's leading experts on all things cowboy. I stayed until about ten thirty, and then Bevin walked out to Old Dirty, kissed me goodnight, and thanked me for such a nice day.

I drove back to the ranch, and it was very dark with nothing but a slight crescent of a moon showing. The darkness of the night allowed the brightness of the stars to shine through, and it seemed like they stretched forth their hands and touched me. I drove along with the window of the driver's door rolled down and my arm resting on the window ledge. The balmy night air washing across my shirtsleeve felt like rushing water from a stream pure and clean. I looked at the brightness of the stars instead of the blackness of the night, and enjoyed the night wind in my open pickup window instead of worrying about the prolonged drought, and I wondered how long I could keep this beautiful girl thinking that I was somebody.

~~

The crew spent Sunday through Wednesday gathering up all the yearlings and cull cows and bulls that we had scattered around the ranch in various shipping traps. We sorted off the cows and bulls, and on Wednesday, Jimmy Duncan came out from town and looked at the cows and bulls and wrote hauling papers on them, and then two semi-trucks showed up. We loaded the culls and sent them to a slaughter house located somewhere in Southern California.

The brand inspector also looked at and wrote papers for all the yearlings that we had to ship, which amounted to three semi loads, but those trucks were supposed to show up the next day, Thursday. We drove the yearlings down an alleyway and past Jimmy Duncan so he could get a good look at the brands and then turned the yearlings out into a holding pasture which we would regather early the next morning. That finished, we all headed to the bunkhouse to eat lunch and drink coffee. Pete and Jimmy Duncan made plans for Jimmy to return in a week on July second to write hauling papers on some more cattle that would be going to California. We were all sitting at the kitchen table in the bunkhouse while Mitzi was cooking lunch as this conversation between Pete and Jimmy Duncan took place. I knew they were talking about O R O and Double O cattle because all of the Cow Creek cattle that we had to ship would be gone by the next day, Thursday, June twenty-seventh. I thought about all this as I sat and drank my coffee that I had doctored up with plenty of canned milk and sugar. I remembered Dale telling me that I was only following orders. I would be doing what older men told me to do.

The next day we gathered the yearlings early in the morning, and when we got them in the corrals, we went to sorting them. Heifers went one way and steers the other way. We did the sorting in a big wide alley in the shipping pens and used the in and by method: one kind of cattle were turned through a gate out of the alley and deposited into a corral, and the other class of cattle went on down the alley and into a separate corral. I was riding Cowboy, and Pete put me in a gate where I had a considerable amount of action either turning cattle in or allowing them to go by, and always needing to be on my toes so I wouldn't make a mistake. I loved the work, and Cowboy moved like a well-greased shotgun jumping out into the alley and turning cattle and ducking and diving. I decided I wanted to do this kind of work for the rest of my life.

When we got the yearlings sorted, we weighed them and then loaded the three semis with a total of 247 head of cattle, all of which were going to the big Harris Feed Yard in Coalinga, California. The trucks were loaded and gone by eleven in the morning. We took a couple hours off to eat lunch and lay around, and then we all shod a couple of horses apiece. Pete told us that we had a big week ahead, and we needed to have our horses in good shape to do some hard and very important riding. "Ain't gonna be a good time to have a crippled horse," was Pete's comment. So we busied ourselves putting new shoes on any horses in our strings that had long grown-out hooves and thin or rattling horse shoes.

The next morning, which was Friday, Pete turned me loose and said that I could go to town, but he wanted me back no later than two in the morning the next day. "We're gonna get a real early start, so don't be late, kid. You understand?" Pete told me as he said I had the day off. I assured him that I would be back by two the next morning.

I drove into Seligman and picked Bevin up at ten, and we headed east to Ashfork and then turned down highway 89 toward Prescott. It was nothing but open cow country all the way to Chino Valley, which was a hole in the road having an old country store with a gas pump outside, and then a little farther was the Log Cabin Bar, and across the road was an old stone building that was some kind of church. All in all, Chino Valley was a total of twenty buildings, and I never slowed Old Dirty down.

I had a paycheck that I needed to cash so I asked Bevin where a bank was located, and she told me about a new one that had just opened; and since she knew Prescott better than I, she gave me directions on how to get there. It was a real modern affair with a two-lane drive-through teller. I started to park in the parking lot and walk inside, but

Bevin stopped me and told me to use the drive-through teller. "Just pull into that right lane and pull up to where you're supposed to stop. You won't even have to get out.

I had never been through, or even seen, a drive-through teller. "Where do I stop?"

"Just pull in there and I'll tell you when to stop."

I pointed Dirty down between the yellow lines and drove slow until Bevin said, "Okay, now stop!" She was laughing. I looked out my door window and saw a pipe about five foot high coming out of the concrete. Off in the distance and across another lane, where another occupied car was parked, was a big plate-glass window in the side of the fancy new building. The window was elevated above ground level by several feet, and I could easily see inside. There were two very beautiful girls seated at a counter staring out at the cars. The girls looked to be college age, maybe three or four years older than Bevin and I. Suddenly one of them spoke through a speaker that was hanging off of the big pipe going downward into the cement.

The beautiful brunette on the other side of the window said, "Good morning, sir. What can I do for you?

I hesitated wondering if she meant me. I looked at Bevin. "Talk to her," she whispered.

"Ah, yeah, I'd like to cash a check."

"Is it a personal check, sir? Do you have an account with us?"

"Uh, no. It's a paycheck."

"Okay, is it signed, sir?"

I raised the check up to the steering wheel level and stared at it." Yeah! The fella that wrote it signed his name to it!"

I could see the other movie star behind the plate-glass window looking at the movie star who was talking to me, and she grinned. Bevin cupped her hands over her mouth and looked toward the passenger window. She was giggling. No, she was laughing but was trying to hide it. She was sitting close to me in the middle of the seat, and I could feel her body shaking with laughter.

"No, sir, I meant, have you endorsed your check."

"Ah, no." I started looking for a pen but knew that Old Dirty contained no pens in her bowels. Bevin put on a straight face and got into her purse and handed me a pen. I signed the check. I held it up in the open driver's door window and showed the movie star that I had signed it.

"Okay great, send it and some ID, preferably your driver's license, down the tube."

I got my wallet out of my hip pocket and got my driver's license out. I looked at Bevin. "What's the tube?" Bevin leaned across my lap and pointed at the pipe going down into the cement. I felt her breasts pressing into my chest. I almost fainted.

Bevin stayed leaned across me while pointing at the pipe and explaining how it worked. I couldn't concentrate. "That big pipe is called a tube. You see that hole in the side of it? You put your check and driver's license into that hole and a big wind will suck it up and carry it into that office to the girl who is talking to you." I looked out the window; we were almost cheek to cheek. I managed to find the hole in the big pipe that she was talking about. Bevin straightened up and gave me some relief. She smiled. Oh man! She was good looking.

I realized I had not parked close enough to the so called tube. I could barely reach it, but I leaned out of the pickup window and managed to put my check and driver's license into the hole. I looked at the movie star and nodded. Suddenly a great gush of wind passed through the tube. The movie star looked up at me and I looked at her. The second movie star looked at the one who had been talking to me, and then they shrugged their shoulders as they looked at each other and then back at me. "Sir, your check didn't come through."

"Well, I put it in the big hole in this pipe."

"Sir, did you put your check and driver's license in the cylinder?"

Bevin leaned back across me again and pointed to the clear plastic cylinder about the size of a quart jar. It had a screw-on lid. "You were supposed to put it in that thing!" She straightened back up and cocked her head to the side and shrugged her shoulders. "I'm sorry, I should have told you."

I looked at the movie star. "No! I guess I didn't put my stuff in the cylinder."

"Okay. Take the cylinder and put it in the tube and send it to me. Your check is no doubt hung up somewhere in the tube and maybe the cylinder will pick it up and bring it out." I leaned way out with my upper body halfway out the window and managed to reach the cylinder. I put it in the big hole in the big pipe and, whoosh, the wind sucked it away.

"Okay, sir, your license came through but the check didn't, so I'm going to send the cylinder back to you. Maybe it will pick it up in your direction!" Whoosh! Thunk! The cylinder came crashing to a stop at my end but was packing no check, so I sent it back. I was beginning to get the hang of it. The movie star shook her head in the negative and whoosh, thunk, the cylinder crash-landed outside my window. No check, so I sent it back. By now another older woman had appeared behind the plate-glass window and was conversing with the movie stars. A superior officer, no doubt.

Finally, after several passes of the cylinder, the movie star waved the check at me, and everyone behind the plate-glass window celebrated. She counted out the money in twenties and tens plus some change. Two hundred thirty-seven dollars and fifty-three cents.

The movie stars were looking at me when the cylinder came back with my money. "Those girls like you! I'm getting jealous!" Bevin looked at me and grinned.

I decided to prove to the movie stars that I had some class. It was undignified to lean way out of a car window to retrieve a cylinder. I opened Dirty's door and started to step out. The movie stars' superior had returned, and they were all watching me. What for, I wondered. I put my left cowboy boot out onto the asphalt and tried to push the door open wider as my body started outward. The door slammed into the tube quicker than I had anticipated causing my head to crash into the door at the top of the window. My good Resistol cowboy hat got crushed by the door and fell off and onto the pavement. I scraped my left shin on the bottom of Dirty's door and got mad and forced my way out through the crack that was too small because the blasted tube was holding the door mostly closed. By squeezing through the crack, I scraped my good white shirt with pearl snaps, and several of them came unsnapped. My belly was now showing. I looked up and saw all three women staring at me with various degrees of merriment displayed across their expression. As they saw me looking back at them, the superior officer whirled and looked the other way, my movie star struggled valiantly to straighten her expression, and her partner sank straight down until she disappeared from sight behind the counter. I managed to get out, and I first retrieved my bruised Resistol and pressed it onto my head. I grabbed the cylinder and unscrewed the lid and got my money and jammed it down into my Levis' pocket I squeezed back through the crack and knocked my hat off again, but I caught it before it reached the ground and threw it into the pickup seat where it landed on Bevin's lap. She was again looking out the passenger-side window shaking with only slightly concealed laughter. I looked up at the plate-glass window, and the movie stars were experiencing convulsions of hysteria. Their superior officer was walking back into the inner sanctum of the bank shaking her head in either disgust or unbelief, I couldn't tell which.

I fired up old Dirty and put 'er in first and proceeded to get out of there—pronto! I was nervous! I hadn't been to a big town in more than a month. I was used to broncs and running off cattle but not fancy banks and traffic. I got to the street and pulled out, turning right without looking.

Tommy and Bevin under the sculpture of Buckey O'Neill. I Love you Bevin.

Immediately I heard screeching tires and someone honking at me from behind. I had pulled Old Dirty out in front of a big Buick, and the guy was really laying on the horn. Bevin sat up and stared out the back window. "You want me to drive?" she asked.

"No! I'm all right. I just got a little flustered!"

We drove down the street for a ways and she said, "Those girls got you all shook up! How come? You wanting a date with one of them or what?" She looked at me and grinned.

"No!" I was trying to concentrate, telling myself that if I didn't I would wreck Old Dirty and kill us. "Where do you want to eat?" I asked her. "How about El Canario?"

"El Canario?! You mean that place down on Whiskey Row where they use house cats for meat in the tacos?

"Yeah!" She looked at me in surprise, so I added, "I like house cats for meat in my tacos!" I drove down the street past the Hassayampa Hotel and the movie theater and then past the statue of Buckey O'Neill and the Courthouse Plaza. After turning south on Whiskey Row, we continued past the Saint Michaels Hotel and the Palace Bar. After thinking about it she said, "Have you really heard they put cat meat in the tacos?"

"Yeah! That's what they say. I've heard you can go out in the alley early in the morning and find cat carcasses in the garbage cans. I don't know because I haven't seen it, but I heard it from a reliable source!"

"Really? Who did you hear it from? Your friend Ray with the glass eyeballs?" She started laughing and then I started laughing. By the time I parked in front of the El Canario, we were engulfed in laughter. "Come on, I don't care what Ray says, I will like the food in here. Buy me some lunch! Or did you lose all your money in the tube at the bank?" She was really laughing now. "You should have seen those girls when you stepped out and smashed your head against the door and knocked your hat off! One of them actually disappeared, I think she fell off of her chair she was laughing so hard!"

We stepped out of Dirty, and when we got up on the sidewalk, she took my hand, and we walked toward the front door of El Canario's swinging our arms back and forth with her laughing. It wasn't mean; she was just happy. She was happy to be with me.

El Canario was on a street corner in an old two-story brick building catty-corner off of the southwest corner of the Courthouse Plaza. To enter we had to walk up a couple cement steps, the floor being several feet higher than the sidewalk. Inside was a long narrow room having a lunch counter extending the entire length fronted by round stools. Just inside, to the right of the door, was an ancient brass cash register that was heavily embossed with floral carving on the brass exterior. Behind the cash register sat the old Greek proprietor, Gust Vagenas, who sat perched on a very high chair, and he had his feet laying on the counter next to the cash register. He had a very large cigar in his mouth, and he sat there surveying everything that went on. In a strong Greek accent he said hello to Bevin and me as we stepped in the door.

On the left side of the room was a row of booths made up of wooden benches and tables, all of which were connected permanently to the wall. The booths were small and four people would have been a tight fit. All the fixtures and woodwork in the entire place was out of date going back to the twenties or perhaps even earlier. Everything was well made but also very old. The linoleum on the floor was old. The light fixtures were old. A Mexican woman came to wait on us and she was old, at least forty-five. She had on a pale blue and white striped sear sucker dress, the type a maid in a large hotel would wear. Her black hair was pulled back in a bun and held in place with a hairnet. She was heavy and seemed to have no humor. I felt that Gust was watching to make sure she stayed busy. She gave us menus. We didn't need them although we did look at them for a moment. We both wanted the combination plate: taco, tostado, tamale, and enchilada with rice and beans. Lots of red hot sauce please! And iced tea. The Mexican lady walked to the west end of the room and spoke to the cook though the open half of a double door. The cook was another Mexican woman who showed no humor, and she took the information from our waitress and then turned her back and returned to work preparing the food.

I could see Gust watching them. He was watching us. We leaned forward and whispered to each other. "He knows we know about the cats!" Bevin glanced at him. She could see him easier than I could. "He's mad!" She giggled as the overworked waitress brought us our combination plates. It was good. We had a couple flour tortillas on the side, and I smothered the whole plate with hot sauce and asked for more.

The Mexican lady brought us the ticket. Two dollars and thirty-five cents. I left her a fifty cent tip. I didn't want Bevin to think I was a cheapskate, and then we walked to the counter, and I laid the ticket on the ancient mahogany countertop. Gust took his shoes off of the counter and leaned forward and picked up the ticket. He took the big cigar out of his mouth with his left hand, "How was your food? Everything good?"

"Yes, it was very good! Thanks, we liked it!" I answered as I handed him a five dollar bill which he took and pushed different keys on the big brass mechanism. A bell rang and the cash drawer opened. He made change and handed it to me.

"You are a cowboy on the big O R O Ranch?" Gust asked me.

"No, I work on the Cow Creek outfit, north of the O R O."

Ahh, I know about that ranch. I can tell you are a cowboy. This your girl?" he asked, pointing to Bevin.

"Yes, she's my girl!"

"Yes, I can tell! You are a lucky man, I say."

"Thanks!" I answered as we headed toward the door. I looked over my shoulder at him and said, "I am a lucky man." He put his feet back up on the counter and leaned his chair back against the wall. His cigar was reinstalled in his lips. He looked at me and waved goodbye.

I took Bevin's hand when we got out onto the sidewalk and turned north and started across the street toward Whiskey Row and its many saloons. We walked north, and when we got to the Western wear store, we walked in. I was feeling flush after winning two hundred dollars riding bucking horses, so I bought myself a new Stetson hat, a silver belly with a four-inch brim, size 7 ¼. I bought Bevin a flower-carved leather belt with a nice silver buckle, and we walked back out onto the sidewalk glowing in our new ornaments. Then we proceeded north past the famous Palace Bar and Matt's Saloon, equally famous, and heard the jukebox blaring some Tammy Wynette song as we passed. When we got to the Palace Barber Shop, I walked in to get a haircut. I was getting shaggy. Bevin said she would walk down the street and window shop while I did my business. I was just in time as a man was getting out of the barber chair as I walked in, and I didn't have to wait. The barber, a black man, was true to his profession, very friendly and full of questions and answers.

"Hello young man, you're a real cowboy aren't you— you work out at that famous O R O Ranch?"

"No sir, I'm on the outfit north of there, Cow Creek."

"Yes sir! I know about that Cow Creek outfit, sure do! You came into town for a day off, I can tell! Got yourself a new hat, too. Man, it's a nice one!"

"Thank you."

"Cow Creek, isn't that where a cowboy, ah, I believe his name is Dale, yes sir, I believe it's Dale. He works on that outfit, don't he? I cut his hair lots of times, yes sir, he been in here lots of times! Yes sir, ole Dale, I hear he's a darn good hand! That's what they tell me."

"Yeah, he is." I replied. And the black barber, he cut my hair and talked and made me think that I was someone important. He told me all kinds of stories about people he knew and things he had witnessed as he gazed out of the big plate-glass window onto the sidewalk. I told him to cut it short, and so he did, and it didn't take long for a basic, short haircut. I thought about getting him to give me a shave, but decided against the wasting of money. There wasn't anything to shave. But he swept me off really good with his big white brush and rubbed lots of smelly liquid all over my head. As he turned the big swivel barber chair around so I could look at myself in the long, polished mirror, I noticed Bevin had walked up and was standing outside the big window.

"Is that your girl standing out there waiting for you?"

"Yes sir, it is!"

"My oh my! I will tell you that you are one lucky man. She's as pretty as a brand-new twenty-dollar gold coin! Yes sir! You are a lucky man!

"Yes sir! I sure am!"

I gave him a dollar and fifty cents and walked out onto the sidewalk smelling like sugar poured out of a bottle and wearing a new Stetson, and Bevin took my arm and suggested we walk across the street to the Courthouse Plaza with its beautiful trees and green grass and park benches. It was almost four o'clock.

We strolled around the park and studied the huge bronze statue of Buckey O'Neill, and then we decided to sit on the grass in the shade of a giant elm tree, and we listened to the cicadas sing and soaked up the refreshing coolness of the shade and the well-groomed lawn. Bevin sat up leaning back with her hands braced behind her back supporting her upper body, and I laid my head on her lap. She stroked my newly cut hair.

"I love you, Bevin."

She looked down at me for a long time. "I love you, too, Tommy Lee."

Bevin and I stayed there in the park for a long time. The sun was getting low when we decided to walk a block east to the theater. We stood in the line and bought tickets to a new John Wayne movie called "True Grit," and when we got inside the lobby, I bought us two bags of popcorn with lots of butter and two boxes of Junior Mints and two large Cokes. We almost couldn't pack it all. We held hands and watched as Rooster Cogburn led Mattie Ross around Arkansas in pursuit of Tom Cheney and Lucky Ned Pepper. Bevin flinched and I squeezed her tighter when Mattie fell into the snake pit.

We left the theater happy about life in general and popcorn and Junior Mints in particular and walked down the sidewalk on the north side of the Courthouse Plaza feeling the cool night air and talked about John Wayne. When we finally reached Old Dirty, where she was still parked in front of the El Canario, we got in and headed north toward Seligman seventy-five miles away. The window on the driver's door was rolled down, and the night air blew in that smell that only the hills of Yavapai County had. There was something special about it and the sound of cicadas in the summertime.

I drove and Bevin sat next to me and talked. And then she rested her head on my shoulder, and we dreamt—wide awake. As we crossed the old iron bridge that spanned Hells Canyon, I said, "Sing me a song."

"Okay."

There's a young man that I know, his age is twenty-one
Comes from down in Southern Colorado
Just out of the service, and he's looking for his fun
Someday soon, goin' with him, someday soon

My parents cannot stand him 'cause he rides the rodeo
My father says that he will leave me cryin'
I would follow him right down the toughest road I know
Someday soon, goin' with him, someday soon

Chapter Eleven

It was half past midnight when I parked Dirty in front of the bunkhouse and shut the headlights off. I walked into the bunkhouse, pulled back the canvas bed tarp, crawled into my blankets, and was asleep in minutes. It seemed like only minutes later when Dale kicked me and told me it was time to get up. It was 2 a.m. Coffee had been made, and everyone was sitting at the table consuming the black liquid and mixing it with cigarette smoke. There was a pan of cold cinnamon rolls on the stove, and that was breakfast. Mitzi was nowhere around. Coffee and cinnamon rolls, but no one was eating much, just smoking. I put two of the rolls on a plate and went to eating them and washing them down with coffee. Lots of coffee. I was sleepy and figured it was going to be a long day. Everyone was silent as if waiting for the hangman to show up, and the atmosphere was tense.

We were out at the horse corral by twenty after two. Pete roped our horses, and we saddled up like we had eaten breakfast—fast and silent. I saddled Red Ram, the first horse I had ridden when I showed up on the outfit, and I realized that now, a month or so later, the horse was acting a lot different than he had on that first morning. We led our horses out the gate and stepped on, and Pete turned south, and we all fell in behind him and rode down into the depths of Cow Creek. There was a full moon, and as we rode down the steep trail, it was eerie to look out across the canyons and ridges and see dark spots: shadows made by cedar trees, large rocks, and cattle that stood still sleeping on their feet in the coolness of the night. We rode on and in an hour we had reached the bottom of the main canyon and were now riding east and upstream. As we rode along, occasionally, in the distance we would hear cattle trotting off, escaping from the sound of our hoof beats with knowledge obtained by instinct that we were humans mounted on horses and our occupation was harassing livestock.

When we reached the salt ground on the ridge where we had made our first holdup the first morning I was employed at the ranch, we stopped and let our horses blow, and everyone smoked except me. But then after one cigarette we stepped back on our horses and proceeded up the steep slope toward the wire gate that was located in the narrow gap in the black malpai rim rock. The gate that led out onto the famous O R O Ranch. When we reached the gate it was getting light in the east.

Pete stepped off of his horse and opened the gate, and we all rode through and stepped on O R O soil. He looked off into the distance and strained his eyes to see if anyone or anything out of the ordinary could be seen. He looked at Dale. "Where's that dirt tank from here?" He was whispering as if someone might be close enough to hear.

Dale was standing next to his horse, and he took his right arm and laid it over the seat of his saddle and pointed straight south across the top of the rocky mesa that we were now standing on. "It's about a mile and a half right through there." He was also whispering.

The gap in the rim rock and the wire gate were located on a rounded corner of the mesa. To the right of the gate, the rim rock and mesa's edge slowly curved southward and to the gate's left the rim rock turned eastward. Pete stood next to his horse in the growing morning light and surveyed the country that lay before us. He had not ridden in the pasture we were about to try and gather some cattle out of, and he was obviously trying to formulate a plan on how to proceed. The mesa was not perfectly flat but held several shallow draws and ridges, an abundance of malpai rocks, and a considerable amount of cover in the form of cedar trees and cliffrose. "So I'm thinking that if we make a quick drive from this east side," he looked at Dale and pointed off toward the rising sun, "and pushed everything we found in front of us, we could eventually get them held up against the rim over that direction." He motioned off to the southwest. "What do you think?"

"Won't know until we try it." Dale said in a low tone of voice.

Pete got back on his horse and everyone followed suit. The first sliver of the morning sun came sliding over the eastern horizon as we struck a trot going east and following the mesa's edge. Nobody said anything, and I couldn't help but notice that the smoking of cigarettes had even ceased. As we slipped along through the black malpai rocks I imagined that even our horses were making less noise than they should have. I wondered why Pete, considering his ignorance of the lay of the land, didn't ask Dale to lead the drive since he had been in the pasture before. But then I realized that Pete, even in this precarious undertaking, wasn't going to relinquish control over to anyone. I also imagined what would happen if someone showed up with a gun, and suddenly we were all looking down its barrel, if he would admit to being our leader under those circumstances. We turned south and away from the mesa's edge, and it came to me that every one of the crew was probably wondering about various scenarios that could unfold at any minute.

Pete stopped his horse, "Why don't you drop off here, and we'll aim to get some cattle stopped against the rim rock a half mile or so south of the gate." He was talking quietly to Dale who nodded his head in a silent reply. "Which direction is the dirt tank?" Pete asked.

Dale pointed southwest, "About a mile or so."

"Okay, you might not need to show up but be out on this side and turn any cattle we start west and be on the edge to stop them."

Dale nodded his head and we rode off going south leaving him behind us. We trotted along briskly, and within three hundred yards we jumped about fifteen Hereford heifers that were off to our right, and they took off in the perfect direction going west/southwest. Pete stopped momentarily and looked at Ben and pointed at the heifers. Ben understood that he was to drop off and follow them.

Pete, Ray and I took off at a trot again, and after a quarter mile we broke through some thick trees and saw off to our right, which was west, that there were a lot of cattle grazing over a stretch of country that was open, having less tree cover. "That's what we're lookin' for!" Pete took his right arm and pointed toward the yearling heifers and nodded to Ray and then took off in a lope, and I followed him like an obedient soldier. We ran our horses at a brisk pace and set the grazing cattle into a high trot going west toward the mesa's edge that was somewhere that direction a mile or two away. At this point Pete and I basically just stampeded the cattle, and Ray flanked behind us, and luck or the devil, I wasn't sure which, was with us. The cattle ran in the perfect direction, straight into the dirt tank where they had been watering, and the farther we went the more we ran into. Within five minutes we had breezed by the waterhole picking up more cattle as we rode. Suddenly Ben appeared bringing more cattle with him, and following Pete's lead we rode hard and kept the cattle out in front of us moving fast.

Within twenty minutes after Pete had dropped Ray off, we reached the mesa's edge and the cattle had to either turn to the left and south or to the right and north because going straight would have meant a thirty-foot drop onto solid rock and certain death. Pete beat them to the rim rock on the left side and the bunch of stirred up yearlings turned north, and we let them go, hazing them to keep them against the mesa's edge and treating them like a band of wild horses. Within ten more minutes we ran right into Dale who turned his horse's hind end to the herd and rode north in a trot staying out in front of our herd that looked to be about a hundred head. We kept going north along the mesa's edge, and with Dale now in the lead, we slowly throttled the herd of heifers down to a slower pace; and presently we were back at the gap in the rim rock and the wire gate and the trail down into the depths of Cow Creek, or Hell, I couldn't help but wonder. We had only left the spot an hour and twenty minutes earlier.

We were all silent now, everyone doing what needed to be done without being told. The cattle were stirred up and panting so we held them against the rim rock and gate giving them plenty of room and time to realize that they had been captured. For awhile they milled, and occasionally a particularly wild one tried to make a jailbreak, taking some companions with her; but we just headed them off and blocked their retreat and were able to keep them from scattering. We played with them in this manner for at least fifteen minutes. They blew and caught their breath, and as every minute passed they acted gentler, and presently they acted completely calm. We sat there for an extra ten minutes.

We were all positioned in the same places as Pete had dropped us off, so I was closest to him. He rode up to me and stopped his horse. "Listen, kid, you're about to do some of the best cowboyin' you've ever done. Three of us are going to have to go out and get in front of these cattle before they start down that trail. If we ain't out there it will take us a week to gather 'em up cause they'll be scattered all over that canyon. That means you and Ben are going to have to stay up here and get them put through that gate, which might not be easy but there ain't no other way to do it." He looked at me. I said nothing. There was nothing to say. Everything he said was true. It wasn't a request, it was an order. He wasn't asking me for an opinion.

He rode around behind me, and when he got to Ray he stopped and talked for just a moment, and then he rode on alone to where Ben sat on his horse. He stopped and talked to Ben for a minute or so. I couldn't hear him but didn't need to as I knew what he was saying. Then he rode around behind Ben's horse and started toward Dale. As he did so he waved at Ray who turned and followed him. Ray caught up about the time Pete reached Dale's horse, and all three of them walked their horses gently along the rim rock's edge, and then they stopped at the gate. Pete quickly stepped off of his horse and opened the gate and threw it wide open. Then the three of them disappeared, dropping out of sight into the depths of the canyon below.

As the three of them rode off leaving us, the cattle became nervous again, and they took a little run to the south, or my direction. I stayed out in front of them and got them held up with Ben flanking for me, but we were now a hundred yards south of the gate so we needed to turn them around and try and get them to see the hole we wanted them to pass through. I looked off to the east and surveyed the landscape and wondered if someone might be watching us. Perhaps they were using binoculars. Maybe they were packing a high-powered rifle with a scope. Ben and I were the fodder that would be caught. I didn't like it.

We put pressure on the bunch of skittish heifers and got them pointed back toward the gate, and Ben managed to stop them in about the perfect spot. But they stood there staring at us instead of at the opening. There was nothing we could do but wait for them to decide to see it and take it. There were too many of them and too few of us to apply much pressure. We would have to wait until they thought it was their own idea. We had no choice but face them with our horses and let our backs be exposed to anything hiding behind us in the trees or behind a rock and watching. For ten minutes we had a showdown with the heifers. They weren't interested in the gate and were determined to squeeze every ounce of patience out of the two of us gunsels, the low men on the totem pole. The obvious top hands had disappeared so they could be in the important leading role when the cattle tipped downhill. We rode back and forth slightly slapping our shotgun chaps with our bridle reins making just a little noise, but we did not holler or make any verbal noise of any kind. Under internal compulsion Ben and I took turns looking over our shoulders at the trees and rocks and shadows in the distance.

Finally a heifer walked over and stared at the open gate, and after a minute she stepped forward far enough to poke her head through, and then several more followed. When two or three stepped through the opening, the rest slowly noticed and began turning that direction; and when they were all pointed that way, we applied more pressure, and all but a half dozen squirted through. The half dozen that turned back at the end, we ignored. Ben and I, without speaking, knew what the other was thinking. "Let's get outa here." We rode through the gate, and Ben jumped off his horse to close it, and when he had dismounted, he pulled his shotgun chaps off and went to swatting the ground around the gate wiping out any tracks.

I didn't stick around. The leaders had picked up speed as they tipped downhill, and I could see Pete, Dale and Ray down the trail three hundred yards and in front of the heifers, managing, because of cowboy skill, to maintain control over them. I fell in behind the drags and hurried them on to catch up. This was no time to be gentle or slow, and I made the cattle close any gaps in the herd. Soon Ben caught up. I told him it was a good idea to wipe out the tracks. He nodded in the affirmative and said that Pete had told him to do it. We both looked back on several occasions trying to find someone who might be watching, but we saw nothing, nothing except haunting shadows.

The trail from the gap in the rim rock to the canyon bottom near the spot where I had roped and tied down the bull the first morning I had worked for the outfit didn't take long. And then we kept moving down through the rocks and brush in the canyon bottom until we reached the Cienega Corrals. We penned the herd there, and when the last heifer walked through the gate, Pete stepped off and shut it. He looked at his pocket watch and announced it was ten thirty in the morning. It had been too easy. We had made record time. The mood suddenly relaxed. We unsaddled our horses to let their backs cool off and sat down leaning against our saddles, and everyone but me lit up a cigarette. For a while it was silent. Ben, after finishing his cigarette, laid his head back and covered his eyes with his black hat. I wondered if he was sleeping or hiding from someone.

"Damn!" Pete said. "I figured it would be two or three o'clock when we got here, maybe later. What do you think, Dale, should we let them rest for a few minutes and then go on with 'em? It will be a long hot ride out of here, but we could make it by late afternoon, and we would be a day ahead of the game. Might be worth it."

Dale smoked and contemplated for a moment and then replied. "Yeah! I say let them rest an hour and then go. We might be glad we did tomorrow, who knows."

He looked at Ray who said, "Let's go on with them, that's what I say."

I could see Pete, Dale, and Ray down the trail, three-hundred yards and in front of the heifers.

Evidently Ben and I didn't have opinions, we weren't asked to present them. We sat for a short while and then resaddled our horses and led them over to an ancient water trough that was fed by an old rusty inch and a quarter pipe coming from a spring in the canyon wall one hundred yards from the corral. Water barely trickled out of the old pipe, but it was cool, and we cowboys drank out of it while the horses drank out of the old trough. The temperature was probably over a hundred degrees in the canyon bottom.

At a quarter past eleven, I rode into the corral, when instructed by Pete, and pushed the heifers out the gate, and the crew turned them uphill toward the Cow Creek headquarters. The heifers had now calmed down and were quite trail-broke, and all of their friskiness had left him. It grew hotter, and there was no wind, and the trail grew steeper as time went on. Went on very slowly. We had to stop the heifers a half dozen times and let them blow, and when they walked they did it very slowly. It was six o'clock when we finally shut the holding pasture gate behind them at the ranch headquarters. Pete had counted them as they filed past him through the gate. We had stolen ninety-eight head of O R O heifers, and with the exception of suffering miserably from the heat as we trailed them uphill and out of the canyon, it had all been done very easily.

It was Saturday night, and by the time we had done our chores, which consisted of feeding one wrangle horse for the next morning, it was seven in the evening. Mitzi had a supper of steak, biscuits, gravy and apple pie cooked and waiting. I was almost too sleepy and tired to eat, but my youth took over when I smelled the aroma of the meat and gravy. They were worth celebrating for. With the exception of Ben and me, the rest celebrated the day's events with Cow Creek champagne, Old Crow. It was a silent celebration, downing the bourbon but keeping one's thoughts to oneself. I ate, drank lots of water, and was in my bedroll by eight o'clock and immediately fell asleep.

We slept in until five o'clock the next morning, and Dale made breakfast for those of us in the bunkhouse, Mitzi having taken the day off. Ben's horse was in the corral, and after breakfast it was up to him to wrangle. As soon as he had the horses in the corral, Ray caught one for himself, saddled it, stepped on and rode south toward the bottom of the canyon, traveling alone. It wasn't said by anyone, but I figured he was riding back to the trail coming down from the mesa and the O R O pasture. Perhaps he was going to do a better job of wiping out our tracks, or maybe look around for any sign of one of the O R O cowboys snooping around. Nothing was ever said.

The horses were turned back out with the exception of Ben's wrangle horse, and Pete instructed us to rest up and take it easy. He informed us that in the afternoon we were going to trail some horses to Badger Flat so we could be ready to get started in the wee hours of Monday morning. I could tell by his body language that Dale was already privy to all this information, and Pete was only giving it for Ben's and my benefit.

At one in the afternoon, Ray rode back into camp on a very tired looking horse which he unsaddled. Pete met him at the horse corral, and they visited while the rest of us watched from the bunkhouse. After talking for awhile they walked to the bunkhouse where Dale was fixing us all some lunch, and we ate. As soon as we were done, Pete ordered Ben to wrangle the horses for the second time that day. When the horses were in the corral, Pete told us all to catch a tough one, so I called for Toddy. We learned that Ben and I were to trail three horses to Badger Flat, one each for Pete, Dale and Ray. Ben and I would ride the same horse that afternoon as well as the next day. We were instructed to trot the horses across to Badger Flat ten miles away, and Pete would drive over in a pickup and pick us up and give us a ride back to the headquarters. The plan was to return to Badger Flat early the next morning.

We were up early and ate breakfast at three Monday morning, and then we all loaded up into Pete's ranch pickup and headed back to Badger Flat. Mitzi went with us to drive the truck back to headquarters because we planned on riding all the way back on horseback trailing a bunch of Double 0 steers in front of us. Mitzi, Pete and Dale rode in the front of the truck, and Ray, Ben and I rode in the back along with a pile of saddles, blankets and other gear. We bounced along the rocky road gazing out into the stars and remained silent, trapped in our own thoughts. I thought about Bevin, and for some reason I remembered the old Marty Robbins song "El Paso" where the cowboy who had committed a crime gets shot by a member of a posse as he makes his way back to his sweetheart, Felina. Was I going to be shot for crimes I had committed and die in Bevin's arms? I mentally shook myself out of those crazy imaginations and reminded myself that I was the kid on the outfit and was only following orders given to me by older men.

The pickup bounced to a stop outside the horse corral at Badger Flat, and we busied ourselves getting a catch rope in hand as well as a bridle, and we took our dutiful places in the well-rehearsed scene of catching and saddling horses. Mitzi and the taillights of Pete's pickup were almost out of sight when we stepped on our horses and rode south. South to the E L Pasture on the Double O Ranch.

We rode quickly, and it wasn't much of a ride to get to a wire gate in the fence that separated the Cow Creek Ranch from the Double O. Pete had ridden in the E L Pasture before, and so had Dale, so they had a good idea how to make a drive and gather some steers. The country in the E L Pasture was rougher than the top of the mesa where we had gathered the O R O heifers. There were deeper canyons and higher ridges and a great many huge granite boulders strewn about, some of them resembling houses scattered around the countryside and mixed in with brush and trees. We were well into the E L and high up on a granite ridge when the sun peaked its head over the eastern horizon. We sat on our horses, hidden among vegetation and boulders, and surveyed the countryside looking for either men, who might possibly see us, or steers that could be gathered. We saw no men but could see many steers, and they were close by. They were all what was known as Mexicans, cattle crossed into the U.S. over the Mexican border. That meant they had been handled a great deal so they would be gentle and easily driven to a new stomping ground.

Where we had positioned ourselves on a high ridge amidst granite rocks, cedar trees and cliffrose plants that were eight to ten feet high, we were well hidden. We sat on our horses, silent and observant, looking east as the sun peaked its head over the horizon. No one about, that we saw. No dust in the distance from a fast moving horse or a vehicle on some dirt road. There was only the coolness of the June morning and lots of Mexican steers lowing in the draws and hilltops that lay before us. A windmill could be seen a mile and a half to the east, and between that windmill and our position there were at least two hundred steers grazing or laying about, not having any idea what was about to happen.

It was two miles from where we gazed at the easy pickings that awaited us and the gate that we had ridden through less than an hour before. A gate that a man on a fast horse could reach in five minutes or less. A gate that was about eleven miles from the Cow Creek Ranch headquarters.

"I'll take Tommy, Ray and Ben and circle around the head of that draw, and we'll cut this whole bunch off before we reach the windmill. You follow up with the tail end, and about the time we get even with the well, we'll whip 'em into a trot and skedaddle to the gate. Make 'em run if we can! We'll make it quick!" Pete was talking to Dale, but we all understood what he was saying. Dale nodded and then Pete took off in a lope, and the three of us followed riding fast. We had gone no more than four hundred yards when Pete looked over his shoulder and motioned for Ray to drop off. But his dropping off was a mere change of directions, for there were Mexican steers scattered in front of him and he hit them in a run, whipping his heavy chaps with his latigo reins. The steers were soon moving at a brisk pace toward the windmill. A quarter mile farther Pete looked at Ben and motioned him to drop off, but like Ray, his dropping off was only a change in directions, and he chased the steers that lay before him.

Now, after only a few minutes, there were somewhere between 150 and 200 steers loping toward the windmill to the left of where Pete and I rode. "All right, Tommy, let's turn their Mexican hind ends north toward the gate!" Pete hollered at me as he whipped his horse into a dead run hitting the leaders and cutting them off before they reached the well. I flanked for him a hundred yards behind, and we whipped and spurred and turned the herd of running steers north as Ben, Ray and Dale came to us riding hard in an arc, all of us hurrying the steers north instead of east. In less than fifteen minutes, we had the herd bunched up and headed to the gate. The steers were gentle and had only run for a short distance because we made them, and before we got to the gate, they settled down to a fast walk three and four abreast, marching like soldiers. Pete loped up to the gate when we got to it and counted the cattle through just as if they belonged to him. Now, for all practical purposes, they did. One hundred and eighty-six of them. After they all filed through the gate, we turned them sharply down into a draw that would help keep us concealed from someone watching to the east on the Double O Ranch. We turned west toward a holding pasture on the east side of the Cow Creek headquarters, about ten miles distance. It was seven o'clock in the morning. We would be there easily by one in the afternoon.

Chapter Twelve

On Tuesday, July first we were up eating breakfast at 5 a.m. Mitzi was in the bunkhouse cooking, and by anyone's casual observance, it was just another normal day on a Northern Arizona cattle ranch. The atmosphere seemed more relaxed than it had for several days. The fact that we had stolen 284 head of cattle from our neighbors had been accepted in our minds. I supposed that Pete, Dale and Ray never lost any sleep over it anyway.

Pete had been on the phone talking to the men in California who were buying the O R O heifers and the Double O steers and had finalized all the arrangements for their departure from Cow Creek and their arrival in the San Joaquin Valley. For the first time he talked openly to all of us who were involved, whereas previously his conversations about it had been with Dale and Ray only. Ben had never been told directly about what was going on and had not overheard the conversation about the cattle stealing plan like I had. He had not had any conversations about any of it with Dale, like I had. He and Ray almost never talked about anything. Ben had just been following orders.

"We've got a little change of plans," Pete began. "We're gonna load those cattle this afternoon instead of tomorrow. They're goin' to an outfit out west of McKittrick a few miles, a little ways the other side of Bakersfield. It's about ten or eleven hours across there, and it will be a lot cooler traveling at night across that cussed desert. Jimmy Duncan is gonna be here at five o'clock to write us some papers. We'll be done by six or seven, and then we can all go to town and celebrate. We are all gonna get a big paycheck in five or six days."

Ray took a big swallow of coffee and chuckled, "Yeaaah! I'm gonna take a few days off and I'm goin' to California!"

"What are you going to do there, Ray? Go to Disneyland and ride the Ferris wheel?" Mitzi asked sarcastically.

"No! I ain't going to no Disneyland, I'm goin' down to the beach and get acquainted with some of those California girls!"

Mitzi took a big drag off of a new cigarette and said, "In your cowboy boots?" Everyone roared with laughter, Ray even laughed, everyone except Ben who sat with his back against the wall acting nervous. He looked like a trapped raccoon.

Pete told us that we could relax all morning. We would eat an early lunch around eleven and then we would gather all of the Double O steers and the O R O heifers and bring them into the corrals. Our conversation centered around what could be done with a large sum of money. There was talk of buying new pickups, new flower-carved saddles, silver bits and handmade boots. Dale showed his age by talking about buying a little piece of land somewhere and building a little house. Mostly I listened. Ben left the room early in the conversation without saying anything. Nobody seemed to notice. He was always quiet.

We ate at eleven like Pete had said, and at a little after twelve, we saddled up and were ready to ride. Pete sent me with Dale, and we gathered a holding pasture south and west of the headquarters where the O R O heifers were grazing. Pete took Ray and Ben and went out east of camp and gathered the Double O steers. Both pastures had been gathered and the cattle penned by three o'clock. Dale explained to me as we rode out to the backside of the holding pasture that Pete had sold the yearlings by the head, not by the pound, so there was no need to weigh them, and we weren't going to worry about how much weight was shrunk off of them while we held them in the corral waiting for the trucks to arrive.

Jimmy Duncan pulled into the ranch at a quarter to four and got out of his pickup and walked over to talk to Pete. No one could hear their conversation, but from where the rest of us sat in the shade of the corral fence, everything appeared to be amiable. After a short conversation the two of them walked back to Jimmy's pickup. The white Chevy truck had a large star emblem painted on each door, the type of star resembling a sheriff's badge. On top of the star were the words written in large black letters, LIVESTOCK INSPECTOR, and underneath the big black star, STATE of ARIZONA.

Jimmy opened the driver's door and reached in and retrieved a large book similar to a tablet with a lot of carbon paper. Pete leaned on the hood of the pickup and filled out brand inspection papers on 98 heifers and 186 steers. I had no idea whom he listed on the papers as the owner, seller or buyer. I was never given the buyer's name, only that they were going somewhere near McKittrick in Southern California. Jimmy Duncan never looked at the cattle in the corral, and he never counted them. After handing Pete the hauling papers, he and Pete shook hands, and he got back in the Chevy pickup with the big black star and drove back toward Seligman.

The dust had barely settled from Jimmy Duncan's departure when the three big semi-trucks came rattling down the road, three cabover Kenworths, each pulling a set of doubles, brand-new aluminum, double deck, side loading trailers that we loaded forty-seven yearlings onto, except two got forty-eight. We didn't worry about sorting anything or keeping the steers and heifers separate. Just get 'em loaded and gone, that was the goal. The cattle

We loaded three trucks and they were headed back to Route 66 by a quarter of six.

were big and framey, but because of the drought they were not packing much fat. They probably weighed a little over five hundred, but we never weighed them. We were done loading all three trucks, and they were heading back toward Route 66 by a quarter to six. It was all done. The neighbors' cattle were gone.

We rode to the barn and unsaddled our horses, and everyone turned theirs out in the horse pasture except me because Pete had told me to keep my horse up so I could wrangle on him the next day. Then we all walked down to the bunkhouse where Mitzi had started cooking supper. Pete opened a new bottle of Old Crow whiskey and poured everyone a drink whether they had asked for one or not. He was very lighthearted and almost talkative. He told us that for all practical purposes the spring roundup was over. We all drank to that. He said to everyone in general that Ray would be going to Badger Flat after the Fourth of July weekend to take care of everything on that end of the ranch. Everyone already knew that was going to happen so it wasn't news. He looked me in the eye and offered me a steady place on the payroll and said I could spend the summer breaking colts to ride right there at headquarters. That was news, and everyone drank to that, everyone except Ben who seemed in no mood to drink. Pete told Ben he ought to go home for the night and have Sharon bring him back in the morning so he could trail his horses back to Black Creek. Nothing was said about Dale's future, but we all knew that Dale had a permanent place on the ranch.

Ben got up, excused himself, and said he was going to load all of his plunder and head home to his family. We all raise our glasses to him and drank another toast. "Tell Sharon hello, Ben." Mitzi said as Ben walked out of the room.

As Ben's truck rolled out of the yard and headed toward Black Creek, we filled our plates with the supper Mitzi had fixed, and the general feeling of camaraderie and merriment continued. We had rib steaks and baked potatoes, accompanied with sour cream that Mitzi had purchased in town, and fresh homemade light bread on the side.

About the time I took the first bite out of my steak, we heard a vehicle pull up to the front of the bunkhouse and then car doors slamming. Everyone was so relaxed no one got up to see who it was. We heard footsteps coming our way and through the kitchen door walked Ken and Dallas from the Double O Ranch. The mood changed instantly, and for a moment I saw electricity in the atmosphere. Pete jumped to his feet and clenched his fists.

"Howdy boys! Evening ma'am. Didn't mean to bust in at suppertime." Ken said in a friendly tone of voice.

"I thought you was goin' to Wyoming on a trip for a few days!" Pete said gruffly.

"Well, I did, I did, and I just got back this afternoon and thought I ought to run over here and bring Tommy my old bronc saddle and all my stuff so he would be ready for Prescott here in a couple days. Didn't mean to surprise ya none, just wanted to see Tommy."

Pete relaxed and his tone softened. "Good to see you fellas! How about a big rib steak? Won't take a minute to cook it, and we'll share a drink with you while it's cooking!"

"No! No! Really we didn't want to intrude on you!" Ken protested.

"No intrusion! Sit down and join us, we're glad you are here," Mitzi said as she deposited two steaks into the large cast-iron skillet. Pete was pouring Old Crow into a couple of glasses while Dale put his hands on the two men's shoulders and pushed them into an honored spot at the table. The mood became festive again, and Pete went to talking to the Double O cowboys like they were relatives he hadn't seen in years. The two visitors made the mistake of finishing their whiskey, and Pete opened a new bottle and poured a triple shot into their glasses.

"By golly, you people are treatin' us downright neighborly. I didn't expect this! I was just bringin' Tommy here my bronc saddle, didn't expect a rib steak and free drinks! Or are you chargin' us for the drinks?" He said the last words as a joke, and everyone laughed heartily at his wit.

"Damn right, you fellas are good neighbors and we're glad you came!" Pete slammed his whiskey glass down on the table as he said it.

"I'll make a toast to that!" Dale said and he took another swallow of Old Crow. He was beginning to glow with happiness.

"I'm glad you came, too, Pete woulda' never opened that other bottle if you hadn't of showed up!" Ray grinned. The nerves in his eye socket that held the glass prosthesis were becoming numb with the Old Crow, and his eye began to roll around. Dallas stared at him in disbelief, and Ray, who was sitting close to him, leaned over and put his face a few inches from Dallas's face and said as gruffly as possible, "What are you staring at!" Dallas was unnerved and obviously intimidated and afraid to say anything.

"He's looking at your damn glass eye, you idiot!" Mitzi said as she put two sizzling steaks in front of Dallas and Ken. Everyone except Dallas roared with laughter. "Don't pay any attention to him, none of us do." Mitzi advised.

"Yeah, but you love me, don't you!" Ray said.

"Yes, I love you just like I loved an old dog I used to have when I was a kid. But he didn't have fleas and you do!" The laughter got louder, and Ray, in his perverted way, relished the sarcastic remark. He was already drunk.

The Double O men dug into the beefsteak, and the merriment and conversation continued until everyone was finished eating. I had remained sober enough to mind my manners, and I offered to do the dishes, but Mitzi turned me down saying she wanted all of us to celebrate the end of the spring roundup. She reminded everyone that she was celebrating also. She wouldn't be cooking for us until fall so cleaning up after supper was going to be no trouble at all.

When Ken finished his steak, he said he wanted to go out to his truck and get his bronc saddle and bring it in for me to take a look at. Dale, Ray, Dallas and I moved into the other room where our beds and living quarters were, and soon Ken came packing in his old Hamley Association saddle and his riggin' bag, and he deposited it all in the middle of the floor. The saddle looked well used and gave a man the impression that it knew how to ride, whether the man sitting in it did or not.

"You ever ridden a horse in one of these?" Ken ask me.

"No, I sure haven't!"

"Well, it's different, a whole new ball of wax. But as good a cowboy bronc rider as you are, you ought to get the hang of it pretty fast. Sit in it and let's get your stirrups set right."

I sat in the seat of the Hamley saddle as it lay on the hard cement floor. The funny looking stirrup leathers laid out in front of it, and I put my cowboy boots in the narrow oxbow stirrups. It seemed to me that the stirrups were too long. Ken was several inches taller than I was so I figured that the stirrups would have to be adjusted. Ken got down on his hands and knees and started unbuckling and adjusting stirrup leathers, first the left side and then the right.

"Now get down deep in the saddle and stretch your legs out and turn your toes out as far as you can." I did what he told me, and the stirrups felt about right. My insteps were pressing into the oxbows as my butt was pressing into the cantle. "Now," Ken said, "take your left foot and act like you're spurring a horse all the way back to the back of the saddle."

I did so and then snapped my foot back forward with my toes turned out. He adjusted a leather strap, which ran through a hole in the front of the skirts and wrapped around the inside of the stirrup leather, by letting it out one hole looser. Then we went through the same process on the right side. Ken went to great lengths explaining all the parts of a bronc saddle and the difference between that type of saddle and a saddle a cowboy would ride every day on a ranch. I was aware that differences existed but found myself to be quite ignorant about the particulars. It was all very interesting to me, but I was also embarrassed about my ignorance. But Ken was nice and seemed genuine in his attempt to help me. Besides his bronc saddle, he also loaned me his rodeo chaps and bronc spurs and a good hack rein, all things that I did not possess.

Dale and Ray had been sitting in on the lesson and adjustment of the stirrup leathers and bindings on the saddle, and Dale had asked a question or two. Suddenly Ray, who had been quiet up to that point, blurted out, "Hell, there ain't nothin' different about ridin' one of those buckers out of a chute. You just rare back and pull on their head and spur 'em!"

"Well, actually, there is a great deal of difference." Ken was going to go on but Ray interrupted.

"Oh crap! You got a man on a bucking horse just like out here in the brush! Only difference is, a grandstand full of ten thousand people! Some horses buck harder and some men ride better, but it's the same darn thing." He was quite drunk.

Ken looked at me and quietly said, "There is a difference. You ride real good, and I know that, but there's a difference. First of all you have to mark your horse out. You have to be spurring him over the point of his shoulders when he hits the ground the first jump or they will disqualify you. I doubt you will have trouble with that."

"Hell, no, he ain't gonna have no trouble; he rides better than anybody else in the country, including you! What'd you ever win?" Ray's drunkenness was now leading to belligerence.

"I heard Ken rode pretty good, Ray." Dale interjected.

"Oh yeah? Good? Tell us where you won!"

"Oh, I never won much, but I know a little about it."

"Well, if you never won nothin', what are you preachin' to this kid for? If you ain't won nothin' then you don't know nothin'!" Ray bellowed and then turned the bottle of Old Crow upside down with the open end in his mouth.

"Tell them the rodeos where you have won, Ken." Dallas said defensively. Ken just shrugged his shoulders but said nothing so Dallas went on. "He won Cheyenne one time a few years back."

"No I didn't." Ken said.

"You told me just the other day that you won Cheyenne!" Dallas was pleading for a confirmation.

"I won the amateur bronc riding at Cheyenne in 1956, the year I turned eighteen. But I didn't win the pro part of it. I've placed there three other times but never first. Just first in the amateur."

"Tell them about the other rodeos you won." Dallas went on. "You won at Calgary and Pendleton and Red Bluff! Tell them about all the places where you competed! Tell them! Tell them!"

"So you've rode in all those big shows, Ken?" Dale said in a very friendly tone.

"Yeah, I went to a few rodeos when I was a kid, but I was never real good. I was just having fun. But I saw a lotta neat stuff. A lotta great bronc rides."

Ray was a little quieter, a little less hostile. "So what's the best ride you ever made? The most money?"

"Well, I won the bronc riding at Red Lodge, Montana, two years in a row. I grew up around there, south of there between Red Lodge and Cody. I guess that meant a lot to me. I had a little buckle they gave me the second time I won it, the first time they didn't give a buckle, just money. But somebody stole it from me. It was my prized possession but it got stolen. I don't know why somebody would steal from a friend. Another time I drew a famous bucker called Miss Klamath at Prineville, Oregon. I saw Miss Klamath buck Casey Tibbs off one time, not to mention several other great riders. I had seen the horse go three or four times and never saw her ridden. The horse would kick straight over her head every time, the darndest kicker you ever saw. I drew her at Prineville ten years ago. It was my twenty-first birthday. Deb Copenhaver was there behind the chutes, and he had ridden her. I asked him about her, and he helped me measure my rein and get out on her. He was a nice man. I rode her and was 88 points, best ride I ever made. Deb came out three rides later on another great kicker from the Christenson and Son string named War Paint. Deb was 89 points. I was second on the best ride I ever made. But nobody can steal the feeling I had."

"Well, hells bells, I didn't know you was such a good feller! Have a drink." Ray passed the Old Crow to Ken.

"Well, Ken, you need to give Tommy some advice. This kid ain't a know it all, he'll listen." Dale said and I nodded in agreement.

"The main thing is lift on your rein, and when your feet blow out of the shoulders, you fight to get 'em back down there before he hits the ground again. Let your feet come back to the cantle and drag some iron across his hide, but you have to charge the front end. Keep getting under your rein and charging the front end! Lift and charge! Lift and charge!"

I hated to sound ignorant, but I had to ask him, "What do you mean—get under your rein?"

"You don't pull on the rein, you lift. If you pull your bronc rein back to your side, your upper body will move forward and out over your swells. You lift, keep your rein out in front of you and keep your upper body back with your chin tucked and stick that rein out and lift up. If you lift on your rein your butt will go down and force your feet forward toward the end of your stirrups and the horse's shoulders. Sometimes when you're doing it right, your body will be under your rein hand. It's backwards to what you naturally think, but it works. You don't pull on your rein and bring your chest forward, instead you lift, forcing your butt down into the saddle, your feet forward, and your chest back. Keep your chest back on the downstroke. Lift, charge the front end with your toes out, and your upper body back. And don't lose control of your neck! Keep your chin tucked and your nose down."

Suddenly I realized that everyone was staring at me with a judgmental look on their faces. They were wondering if I had digested all of that professional advice, or at least I imagined they were wondering. I had not swallowed any liquid courage for at least forty-five minutes, and the buzz was wearing off, and along with that an awareness that I had no concept of what Ken meant when he said to lift and not pull. I had never felt the sensation of being under my rein. I was a fair to middlin' bronc rider out in a cactus patch or a rock pile, and I had no fear, but I had no bearings, or point of reference, in a rodeo arena. The amateur bronc riding at the Prescott Frontier Days was going to be my Genesis. I felt very uneasy.

Ken and Dallas stayed for a while after he helped adjust the bronc saddle to fit me. We all visited and told cowboy stories. Dale and Ray mostly told stories about rough country cowboying and wild cattle, and Ken told a few more good rodeo stories, mostly about Northern rodeos and bucking horses. We could all tell by the stories that he had been around. I could tell by the stories that he was a lot better bronc rider than he would ever let on. He was obviously humble and not prone to bring attention to his accomplishments. At eleven o'clock he and Dallas left and headed back toward the Double O Ranch and we Cow Creek cowboys turned in for the night.

The next morning I woke up at five thirty and went out and fed the wrangle horse and then returned to the bunkhouse kitchen and made coffee. I put on a big pan of bacon to fry. It was my eighteenth birthday, July second. I was feeling better than the night before. I felt like I could ride Five Minutes to Midnight to a standstill. I didn't understand lifting on my rein, but I did know about staying on top. I would rely on that. I would rely on my instincts. When I got down on my bronc in the bucking chute, I would look out across the Prescott rodeo grounds and imagine seeing saguaro and cholla cactus and granite rocks. I would stay on. I drank hot black coffee and hot young blood pumped through my veins. I had the next five days off, Pete had told me so. After breakfast I would drive into Seligman and see Bevin.

I took a shower and put on a clean suit of clothes: new Levis size 32 x 36, a new denim shirt with pearl snaps, my new Stetson hat with the cattleman's crease; and my Tony Lama boots were polished. Me an Old Dirty left the ranch at 10:00 a.m., and I was in Seligman by 11:00, and because of habit I drove by the Conoco service station thinking that maybe Bevin would be there, but the unkempt hillbilly with the dirty shirt was working so I didn't stop. I knew from experience that talking to him would be fruitless.

I drove up to Bevin's house and knocked on the door, but nobody answered. I looked around back of the house. I even peeked into the living room window. No one was there and the family car was gone. I got back in Dirty and drove back to the Conoco service station, parked and walked in to talk to the hillbilly with the dirty shirt. Before I could even ask were Bevin was, he opened a drawer under the counter and retrieved an envelope and handed

it to me. "She said to give this to you when you came by."
On the outside of the envelope was written, Tommy. I took
my pocket knife and cut the envelope open being careful
not to cut what was held inside, one white piece of paper
that was folded:

Dear Tommy,

*We had an unexpected emergency in our family, a
medical issue with my dad's younger sister who lives
in Santa Rosa, New Mexico. I went with my family,
and we drove to Albuquerque to be with my aunt and
her family and try to help in some way while she is in
the hospital there in Albuquerque. I will tell you about
it when I get back.*
*I am hoping to be back in time to see you ride in Prescott
at the rodeo on July fourth. I will make it down there
someway so look for me in the grandstand. I will be
cheering. I am your biggest fan!*

Love you,
Bevin

Well, I won't be seeing Bevin today. I drove up and
down Route 66 from the east end of town to the west. I
turned around and went back east and stopped in front
of Delgaddios Snow Cone and bought myself a milkshake
and sat outside at a table with a canvas cover on it and
watched the cars go by. I sat there a long time with
nowhere to go and no one to talk to, and then I got up and
bought another milkshake and sat down and drank it and
watched some more cars go by. Being too embarrassed
to buy a third, I got up and drove away. I turned around
on the far east side of town and headed west and slowly
drove out to the ranch.

I pulled into the ranch about three in the afternoon and could see Pete, Dale and Ray standing in the shade of a big cottonwood tree near the barn, so I parked Dirty and walked up to where they were. In the distance to the west, I saw a big dust rising into the sky coming off the dirt road that led to Black Creek. Someone was coming.

"Happy birthday, Tommy!" Pete said as I walked up. "Did you see your girl?"

"No, she wasn't home. Had to go to Albuquerque to see an aunt who is in the hospital there."

"So did you go down to the Black Cat and get drunk, Peckerwood, beings your little church-mouse wasn't around to keep you out of trouble?" Ray asked.

"Actually, I downed a double shot! I downed two milkshakes at the snow cone." All three men laughed at that. The dust was getting closer, and around the corner of the barn came Ben, Sharon and Cheyenne in Ben's old Chevy pickup that was hooked to an old stock trailer. The pickup and the old trailer were piled high and stuffed full of furniture and everything else Ben and Sharon owned. There were mattresses, a table and chairs, boxes of pots and pans, and pillows and blankets stuffed into the cracks. There was Cheyenne's old wooden highchair tied onto the side of the trailer with a nylon piggin' string. On the other side of the trailer was a homemade wire cage with a half-dozen chickens captured inside. The front half of the makeshift cage was lined with cardboard in an obvious attempt to keep the wind from blowing all the chickens' feathers off. In the back of the trailer in a small crack several inches wide that was between a thick layer of household goods and the metal trailer gate were Ben's two hound dogs who stood on their hind paws, and their front paws and muzzles were sticking out of the cracks between the steel rails in the gate. The hounds went back and forth between fits of barking as if they had a lion bayed up in a tree and panting and whining like they might die of thirst or neglect.

"Well, lookie there, a couple pilgrims leaving Egypt and headed toward the Promise Land. I ain't surprised." Pete said.

Ben parked between the bunkhouse, the barn, and the cottonwood tree, about a hundred yards distance from where the three of us were standing under the tree. He got out of the truck and cautiously approached.

"You want me to kick his ass, Pete?" Ray said in a whisper. "He and that holy roller he's married to will do a lot of talkin'!"

"Naw. I'll do the ass kickin' if it needs done, but he'll never say anything to anyone. Besides, what's he gonna say? I've got haulin' papers. The only brand recorded on the haulin' papers is the P O Bar, my personal brand."

Ben was now close enough to hear what was being said so Pete and Ray became silent. Ben approached slowly, warily, as if he expected some kind of trouble. We all remained still, like Kawliga the wooden Indian who stared off into space at nobody. Or everybody. He slowed down and stopped without entering the shade of the cottonwood. "I guess I'm going to be leaving, Pete." He kicked a rock near his cowboy boot, and he stared down toward the dust and several seconds of silence passed uneasily. After slowly raising his eyes, he managed to get some words out of his mouth, "I'm sorry if I'm leavin' you in a tight spot, but I gotta go."

"When you leave, Ben, I'll be all caught up." Pete said in an octave so low that his vocal cords rumbled like great stones rolling down a mountainside. They stood there staring at each other—one in derision and the other in mortal fear.

I walked away and went down to the shady side of the Chevy truck that resembled a vision of the *Grapes of Wrath.*

Sharon sat there with Cheyenne crawling all over her and both of them perspiring. The hens in the cage cackled and the hounds howled in misery. "Sharon, I'm sorry you're leaving!"

She looked at me with her Mona Lisa eyes. A drop of sweat slid down her forehead, and she used the back of her hand to wipe it away. "Tommy, you need to leave here."

I faltered for words and looked down at the ground for a moment, and then in a forced exhibition of courage, I challenged her statement, "I'm doin' fine, Sharon. I'm not going anywhere. I've got a job."

Ben had walked back to the truck. He opened the opposite door, slid in the driver's side, and started the engine. He put the gearshift into first, and looked at me, "I enjoyed working with you, Tommy. Thanks for being a friend." He stretched his arm past his wife and offered me his hand. I shook it, and then they were gone in a cloud of dry July dust.

Chapter Thirteen

On Friday, the Fourth of July, we set out for Prescott and the Frontier Days Rodeo, which was supposed to be the oldest rodeo in the world. I didn't know if there was any truth to that claim or not, but we were going to be there, and I was entered. It was the three of us, Dale, Ray, and me, traveling down the dusty road in Old Dirty. Ray didn't own a vehicle, and Dale still had his nice Chevy pickup loaned to Wanda, whose truck had not been repaired yet. Then to top it off, Wanda had announced that her old mama, who lived in Las Vegas, Nevada, had come down with an illness. Could she use Dale's nice Chevy truck to travel to Las Vegas to minister to her sick mother? Of course! Dale couldn't say no. He was a man who would give someone he liked anything or everything and never complain, so Wanda had the use of the Chevy, and Dale was afoot and womanless. Neither deficiency seemed to bother him. A pickup in his mind was no more than a hunk of iron that could be replaced. He seemed to like Wanda, but there was no doubt that she was replaceable also. There were always lots of women in Prescott on the Fourth of July.

About eight miles west of Seligman, we turned south on the road that took us down by the H's Camp on the Double O and then past the small Anvil Rock Ranch and then the E L Pasture where we had stolen almost two hundred steers a few days earlier. After a dozen miles or so, we drove past the Oaks and Willows, which was what the O R O headquarters was named. And then on down the north fork of Walnut Creek and the famous K4 Ranch, and finally thirty-seven miles after that, we reached the outskirts of Prescott. I had never come into town on those backroads before, and I enjoyed the drive. It was hot and humid when we reached the rodeo grounds at ten thirty, and a few big thunderheads were starting to build. Everyone was hoping it would rain.

The famous rodeo arena was located in the infield of the racetrack. I drove across the track and parked with the other contestants, who filled up every bit of the space that wasn't taken up by the arena itself. The huge grandstand was empty, but there was lots of activity. Pickups and big cars hooked to horse trailers were as thick as flies, and cowboys and cowgirls were walking around or huddled in small groups visiting. There was lots of laughter and I could feel the excitement and expectations of the afternoon performance even though it was still two and a half hours away. I needed to find the rodeo office so I could pay my entry fees, so I parked behind the corrals and bucking chutes and set out to tend to my business. Dale and Ray told me they were going to go find the beer stand but would return in plenty of time to help me out with my bronc.

As I walked around the west end of the arena, which was the end where the roping chute and boxes were located, I asked a cowboy where the entry office was, and he pointed toward a rock building across the racetrack and west of the big grandstand. I walked on and passed several famous rodeo cowboys who were standing around in bunches swapping stories. There was a great deal of laughter and camaraderie among everyone, some of whom I recognized from pictures I had seen in magazines. The Camarillo brothers were gathered around their big Buick car talking to John Miller, who was partnered up with them in the team tying. Standing by a Ford pickup and horse trailer, I saw

Billy Hamilton, whom I knew because my dad had broke several horses for him. I waved at him, and he waved back saying, "Howdy, Tommy, how are you?" He was visiting with Joe Glenn and Art Arnold, and all of them were past world champion team ropers. It felt good to be recognized by someone as famous as a world champion.

I walked up to the rodeo secretary's office and almost bumped into Cody Bill Smith and Larry Mahan who were walking out the office door as I tried to enter. Inside the office were more top cowboys standing in line and paying their entry fees. When I walked up to the secretary and told her my business, she said that she remembered seeing my name on the amateur bronc riding list. She ran her finger down through the names, and when she came to mine it read, Paid. "Keep your money, cowboy, somebody already paid for you." By the stroke of her hand, she dismissed me, and began dealing with the cowboy behind me. No doubt Mr. King from the Double O Ranch had paid the entry fee when he had my name written down on the list.

I left the rodeo secretary's office and walked up into the huge grandstand that was elevated a few feet above the rodeo arena. The arena and oval racetrack that circumvented it sat below a granite hill, and the covered grandstand was built on the slope of that hill. There were lots of pine trees and brush visible in a beautiful natural landscape. Big cumulus clouds were building, which cooled the atmosphere with their shade and humidity. Cicadas were making noise, and the whole fairground smelled like pine. I walked along the upper level of the grandstand sucking in the air and reveling in the thought that I was about to ride in the Prescott Frontier Days Rodeo. I had been here as a spectator many times when growing up but had never dreamed that I would be down there in the arena in front of a roaring crowd. I was excited, even euphoric. I wandered through the growing crowd of rodeo fans and looked for Bevin but couldn't find her. I found Dale and Ray, instead, at the beer stand talking to a couple of, what my dad called, chippies.

"Hey, Tommy, come on over here. Let me introduce you to a couple of old friends!" Dale was waving his arm at me. "Well, they're young beautiful friends, but I've known them a long time! Let's put it that way. Tommy, this is Kay and Veronica." He pointed at them and then at me. "Kay, Veronica, this is Tommy Lee, the best young cowboy I've worked with in forty years! I love him like a son!"

Kay and Veronica smiled, "So you are Tommy Lee, we've heard a lot about you!" Kay held out her hand, suggesting that I shake it. I did so with as much style as I could muster. Veronica, who was sitting on a bar stool close to Ray, simply stared at me and smiled. Her bedroom eyes smoldered, and when she was sure I was staring at her, she turned sideways and posed in the perfect position to make her large breasts, which were encased in a white blouse, create a sensuous silhouette against the dark wood of the bar. Ray attempted to suspend the electricity that had suddenly been created by her moves. "Where's your little church mouse, Peckerwood?"

Ray's crude question shook me out of the spell that Veronica's shape and smile had put me under. She addressed me for the first time. "So cowboy, you got yourself a sweetheart, huh?"

"Uh—ah, yes, ma'am, I do!"

She lifted her thick brown eyebrows and grinned at me and said, "Yes ma'am... you are the cutest little gentleman I've been around in ages! You're like a teddy bear; I'd like to take you home and see what else you can do!"

"Hell, that kid is as dumb as a post!" Ray roared. Kay started giggling.

"I'll bet I could teach him a thing or two!" Veronica said and then she winked at me.

Ray raised his can of Schlitz beer and tilted his head back and swallowed ten ounces and then crushed the can with his hand like it was paper. The crushing was loud, and Veronica looked at him and said, "Ho, Egor, settle down!" He turned his back to me and ordered another round of beers for everyone but me. "Tommy, you want a beer?" Varonica asked.

"He ain't old enough to drink beer!" Ray said loudly, and then the bartender stared at me in a menacing way.

I decided to make my exit. "Nice to meet you girls, I gotta get going."

"See you, Teddy!" Veronica waved.

"His name is Tommy!" Ray said.

I walked quickly away and looked through the crowd as I drifted toward the west end of the grandstand. I didn't see Bevin or anyone else that I knew, so I walked down and across the racetrack and entered the infield where all the rodeo contestants were parked. The ropers were saddling their horses and some were riding around warming them up. Bronc riders and bull riders were walking toward the back of the chutes packing their bronc saddles and riggin' bags, so I went to Old Dirty and got Ken's Association saddle and all the stuff he had loaned me and followed the cowboys. A large bunch of rough stock riders had accumulated behind the bucking chutes, and most of them were checking their gear and making adjustments or repairs or just visiting. I recognized several more famous cowboys, Clyde Vamvoras and Doug Brown were there, and like Mahan and Smith, I recognized them from pictures in magazines. There was no one around that I had ever met. Most of the famous guys all seem to be laughing and enjoying themselves while some others were serious and totally engrossed in their thoughts. I found an empty space of dirt and threw the Hamley bronc saddle down along with the riggin' bag. I tried to act like

I knew what I was doing. I could see some saddle bronc riders sitting in their saddles that lay on the ground, and they seemed to be checking the length of their stirrups and their binds. Several were rubbing rosin on the inside of their chap legs and the swells of their saddles. I imitated some of the things they were doing and tried to fit in.

"What'd ya draw?" A bronc rider who was sitting close to me said.

"I don't know, haven't checked." I replied.

"I've got a good one, so I hear."

"Where do you find out?"

He looked at me like I had asked a dumb question. "The draw is posted over there on the fence." He pointed at several pieces of white paper that were stapled to a board on the corral fence a few feet away. I walked over and looked at the paper. Everyone who was going to ride that day was listed, and the horse or bull they had drawn was written alongside their names. The list said that I had drawn a bronc named Red Pepper. I also learned that there were seven other men entered in the amateur bronc riding which would be run between the bull dogging and the barrel racing.

"I gotta horse named Red Pepper." I said to the cowboy who had talked to me earlier.

He looked at me and shrugged his shoulders, and for a second he concentrated on adjusting his stirrup leathers. "Anyone know anything about a horse called Red Pepper?" He hollered to everyone in general and went on working on his saddle.

"Don't know him," someone said.

"Nope," came from someone else.

"Who's got 'em?" someone else hollered the question from down at the far end of the chutes.

"What's your name, kid?" asked my new acquaintance.

"Tommy Lee."

"This kid here is named Tommy Lee."

"Is he in the broncs?"

"I'm entered in the amateur saddle bronc riding."

"He's in the amateur," my friend hollered back to the crowd of cowboys while he continued to concentrate on his saddle.

"Hell, they don't put any campaigners in the amateur! It will be a bunch of colts nobody ever heard of." They all agreed Red Pepper and all the broncs in the amateur bronc riding were probably young horses that had not been ridden much, if any.

I hung around the back of the chutes, and for the most part, I just watched and observed what the veteran rodeo hands were doing. They adjusted their saddles and bareback riggings and applied rosin to chaps, swells, gloves and bull ropes. They talked about the horses or bulls they had drawn for the day's performance. They joked and laughed and told stories. They were a clique and I was not a member. I felt no animosity, and I figured that I could become a part of the rodeo fraternity if I became a regular participant, but I realized for the first time that rodeo cowboys and cow hands fresh out of the brush were not necessarily the same species. I was swimming in deep water with no lifejacket, but when the announcer came over the PA system and said that it was only five minutes until rodeo time, I got excited regardless if I was part of the club or not. There was something about a Fourth of July rodeo in a cow town like Prescott.

At one o'clock straight up the announcer said "Ladies and Gentleman! Welcome to the world's oldest rodeo, the Prescott Frontier Days!" The audience had swelled to standing room only, and when the announcer shouted, "Are you ready to rodeo?" the cheering and clapping could have been heard in Wickenburg, sixty miles to the south. The arena gates opened and the cowboys and cowgirls began riding in carrying the American flag, the Arizona state flag, and other flags too numerous to count. A big summertime thunderhead had formed over the grandstands cooling the atmosphere to a comfortable seventy degrees, and a slight breeze blew the smell of piñon pine down into the arena, and it soothed the soul of every rodeo fan present. With the sound of the national anthem, which was sung by some local girl with a beautiful voice, excitement and static electricity oozed down out of the grandstand, and by the end of the song, I felt like I was somebody.

The bareback riding was first, and I claimed a spot to watch on the top rail beside chute number six. The broncs kicked at the gates and refused to stand still, and when they blew out of the chute, they bucked. After several horses had come out of the chutes, I couldn't help but think they made Don Kambitch's buckskin outlaw look like he didn't even know how to buck. There were nine bareback riders and only three of them lasted until the eight-second whistle blew.

About the time they bucked the seventh of the nine bareback horses, Ken showed up. I was glad to see him. He said he would stay with me and help me get down on Red Pepper. I had noticed as he entered the area behind the chutes where all the rough stock hands were hanging out that several of the old veterans shook his hand and said hello to him. It was obvious that they respected him. I felt good to have him hanging around with me.

When it was time for the saddle bronc riding, they ran the professional bronc riders first. The whole bunch made great rides. Mel Hyland asked Ken to help him saddle his horse and get out of the chute on him. As we watched, Ken critiqued the rides and told me technical stuff to watch for. Hanging out with a pro like Ken made me feel comfortable and like I was part of the cult.

Then it was time for the amateur bronc riding. They moved from the pros right into the amateurs without a break, and it caught me off guard. The horses were run into the chutes and a man walking down in the arena in front of the chute gates started hollering at us, "You kids get 'em saddled! Get your asses ready! This is Prescott! You're not in kindergarten anymore!" He walked down in front of the chutes with a clipboard and paper in his hand hollering names and telling us riders what chutes our horses were in. Ken said he was the stock contractor and arena director. He had a big cigar sticking out of his mouth, and he was in a foul mood, or it seemed that way to me.

My horse, Red Pepper, was in chute number four which, according to the cranky man with the cigar, meant I would be fourth out. Ken sprang into motion, which saved my bacon, and started saddling Red Pepper while the arena director paced back and forth. "Get your saddles on, boys, we ain't got all day!" We got the saddle on Red Pepper, and because of Ken's know-how, we got the cinches adjusted evenly. We put the halter on, and Ken asked the cursing, cigar-smoking arena director how much rein to give him. "Oh hell, give him an average plus two. It don't matter, he ain't gonna ride him anyhow," was the cigar smokers answer.

The first two amateurs had gone out into the arena and had promptly been launched into the Prescott sky much earlier than the eight-second whistle. Now there was one before me: a man several years older than I was and having the look of a seasoned hand. The stock contractor's orders didn't seem to faze him, and he took his time getting down on the bronc and got everything right before he nodded his head. And then when he was ready, they opened the gate and the bronc, a big bay, blew out of there jumping and kicking, and the cowboy stayed with him and spurred him in style. He proved that an amateur could ride at Prescott. They scored him 76 points.

Suddenly all eyes were on me. "And now, ladies and gentlemen, we move to chute number four and a horse named Red Pepper. The cowboy is Tommy Lee from Seligman, Arizona!" The PA system speakers seemed louder than usual as the announcer produced more information than I was ready for. "Get on him, kid! I got a rodeo to run here!" the stock contractor shouted at me from in front of the chute gate. Another man that I had seen hanging around the back of the chutes suddenly appeared beside me and wanted to help.

"You can ride him, kid! You can ride him! Don't pay any attention to the horse, kid, just ride that saddle, just ride that saddle!" the stranger said as he slapped my back. "Don't pay any attention to the horse!" I thought to myself, *That's crazy!*

I stood over Red Pepper with my left foot in the seat of the saddle and leaned over hanging onto the hack rein at the exact spot that Ken had told me to. I eased downward slipping my right leg between the gate and the right stirrup.

"Hurry up, kid! We ain't got all day!" The stock contractor snarled at me.

"You want to watch this next horse, ladies and gentlemen. The rumor is he is one of the best young broncs we've got coming on!" The announcer's words blared over the airwaves.

"Don't worry about that horse, kid! Just ride that saddle! Just ride that saddle!" My new-found good Samaritan was talking right into my left ear as I eased my left foot into the left stirrup.

"You folks remember that tomorrow morning you need to be downtown to watch the big rodeo parade at ten o'clock," the announcer declared.

"Damn it, kid, come on!" the cigar smoker hissed.

"Remember, Tommy, lift, don't pull, lift on your rein!" Ken said.

"Don't worry about that horse, kid! Ride that saddle! Ride that saddle!"

I nodded and the gate opened and the roan horse blew out of there like a gigantic torch was gushing out from underneath his black tail. I pointed my toes out and dug my spurs into his neck, and we were airborne. The first jump, I didn't need to worry about keeping my upper body back because the G forces of the tremendous forward motion snapped my chest and head backwards. I fought to keep my chin tucked. The power was overwhelming, but somehow I managed to keep my spurs in his neck. Then the second jump came quicker than I was ready. He broke upwards a second time, and in my mind I remembered I was supposed to move my feet, but I was late and the lateness made them move out of control. My feet blew out of the neck and went back to the front cinch, and before I was ready he was breaking over and coming back down. The power and speed confused me. I felt my upper body going forward and out over the swells of the saddle. I thought about lifting on my rein, but instead I pulled my left hand with the bronc rein back to my side. My chest passed my head and was over the front of the saddle and WHAM, his front feet hit the ground. My legs were forcibly spread apart by the tremendous jar, and I realized my knees were up too far and rubbing against the outside of the saddle swells. Red Pepper went upward into the sky with the power of a rocket while I tried to push my body back, and then at the peak of that third powerful jump, my fanny crashed out of control into the cantle of the Hamley bronc saddle. The connection of Levis' rear pockets and the cantle board was bone jarring and painful. It had, by fate or bad luck, the same effect as a baseball connecting

The power and speed confused me, I felt my upper body going forward and out over the swells.

with a fast-moving bat. I was suddenly being driven like a lead bullet, with powder burning behind it, downward toward the sand on the floor of the Prescott rodeo arena. I felt Red Pepper jerk the bronc rein out of my left hand right before my face crashed into the earth. I slid sideways, and because of the shock of what was happening, I had my mouth wide open. When my face hit the arena floor it slid sideways, and at least two cups of arena sand and horse manure went into my mouth. Luckily for me, Red Pepper bucked on and did not step on me.

"Yes sir! Ladies and gentlemen, you can be proud of the stock here at the oldest rodeo on earth. They bring the best to Prescott every year. Give that young man a hand. That's all he's going to get today!" I lay there for a moment listening to the announcer, and then suddenly I sensed vibrations in the earth, and I opened my eyes, and Red Pepper and the two pickup men thundering toward me. I started to get up and run, but it was too late. I lay down flat on my stomach and covered my head with my hands.

I felt the sensation of horses running over me as a pickup man screamed as he loped by, "Get the hell out of the arena, kid, you're gonna get run over!" I jumped up and realized my hat was gone. I was confused and turned around looking for it while spitting globs of arena sediment out of my mouth. The announcer was saying the next horse was about to come out! Where was my cowboy hat? I saw it forty feet away and ran toward it as the next bronc rider came out on another demonized, fire-breathing bronc that came smashing the earth as it bucked forward. I grabbed my hat and ran toward the chute feeling sure that everyone in the grandstand was laughing at me. The pearl snaps on my cowboy shirt had come undone and my bare chest was showing. My shirttail was out. My hat had horse manure all over it. I had not made the whistle.

I ran and jumped over the bucking chutes and joined the bronc riders who were all still hanging out talking about the way their various horses had bucked and how they had ridden or, in some cases, not ridden. I was immediately given a play-by-play recount of my ride, but that didn't take long because I hadn't stayed on long, but simply coming out of the chute on a first-class bucker had made me an automatic member of the fraternity. There were no laughing mockeries of anyone's failures, just excited dialogue concerning the finer points of saddle bronc riding and how one might become more proficient at it.

Ken was slow to speak but finally gave me his professional opinion of my outing: my failure to lift on my rein, my slowness to react and get my feet moving, and my failure to keep my upper body tucked and leaning back. He told me I had marked the horse out perfectly, but after the horse hit the ground on the first jump, everything went wrong, and there was no forgiveness when you're on a horse of that caliber. In the end he slapped me on the back and said better luck next time. We got his gear—the saddle, chaps, spurs and riggin' bag—wrapped up in the same fashion as the other bronc riders, and we all began to file out toward the parking lot behind the chutes and corrals. The bull riders were the last rough stock boys to go, so we gave them all the space they wanted. We were done for the day.

Ken had parked his truck near mine, and we deposited his gear in it. I found a hose going to a water trough for the bucking horses and bulls, and I washed as much of the dust and mud and grime off of me as possible and then brushed myself off and tucked my shirttail in. We walked together around the west end of the rodeo arena and then across the racetrack and up into the grandstand. There were several thousand people there, maybe as many as five thousand, I couldn't tell. The team roping was in progress now, and the announcer kept up a continuous flow of commentary coming through the PA system, and rodeo fans were laughing, cheering and talking. It was a lively crowd.

Ken and I walked on the cement walkway above most of the seats. He seemed to be strolling for no particular reason, I was hunting for Bevin. We were about two-thirds of the way around toward the east end of the grandstand when I heard her holler at me, calling my name. She was three or four rows below where we stood and in the middle of a long row of crowded seats, standing and waving at me. Next to her were Ben, Sharon and Cheyenne. They all waved and motioned to me that there was room for one more. I looked at Ken and said, "I'm going to go down and sit with my girl."

"I understand. I'd go down there, too, if I was you. See you later." He walked off toward the beer stand where I had last seen Dale and Ray a couple hours earlier.

I nudged my way through the crowded seats and finally reached her. She had on an orange Western blouse and blue jeans and the belt I had bought her. A Navajo Indian squash blossom necklace with beautiful turquoise stones hung around her neck. It had been polished and along with her green eyes and carrot hair shone like the stars. When I got close to her, she got up and hugged me and kissed my cheek. After shoveling a mouthful of arena sand into my mouth and losing my hat, I had felt like the dumbest human being on planet earth. Now, thirty minutes later, I felt like I was surely somebody. I was sitting next to her and the rest didn't matter.

As soon as I sat down, Billy Hamilton and his partner came out and tied a steer down in 11.7 seconds. I mentioned to Bevin, Ben and Sharon that I knew him, and we had spoken to each other before the rodeo. Their 11.7 second run was the fastest of the performance. No one asked me why I had gotten bucked off. We talked about the roping, and then the bull riding was next. Bevin sat with her arm curled around my elbow. It was good to be alive.

The bull riding was rank, the bulls winning 10 to 1. The only cowboy who made the whistle was somebody named Gary Leffew who was rumored to be a hippy from California. Ben said that he had heard that rumor, and Bevin asked me if a California hippy could be a cowboy. We all laughed, and I answered her saying anyone could be a bull rider, I guessed, but I hadn't seen any California hippies on ranches.

Far too soon the bull riding was over and that meant the rodeo was over. It was almost four o'clock and the crowd began to disperse, many of them headed downtown to visit Whiskey Row and the string of cowboy saloons that were there. Ben, Sharon, Bevin and I stepped out onto the cement runway at the top of the grandstand stairs and visited. Ben told me that he had found a new job on a ranch south of town near Walnut Grove. He and Sharon were already moved in and getting their camp in order.

"Are you going to stay at Cow Creek?" Ben asked.

"Yeah, I reckon. I've got a bunch of colts to start this summer, so, yeah, I reckon I'm going to stay."

Bevin looked at me seriously, and then Sharon spoke up and reminded Ben that they needed to get going. They had important things to do before they got started toward their new home. Sharon gave Bevin a big hug and said goodbye, and then she stepped toward me and hugged me also. Ben shook my hand and said adios, and they headed toward the parking lot.

Bevin looked at me and smiled. "I'm sorry you didn't get your horse ridden."

"Yeah, well, chalk it up to experience I guess. You can't ride them all, especially when you're as young and green as I am. Riding here in a different saddle and in front of thousands of people isn't the same as what I'm used to. Maybe I'll get another chance someday."

She smiled, "I'm sure you will! Everyone says so."

"What do you want to do? Where are you parked?"

"I'm just out here in this parking lot on the hill. Where are you parked?"

"Old Dirty's parked down there behind the announcer's stand. You want to go somewhere? Maybe get something to eat and go to a movie?"

"Maybe, but first let's talk. I want you to tell me something." She paused and looked at me kind of serious. We were leaned up against an iron pillar that supported the roof over the grandstand. We were at ground level with the upper parking lot because the top of the grandstand was level with the top of the hill and the arena floor was much lower than where we stood. People were walking by, hurrying to get to their cars.

"Sure! What do you want me to tell you?"

"Well, I don't know. I don't even know what the question is, but Sharon said that you should be honest with me." She continued to look at me while leaning her back against the iron pillar.

I looked back at her and our eyes met, and then I glanced away and stared at the cars out in the parking lot area. "What do you want me to tell you?" She was silent. But she wasn't mad, instead I could tell she didn't know what to say. We stood that way for a minute. "Look!" I said. "Everything is going to be fine! I don't know what Sharon said to you, but everything is fine! I'm doing fine! Let's go out to eat or something."

She looked away for a minute, staring at the crowd of rushing people, or the storm clouds, or something, I didn't know what. When she turned back and looked at me, she was crying. Not much, but a small tear was falling down one cheek. "Tommy, Sharon told me that something had taken place out at the ranch, and there was going to be big trouble. She said that was why they left and found a job somewhere else. She said that if you didn't get out of there you might be in some really hot water. Hot water! That's the word she used. She said that you knew that you should leave. She also said that if you were being honest with me you would tell me about it." Now there were tears on both of her cheeks.

I reached out with my hands and tried to take hers. "No!" She shouted. Several people looked at her as they passed by. She turned her head again and looked off into the distance. Her nose had begun to run and tears were falling off her chin. I got a handkerchief out of my Levis' pocket and handed it to her. She took it without looking at me, blew her nose, and collected herself. We stood there close to each other but staring off at something neither one of us wanted to look at. She blew her nose a second time and then turned toward me. "You told me that you loved me. I believed you, but you won't tell me what's going on. You won't tell me why you are about to be in hot water, whatever that's supposed to mean. Is that how you love a girl? Is that how you're going to love me?"

"Look, Bevin! I do love you and everything is fine. I'm going to be all right. Really, everything is going to be all right!"

"No, Tommy," she handed back my handkerchief, "everything is not all right!" She started walking south out into the parking lot.

"Look... where are you going? What minute! Where are you going?"

She walked, her head straight ahead, and she put her right arm behind her without looking back and spread her fingers wide as if to push me away. "I'm going home! Go down to Whiskey Row and be with all your cowboy friends! I'm going home!"

"Bevin!"

She was gone. I had lost her.

Chapter Fourteen

I stood there by the iron pillar that supported the roof of the grandstand where Bevin had asked me to level with her about the cow thievin' going on at the ranch. I went over our conversation in my mind and reminded myself of all the reasons I couldn't tell her everything. I was only involved because I was following orders. I justified my refusal to communicate with her as I stood there alone and looked out into the parking lot hoping I would see her walking back to me. I saw other couples walking hand-in-hand laughing and enjoying the Fourth of July atmosphere and realized I was lonely. She wasn't coming back.

I meandered downward through the concrete steps under the grandstand roof and then walked across the racetrack at the west end of the rodeo arena and reached Old Dirty. I fired her up and headed toward downtown Prescott and Whiskey Row. If I couldn't have Bevin, I would settle for second best. I would go tie one on like a real cowboy.

Amazingly I found an empty parking space on Whiskey Row a few doors south of the Palace Bar. It was late afternoon, about five thirty, and the sidewalk was crowded with rodeo fans and cowboys. I walked up to the swinging doors of the famous Palace Bar and stepped inside. It was wall-to-wall cowboys and cowgirls, all of whom seemed to be talking loudly or hollering in celebration. Every table was loaded with beer bottles, beer glasses, and highball glasses and every chair around those tables was occupied.

I shoved my way through the crowd, and about four tables deep into the room, I spied Pete and Mitzi sitting with Dale and Ray at a table. Kay and Veronica were also there, as well as several cowboys I didn't know.

"Tommy! Get over here and join us!" Pete hollered when he saw me. Everyone else at the table saw me and joined in the salutations and invitation to sit down. I walked up and said hello and looked around for an empty chair, but there wasn't one. "What are you drinkin'?" Pete asked.

"Coors."

Pete went to waving at the barmaid, hollering for another round. The place was loud and then got louder when a band at the back of the large room started playing a Merle Haggard song.

> *I'd like to settle down but they won't let me*
> *A fugitive must be a rolling stone*
> *Down every road there's always one more city*
> *I'm on the run, the highway is my home*

Veronica stood up and took my hand and said, "There's no chair for you to sit in so you'll have to dance!" She led the way to the dance floor that was crowded. We skimmed across the floor, and she put her head close to mine. "So are you hurt too bad, cowboy? You don't act like you're hurt!" We two-stepped for several stanzas and then I answered.

"No, I'm not hurt at all."

"Good! I wouldn't want you hurt." She held me closer and we danced on.

When the music stopped we walked back to the table, and new drinks had arrived but no new chairs. "You'll have to stand at the bar, Peckerwood, there ain't enough chairs for you here." Ray said

Veronica pushed me into her chair and said, "I'll sit on his lap." She sat down and put her arms around me and smiled at Ray whose glass eye was beginning to roll around in his head. He glared at me. Kay giggled at the goings-on between Ray and Veronica and was obviously having a fine time being partnered up with Dale who was smiling from ear to ear. He was enjoying himself immensely.

No one cared how old I was. I was a bona fide Arizona cowboy with my hat creased just right sitting at a table with Pete Kramer who was one of Northern Arizona's better known cowpunchers. He was also a man that nobody messed with. The crowd was rowdy and getting louder, and we were right in the middle of it. I drank all the alcohol I wanted, and besides that I had a very attractive woman, probably fifteen years older than I was, sitting on my lap with her arms around my neck. I forgot about Bevin. I forgot about getting bucked off in front of ten thousand rodeo fans, but I didn't forget how to dance. Veronica and I danced two out of three songs for three or four hours, I lost track of time.

Ray had given up on any chance of romance with Veronica, so he began to prowl through the crowd looking for another victim. He danced with several and even got several dances with one or two but couldn't come up with a steady partner. He came back to our table and hung out in between his various pursuits of possible female companionship. He became loud and obnoxious.

Pete and Mitzi danced and drank and visited with numerous cowboys and cowgirls who happened by our table. Dale and Kay were doing the same, dancing and visiting with lots of people. I was introduced to half of the cowboys in Northern Arizona and was having a good time. By ten thirty Veronica had convinced me that she was in love with me. She acted like I was the first man she had ever met. She kissed my ear while we danced and made me hope the night would never end.

Around eleven o'clock, Ray went over to a table near the jukebox about halfway down the north wall of the long narrow room that was almost a half city block in length. There were three couples sitting there minding their own business. They were probably the only people in the saloon who were not cowboys. Two of the men had long hair, and they were dressed like hippies, at least like urban city dwellers who were more inclined to listen to the Rolling Stones than Loretta Lynn or Bob Wills. They didn't fit into the surrounding crowd. All of the women, who were in their mid-twenties, were very attractive. In an aggressive fashion, Ray tapped one of the women on the shoulder and asked her to dance. He was behind her, and she had to turn around in her chair to see who was introducing himself into her space. She looked genuinely shocked when she saw Ray with his rolling glass eye staring down at her, and her negative reaction was obvious. She turned him down.

Ray was too drunk and too bored and too frustrated to let it slide. He said something back to her that I couldn't hear, but it was obviously insulting. She got out of her chair and started to point a finger at him and give him a lecture, but the long-haired man sitting next to her was up and in Ray's face immediately. By now everyone within thirty feet was watching, including Pete who was a lot more sober than any of the rest of us. He had a strange way of drinking without losing his wits.

Ray called the hippy a long-haired so-and-so, to which the hippy replied that Ray was a moron. "This is a cow town you long-haired faggot! I think I'll just give you a haircut!" Ray stuck his right hand into his Levis pocket and came out with a Case pocket knife, but before he could open a blade to do any barbering, the hippy hit him with a powerful right hand and knocked him down.

Pete jumped up and ran to Ray's rescue. I supposed it was out of boredom more than a feeling of obligation to help Ray. But whatever the reason, he was there and swinging in a flash. The hippy crew backed up against the wall with their three women crammed behind a nearby jukebox, and they all played defense. They played it very well. Pete was a fighter and knew how to use his fists, but the hippies were scrappers and obviously had some serious combat training. Ray was up for a moment and attacked like an insane barbarian but got knocked down almost as fast as he got up. Several of Pete's friends from nearby tables got into the action, and there was a considerable amount of yelling about cutting the long-haired so-and-so's hair off. Someone hollered, "Don't cut their hair, cut their damn throats!"

There were at least five cowboys attacking the hippies including Ray who was down as much as he was up. Pete was doing hand-to-hand combat with the man who had knocked Ray down the first time but not necessarily the times after that. The longhairs could fight, and with their backs against the wall, and the enemy out in front, they were having no problem. Tables were knocked over and beer bottles broken and several cowboys threw chairs at the long-haired crew who, in the cowboys' minds, had invaded sacred ground: the Palace Bar. And to top it all off, they had committed their sacrilege on the most holy of all cowboys' holy days, the Fourth of July.

Dale had remained in his chair for most of the fight, but then, for some reason, he decided to get up. He staggered northward toward the action. Dale was not a fighter and never sat around bragging about all the fights he had been in. He didn't brag about being tough, but he approached the edge of the battle and seemed to be wading into the middle of it. Perhaps he was going to try and break it up, but he was there, for some reason unknown to me, when a cowboy from a nearby table picked up a chair intending to swing it and club a hippy over the head. But instead, because he was drunk, he swung, missed the hippy, and clobbered Dale over the top of the head. He went down and stayed there, out cold.

Then suddenly the swinging doors blew open and a couple of Prescott city policemen entered the room. Pete saw them and retreated to our table and grabbed Mitzi. They ran across the dance floor to the west end of the building and out the backdoor into the alley. The fight was over. Dale was slowly coming to but couldn't get on his feet for several minutes. Ray was up but staggering and bleeding from multiple wounds about his head. With Pete and Mitzi gone, all of the other cowboys who had sided with Ray seemed to become invisible also. Everyone disappeared but Dale and Ray, who were too wounded to maneuver anywhere very fast. The policemen immediately sided with the hippies.

The long-haired young men who didn't fit into the cowboy crowd turned out to be Vietnam veterans. Two of them were Green Berets and all three had combat experience. They had been fighting Viet Cong and had only been released from duty several months earlier. They weren't afraid of cowboys. One of them also happened to be the police chief's little brother, and he had met both of the policemen who had come into the Palace to break up the fight. When the policeman asked the so-called hippies who started the fight, they pointed out Ray and Dale who were both having a hard time standing up. The policemen cuffed them both, even though Dale had never actually taken a swing at anyone.

Leaving Veronica behind, I decided I needed to try and rescue my friends out of the arms of the law. I told her I would return momentarily. The policemen were pushing my two handcuffed friends toward the front door, and I followed. I could see flashing lights out in the street beyond the cars that were parked at the curb.

"Sir, if you want, I'll take those fellows home and get them out of here!" I said when we reached the sidewalk.

"You can probably get them out of jail tomorrow about noon." One of the officers replied as he pushed Dale on toward a squad car parked in the street.

"Really, that older fellow, Dale, didn't have anything to do with it! He never even hit anyone! I saw the whole thing! He didn't do anything!"

"Yeah, they all say that." We had reached the police car and one of the policemen opened the back door on the driver's side. He pushed Ray inside and then pushed Dale in also.

"Really, officer, I'm being honest! Dale didn't do anything!"

The policeman looked at me and didn't say anything for a moment, and then he put his hand on my shoulder. "You want to help your friend?" he said.

"Sure! He didn't do anything wrong!"

"Then why don't you ride down to the station with him and tell the sergeant!" He pushed me down and into the back seat next to Dale, and then he shut the car door.

I immediately noticed that the back door had no door handle on the inside. I couldn't get out. "Hey! Let me outta here! Let me outta here!"

The cop was getting in behind the steering wheel, and he turned and looked at me, "I thought you wanted to help your friend?"

"Look, officer, this kid ain't done nothin' wrong. He wasn't in the fight. Let him go! He ain't done nothin'!" Dale spoke for the first time.

The police officer looked at me and said, "So, do you like the inside of a cop car? Do you want to go down to the station with your friend or not?"

"He doesn't want to go." Dale said in a very respectful tone of voice.

The policeman got back out of the car and opened the back door. "Get out!" he said.

I stepped out to freedom and Dale said to the policemen, "Sir, could you please take these cuffs off so I can get my hotel key out of my pocket and give it to this fellow?" The officer let Dale get back out of the car, and he unlocked the handcuffs freeing Dale's arms. He reached into his Levis pocket and pulled out a key to room number 217 in the St. Michael's Hotel. "It's paid for, Tommy; you just as well use it. Come and get us about noon tomorrow."

"Okay, I'll do it."

As the policeman was shutting the door, Dale said, "Go find that girl Veronica, she'll keep you warm tonight!"

The cop slammed the door in Dale's face and looked at me, "You old enough to be in that bar, kid?"

"Yeah! I guess so. I mean, yes. I have to be going. Thank you, sir!"

I ran in between two parked cars directly in front of the swinging mahogany doors of the Palace Bar. There were cowboys everywhere as thick as flies, and when I was fifteen feet from the doors, they swung open and out burst Kay and Veronica arm in arm with two cowboys that I did not know. The girls' two new acquaintances were twice my age and in full possession of a prize they had come seeking. They were all headed to some destination where I was not welcome. "Nice to meet you, Tommy Lee. Be seeing ya." Veronica said as she passed by.

Chapter Fifteen

I woke up alone in Dale's room in the St. Michael's Hotel on the corner, a few doors north of the Palace Bar. It was 5 a.m., and I was in bad need of some coffee and breakfast but had no idea where I could find some at such an early hour. I cleaned up, and when I got myself downstairs, I asked an old man who was the night clerk at the desk where I might find breakfast. He directed me west toward Miller Valley Road, and a working man's café that opened early. I got there at six and ordered bacon, hash browns and eggs, and lots of coffee. I stayed there until seven thirty and then ventured back down to Whiskey Row and hung out at a Western wear store and saddle shop until the parade commenced at ten.

The rodeo parade was huge and long and full of fancy horses and beautiful girls dressed up in shiny cowgirl costumes and new hats. There were marching bands and dozens of old vintage cars dating back to the teens and twenties, plus every red fire engine in Yavapai County. The whole event lifted my spirits, and I enjoyed the morning, but my luck was bad because I saw nobody I knew or recognized. All of the people watching from the sidewalk in front of the Palace were town people or would-be cowboys with gaudy hats and twenty-dollar pants that had been recently purchased at the store a few doors down. No man I saw had ever breathed the dust of a branding corral or pushed the pointed toes of his new cowboy boots down into a freshly deposited cow pie.

I wandered up and down the street looking for a familiar face but found none. I was lonesome for a friend and wished I hadn't made Bevin mad but figured there was no chance of making that right, so I set my sights on getting my old friend Dale out of jail. I would put up with Ray's belligerence to acquire the company of someone I knew was a friend. I got in Old Dirty and fired her up and set out to make a jailbreak.

It was one in the afternoon when I walked in the front door of the Prescott city jail, and when I inquired about my two friends, I was told they would gladly let them go. The jail was overflowing with Fourth of July partiers who had partied too much. The jailer sent a man in uniform down into the bowels of the building, and he quickly returned with Dale and Ray. We were told that it would be best if we got out of town and didn't come back for a few days; they didn't want to see us again. At least not anytime soon.

I drove north on Highway 89. We were a forlorn bunch: my new Stetson hat had been exposed to a lot rodeo arena dirt and no longer looked new. But I looked like a million dollars compared to my companions. They were both filthy and smelled like the drunk tank, but Dale was smiling and generally glad to be alive. Ray was a different story. He had been whipped by the hippies worse than I had realized. The hide around his glass eye was swollen and black, and his lips were cut and bruised, plus he had a lot of carpet burn on various spots all around his head. I couldn't help but think to myself that for all his reputation of being a tough guy, he hadn't performed well lately. Every fight I had seen him in had turned out badly for him. He was in an especially foul humor, which when he was sober meant he was silent.

When we reached Chino Valley, we stopped at the Log Cabin Bar. Dale and Ray were both insistent about the stop, and they both started drinking heavily. I drank a beer but stopped at one not wanting to get arrested for drunk driving. Almost no one was there so I was able to talk them out of staying long, suggesting to them that there would be a bigger crowd in Seligman. Dale bought a bottle of Jim Beam, and we left and headed north again.

Ray started getting mouthy as the alcohol hit him. He said that I had let him down by not getting involved in the fight with the hippies. He implied that I was a coward. Dale argued with him and stood up for me. I said nothing as I drove on toward Seligman.

We drove into Seligman about four o'clock, and as we passed the Conoco service station, I strained my eyes to see if Bevin was there working. Instead, I saw the hillbilly with the dirty shirt. "Is your little church mouse there, Tommy?" Ray asked snidely. "What's she like, anyway; you know, when you two are alone, you know what I mean!"

"Shut up, Ray!" It was the first time I had ever directly stood up to him.

"Don't tell me to shut up, you little peckerwood you!" He was sitting in the middle between Dale and me, and he punched me in my right ear. The punch was a serious attempt at hurting me, and it knocked my hat off, and as it fell off my head, it blinded me momentarily as it slid down in front of my face. The punch also knocked my whole head sideways. Between the punch and my hat blinding me, I jerked the steering wheel and ended up in the left lane, facing oncoming Route 66 traffic. I jerked the wheel back and almost overcorrected to the point I came close to hitting a parked car to the right. Cars honked their horns at me, and people on the sidewalk by Delgadillo's Snow Cone stared at us. "Yeehaw! Cowboys in town, trouble expected!" Ray bellered as I managed to get control of Dirty. Within a half block we reached the Black Cat and came to a stop in the parking lot.

Without asking my companions' opinion, I headed across the street to the Copper Cart to get something to eat, and to my surprise they followed. I was going to order a cheeseburger, but Dale insisted that we all order a rib steak, which was the most expensive thing on the menu. He said he wanted to buy.

"I'm coming into some good money in a day or two, and I want to treat my friends to supper tonight!"

"What are you going to do with your share of the money, Peckerwood? Probably give most of it to the church, I suppose. Maybe save some to buy you and your little redhead a honeymoon cottage?" Ray said

"I don't have a redhead anymore." I answered.

"Ah, really? Did she leave you? I wondered why you been so low down and nasty!" Ray started har-haring, which was supposed to be a laugh.

"Don't worry about it, Tommy, there's lots of girls out there! You're only eighteen. So what are you going to do with your money?" Dale asked.

Ray was smiling.

"I don't know, I suppose the first thing I'll do is order a new flower-carved Ray Holes saddle. Just like yours! And a new pair of Paul Bond boots. And then I might get a new pickup." I answered Dale's question.

"What about you, Ray?" Dale said. He was drinking hot coffee, and we were all waiting for our steaks.

"I'm gonna take a week off and go up to the chicken ranch, up by Tonopah. You know what the chicken ranch is, Tommy?" Ray asked.

"No, guess not."

"Well, it'sa ranch with lots of girls! My kinda girls!"

Our steaks came and interrupted our conversation. I was glad. I had an odd feeling that Ray and I were headed into new territory in our relationship. I was getting to where I disliked him very much, and I was sure the feeling was mutual. I ate my steak and tried to talk to Dale and ignore Ray. When Ray was eating you could ignore him. He was crude, and as long as food lay before him, it was all his cerebrum could process. Good conversation during mealtime meant nothing to him. Dale and I talked about the details of ordering a new saddle. We discussed gullet heights and widths, and the length of saddle seats, and what horn to order. Ray devoured his steak long before Dale and I were finished and got up. "See you pilgrims next door." he said as he left. I was happy he was gone.

For a while we ate in silence. Dale and I agreed that a rib steak, cooked with the bone still in, was our favorite piece of meat. The steaks were big, and we also had a large baked potato and lots of butter and sour cream to go with it. We took our time and satisfied our appetites. Dale ordered another cup coffee for both of us, and we sat for a moment enjoying each other's company. "This coffee is a good appetizer for all that good whiskey we're going to drink tonight. Me and you haven't done much Fourth of July celebratin'. Gettin' thrown in the juzgado didn't help much!"

"No. Kinda shut the party down for me, too!"

"Ah, who cares? It's still Fourth of July weekend."

"Yeah."

"So your gal pulled out on ya, huh?"

"She wanted me to tell her about what all happened out there. She wanted me to explain everything about the O R O and the Doubled O cattle and how we got 'em, and what we did with them. The whole thing. I didn't know what to tell her." I paused for a moment and then went on. "How the heck was I going to explain all that?"

Dale stared out the window at the cars driving by for several minutes before he answered. "That's a tough one!"

"No kidding!"

"Listen, Tommy!" Dale leaned across the table and got closer to me. "There ain't a darn thing anybody can do about them cattle! Those outfits ain't gonna know they're gone until this fall, and there won't be no trail to follow! Nothin'! The only thing we need to watch is too much talk. There isn't any worry about Ben... I don't think... what's he gonna to say? I ain't worried about you, but Ray's another issue. Ray isn't gonna doublecross anybody, but when we get our money in a couple days, he's gonna go on a big bender, and when he's partyin', he might say anything. He's stupid, so be careful. When that money shows up, which will be about Monday, two days from now, let him go off partyin' by hisself! Don't be pallin' around with him! That's some free advice from your old friend Dale. And quit worrying about your girl, she'll come around. If she doesn't, there will be another one." He got up and walked to the counter and paid for the three steaks and then headed across the street to the Black Cat bar, and I followed.

There were a half dozen local people inside, most of whom Dale and Ray knew. Everything was peaceful. Dale continued drinking whiskey, which was his drink of choice for the night. Ray and I drank beer, he a lot more than I. We played pool with the locals and put money in the jukebox, but mostly we drank and told cowboy stories, at least Dale and I did. He told me about some of his travels and some of the big ranches he had worked on and the good horses he had ridden. Ray got smart-alecky and loud, first to one person and then another, but everyone pretty much ignored him. We drank from six until ten thirty, and by then we were the only ones left. The bartender, a new one that I had never seen, wanted to close up and go home for the night, so he asked us to leave. Dale weaved as we walked across the parking lot to Old Dirty, and he sang "San Antonio Rose" as we walked along. Ray was sullen, obviously searching for something more, something that he wasn't going to find in the Black Cat parking lot.

Old Dirty needed gas, so I drove to the east end of town to the Conoco and parked next to the pump that read, regular 29 cents per gallon. I cleared the pump, put the nozzle in the gas tank and started filling my old Ford truck. About twenty feet away, parked at another pump, was an old Volkswagen van painted with flowers and rainbows and all kinds of pastel-colored decorations. There were numerous bumper stickers glued on the bus's exterior that read, Jesus Saves and God Loves You. The bus had a California license plate.

There were three or four hippies that belonged to the bus. One of them was filling the gas tank and several were standing around just hanging out. I wasn't sure how many there were, at least one was a girl, and they were dressed like San Francisco flower children. They all smiled at us and said hello.

Ray couldn't stand it. "You hippies are in the wrong territory! You better get movin' or I'm gonna move ya!" He staggered toward them and dug his pocket knife out of his Levis.

"Listen, man, we've no quarrel with you!" the man pumping gas said.

"Well, I'm quarrelin' with you! I'm fixin' on cuttin' your hair! How do you like that, hippie?"

"Listen, cowboy, my friend told you, we're not looking for trouble!" The biggest one of the bunch had cut Ray off and stood unintimidated in front of him.

"Come on, Ray! We don't have a fight with these people! You are fixin' on gettin' all of us in trouble! Come on!" Dale staggered out of Dirty and was ordering Ray to retreat.

I ran inside the office and paid the hillbilly with the dirty T-shirt for my gas. The hillbilly was staring at the telephone hanging on the office wall. I didn't want to get arrested right there in Bevin's gas station so I ran toward my truck.

"Jesus loves you, man!" one of the hippies hollered at us as I got in. Dale had managed to get Ray loaded, and I got Dirty going and headed toward the west end of town. "God loves you, man!" I could hear them shouting as we drove off.

"Squeaky clean, dirty bastards! I hate 'em!" Ray said as we passed the Black Cat.

"Squeaky clean, dirty bastards!" Dale roared with laughter and uncorked a new bottle of Jim Beam. "Now how can you be squeaky clean and dirty at the same time? Explain to me how that's done, Ray old buddy!"

"They're so wholesome they squeak! Just like that redheaded slut that Tommy's so proud of!"

"Shut up, Ray!"

"Don't tell me to shut up you little spoiled brat! I'll kick your ass from here to breakfast!" Ray slapped me across my right temple as he said it. I swerved and lost control of the steering wheel as I ducked my head trying to avoid Ray's abuse. For a second time I was in the left lane and staring into the headlights of oncoming traffic. I overcorrected and ended up in the bar ditch on the right side and fought to regain control of old Dirty. The drivers coming toward us honked loudly as they passed, and when I slowed down to regain control, the cars behind us passed with the people yelling out their car windows at us. "You idiot, watch what you're doing!"

Ray hit me again as I drove twenty miles an hour with the right wheels down in the bar ditch. I flinched and shoved him as hard as I could with my right elbow trying to get him off of me. And then suddenly there was a loud explosion. My right front tire had blown out with a bang after passing over a sharp malpai rock lying off the edge of the pavement. We rolled to a stop with the passenger side of my pickup leaning downhill and unlevel as a result of our right side being in the ditch.

Ray cursed me while I got out and climbed into the pickup bed to retrieve a Handyman jack and a lug wrench. I also threw out the spare tire. Dale staggered out, picked up the lug wrench, squatted and then sat down on his hind end. With the wrench he started loosening up the lug nuts on the flat tire. I drug the long jack around the left side of the truck and then around to the front of the grill and stuck the flange underneath the bumper and began pushing the long handle down and up like a pump jack, causing the jack to go upward taking the right corner of the pickup with it. I lifted the truck about two inches and stopped. "You need some help, Dale?" I asked and looked at him as he sat beside the tire with the lug wrench in his hand.

"I got a couple of 'em loose. Just give me a minute or two to get the rest."

Ray stood behind me glaring at me. "Why don't me and you just have it out, Peckerwood! I don't like you, never did!"

"Hells bells, Ray! Quit fighting! It's the Fourth of July weekend!" Dale looked around the corner of the truck. His head was about as high as the axle because he sat in the ditch. "Leave the kid alone, he ain't done nothin' to you!"

Ray shoved me up against the front of the truck. "What's she look like, Tommy? You know, when she's got no—"

"Shut up, Ray!"

He went to push me again, but I ducked under his arm, stepped behind him and hit him in the ear. He turned around and lunged at me, and I stepped sideways as he passed me. I didn't know anything about fighting, but I was quicker and I had sobered up. I told myself, *Whatever happens, don't let him get his hands on you.* He turned again and took a big roundhouse swing at my head, and I ducked and tapped him on his right ear as I stepped by him. He turned around and fell against the front of the truck. He cursed and swung at me again. I was gaining confidence, and I brought my right hand up and hit him squarely in the jaw. Just as my fist connected, Dale stuck his head out in front of the pickup again, about axle high. "Quit fightin'!" My punch was a good one, and it knocked Ray off balance, and he fell to his right into the long upright shaft of the Handyman jack that was tight and sticking upward in front of the right headlight. When Ray fell into it, the whole pickup shifted to the direction of the bar ditch and the jack came out from under the bumper with a snapping sound. It crashed downward toward the ditch with tremendous speed. Dale's head and shoulders were in the Handyman jack's path, and the heavy shaft struck him about three inches under his left ear. Because the truck was unlevel, it fell farther down into the bar ditch, and the tire from which Dale had just removed the last lug nut was pushed downward and landed on top of Dale's legs. The spindle and brake drum ended up sitting on top of the tire, and all of the weight of that corner of Old Dirty had Dale penned tightly to the ground. It didn't matter. Dale was very dead.

At first we couldn't make out what for sure had happened. We quit fighting and hollered at Dale. There was no response. I had turned the engine off and the headlights with it, and we had been working in the dark, but we could make out the jack lying across Dale's neck and ear.

"Strike a match so we can see!" I told Ray. He dug down into his shirt pocket and pulled out a wooden match and struck it against the bumper. Dale's head was obviously dislocated and cocked off to one side by at least two inches, the result of a broken neck.

Ray stood up, stiffened, and threw his fists up to his head and screamed, " Ahhh, he's dead! He's dead!"

He slammed his head down onto the hood of the truck repeating, "He's dead!" I stood numbly staring into the darkness pierced by the oncoming headlights. Ray continued screaming, "You killed him!" then suddenly turning toward the pavement, staggering and screaming, "aahhh!" he walked out onto the highway totally oblivious to Route 66 traffic, and soon he was in the middle of the road holding his head and moaning. Cars passed within inches of him at fifty to sixty miles an hour. Horns honked and people leaned out of their windows hollering at him. "Get out of the road, you moron!"

I ran forward a few steps and yelled at him, "Ray, come back! Help me jack the truck up and get it off of Dale!" He ignored me or maybe was unable to hear me, but he continued on for fifty yards right down the middle of the highway with cars passing him going east and west, swerving and honking at him as they drove on by. I watched Ray until he crossed all the way to the other side of the highway and headed west on the side of the road, facing the oncoming traffic. He finally disappeared into the darkness.

I was confused. I was numb. I didn't know what to do. Should I try and jack up the truck and pull Dale out from under the weight. But the truck had now shifted sideways more, putting the passenger side even farther downhill. I thought that if I jacked it up again it would only fall downward again and be on top of him more. I needed help. I knew that Dale was dead. There was no changing that.

I stepped out onto the side of Route 66 and started waving my arms at passing cars and several drove past me without stopping. Then I realized that I needed to stop someone going into town, so I ran over to the other side of the road and commenced trying to stop someone going that direction. Finally a car stopped and a man asked me what the problem was.

"I've been in a bad accident! Could you please drive into town and call someone for me?"

"Okay, is there a police station in town? Or do you need tow truck?" the driver of the car asked.

"No, but call 422-3116 and asked for Bevin. If she is not there ask for her dad, Mr. Magennis. Tell them Tommy is in a wreck on the edge of town out by the airport turnoff. Tell them I need help."

The driver said he would do it for sure. For some reason I never doubted him. I never thought about telling him to call the highway patrol or the sheriff. Maybe it was because the only number I knew was Bevin's. It was funny because I had never actually talked to Bevin on the phone, but I remembered her number.

I slowly walked back across the highway and leaned against the front of the truck. I wondered if I should do something. I wondered if I would be blamed. I wondered if I would be in trouble for not getting the truck off of Dale's body. I wondered what I should tell them. I remembered the whiskey and got in the cab of the truck and found the open bottle of Jim Beam and threw it out in the cow pasture as far as I could. I tucked my shirttail in and took my handkerchief and wiped the sweat and dirt off of my face. I felt dirty, all over.

Finally several vehicles pulled up behind Dirty and stopped. Out of the first stepped Bevin from the passenger's side, and her father out of the driver's side. Almost immediately Jimmy Duncan, the brand inspector, came walking up from the second vehicle.

"Tommy! Are you all right?" Bevin said from ten feet away.

I started to answer her but Jimmy Duncan interrupted. "What's the problem, young man?"

"Dale's dead, the jack broke his neck when it slipped. We were changing a flat tire. He's laying down there in the ditch."

"Oh, Tommy!" Bevin said.

Jimmy Duncan had a flashlight, and he walked up the right side of the pickup and pointed his light down on Dale's body. Bevin's father had walked along side of him. I stood by the tailgate staring back toward the lights of town that seemed miles away, but in reality were only a short distance, maybe a quarter-mile or a little farther. Bevin stood ten feet away holding her hands up to her cheeks and crying.

Jimmy Duncan came back and shined his flashlight in my face. "When'd this happen?"

"I don't know, a little while ago. A few minutes."

"Just you and him?"

"No, Ray was with us, but he took off running."

"Why was he running?"

I hung my head and held my hands up in a how-would-I-know gesture. That was how I felt, how would I know what was going through Ray's mind.

Jimmy Duncan walked back to his truck and used the two-way radio that was in it, and then he returned. "I want to know what happened, young man. Is there something you need to tell me?"

Bevin's father stood by my side and patted me on the back. "The truth is always best." he said.

I stared at the ground for a while and decided it didn't matter one way or the other. Was it my fault? Was it, Ray's? I didn't care. "We were going home, back out to the ranch, and I was driving, and I had a flat tire so I pulled off, and I got my Handyman jack and handed Dale the lug wrench. He walked up there and sat down beside the flat tire and went to loosening the lug nuts while I started jacking the front of the truck up. When I had lifted it several inches, I stopped so Dale could finish getting the nuts off. Ray was mad at me about something and was wanting to fight, and he hit me. And then I hit him back, and it knocked him off balance, and he landed on the jack, and it came off the bumper and hit Dale upside his head and killed him. It's as simple as that. I guess maybe I killed him. I don't know, it just happened."

"And then Ray took off running?" Jimmy Duncan asked.

"Yeah, I think he thought it was his fault. I really don't know what he thought. He just took off running out that way." I pointed toward the west.

"Do you think it was Ray's fault?" Jimmy Duncan questioned.

"No!" I paused, thinking to myself. Tell the truth, Bevin's father had said. "It was both of us. Our fault. It was my fault! I don't know! What difference does it make? Dale's dead. The best friend I had and he's dead. I don't care whose fault it is."

A tow truck pulled up with the lights flashing, and he backed up to the front of Dirty and soon had the pickup lifted straight up. An ambulance showed up a few minutes later, and they checked for a pulse, but Dale was already cold. The ghost had flown away. They put Dale in the ambulance, and then I put my spare tire on, and the tow truck set Old Dirty back down on the ground.

Finally more flashing lights showed up, and an Arizona State highway patrolman stepped out of his black and white car. Jimmy Duncan intercepted him and pulled him off to the side and talked to him for a while. The patrolman then walked to the ambulance and viewed Dale's dead body and talked to the people driving the ambulance, and then the ambulance drove away. I never saw Dale again. The patrolman walked up to me. "I understand that the deceased man was your friend?"

"Yes, sir, he was."

"Can I see your driver's license?"

I got my wallet out of my Levis pocket and took out

my license and handed it to him. He looked at it and wrote some numbers down on a piece of paper. "So you had a flat tire, and you stopped to change it, and your friend was sitting down taking the tire off while you jacked the front of your truck up? Is that right?"

"Yes, sir."

"And then after you raised the truck up a ways, the jack slipped and fell on your friend and killed him. Is that right?" the officer said.

"Yes, that's right." I answered and waited for more questions, but he asked none. Instead he walked away and began writing out a report.

Bevin and her father had stayed nearby and watched while I talked to the highway patrolman. When the patrolman walked back to his car to fill out the paperwork, Bevin walked up to me and reached out and touched my arm. I looked at her and realized how much I thought of her. I also realized how far apart we were. She looked at me and said, "I'm very sorry, Tommy. I'm really very sorry."

I looked at her, and for the first time I wanted to cry. But I didn't. "Thanks. I appreciate it."

Bevin turned and walked away, and she and her dad got into their car and drove away.

Chapter Sixteen

At five o'clock in the morning, I woke up after a fitful two hours of sleep. For a moment I didn't know where I was, and then in a flash I remembered that I had reached the ranch at 3:00 a.m., and I remembered the flat tire and the Handyman jack lying across Dale's neck as he lay dead in the bar ditch. And then a thought passed by all those thoughts like a high-powered racecar going by a Volkswagen on a wide highway, and I was suddenly overcome with fear. I remembered Ray and the knowledge that I had last seen him walking in the direction of the ranch. I jerked upward, lifting my head off of my pillow, threw my bed tarp back and glanced nervously around the bunkhouse expecting to see him staring at me. But he was not there. I was alone.

I froze, still searching for sounds of someone who might be close by, but there was only silence. I got up and pulled my Levis on and looked out a window and saw nothing. I went to the door and peered outward toward the barn and saw nothing. I stared down the dirt road that led to Seligman, forty miles away, and saw nothing. I told myself to settle down and think about my situation. I realized that I had already subconsciously decided that I was leaving the outfit. And now that the decision was out in the open for viewing by my mind's eye, I needed to decide how I was going to leave. Should I scrape up all my belongings and toss them in Old Dirty without so much as rolling my bed or changing clothes? Or should I muster up enough courage to leave like a man, looking everyone in the eye as I made my exit.

Walking into the bathroom, I relieved myself and then went to the wash basin to wash my hands, and there staring back at me in the mirror was the face of a coward. It was then, while I stared into the mirror, that I decided that I wasn't going to crawl off the Cow Creek Ranch like a snake eating dust and being kicked at by some antagonists, by someone who planned on beating me half to death just because I was a dumb kid. I told myself that maybe I wasn't a man, but I sure as hell wasn't a dumb kid anymore. The last couple days had changed all that.

I had no desire to get in a fist fight with Ray, or Pete, whom I suddenly feared more than Ray. I could outsmart Ray, but Pete was truly dangerous to anyone who crossed him. He would keep his cards close to the table and protect them and himself. He would not be friendly if for some reason he thought I would talk too much. I had no idea how he would feel about me leaving the ranch, but the concept worried me. I told myself that there was no reason to worry. I had never shown any disloyalty to Pete, but still, I wasn't sure.

What I needed was an equalizer of some kind. I remembered that Dale had a Ruger Blackhawk .45 caliber pistol rolled up in his bedroll. I got into the bedroll and retrieved the pistol. I also found a box of shells hidden in a suitcase next to his bed. I took the ammunition and pistol to where my bedroll and belongings were and laid them down within my reach, but told myself that, if possible, when someone showed up, I would keep the gun hidden until I should need it. Hopefully the situation would never go that direction.

I was filthy dirty, so I gathered up some new cloths and my shaving kit and went to the bathroom to clean myself up. I kept the Ruger pistol within reach while I was in the shower. I had seen that in a movie, and so I acted like the gangster in the film who was always ready to shoot anyone who might attack him. When I walked out of the bathroom, I was clean shaven and freshly clothed and had applied a healthy dose of aftershave. I kept moving.

After rolling my bed I got all my clothes stored away in a couple canvas war bags that made up the only luggage I possessed. I packed it all up and took it outside and neatly loaded it in the back of Dirty. Then I started the pickup and pulled over to the barn and gathered up all my horse gear, which wasn't much. My old N. Porter saddle and chaps and what few bridles I owned, three to be exact—a curb bit, a snaffle with latigo reins, and a hackamore. I loaded it all up and stacked it neatly along with my other belongings, such as they were.

I looked over at the rock house were Pete and Mitzi lived and could see no vehicle so I knew they were still in town but figured they would be home today. I had no idea where Ray was. I wanted to see Pete before I left so I drove Old Dirty back over and parked in front of the bunkhouse and went in. By the time I did all this, it was seven thirty, and the sun was well up in the sky. I was hungry so I went into the kitchen and boiled a pot of strong coffee and fried myself some bacon and eggs, which I consumed quickly, and then I washed the dishes I had dirtied. I walked back into the big room where we all slept and did most of our living. I packed the coffee pot with me and my cup. I also had my Levi jumper, and I laid the Ruger pistol on a small table and then laid my Levi coat loosely over it, hiding it. I sat in a chair close to the table drinking coffee and waiting for someone to show up.

Reflecting back on the events of the night before, I remembered the highway patrolman had filled out the accident report, and in the place on the form that said Cause of Accident he had written, "Vehicle fell off of a high lift jack during an attempt to change a flat tire. The jack struck the deceased man in his head killing him. Incident deemed accidental." I saw on another line the question: Arrests Made, and on that line the officer had written: None.

Evidently neither Ray nor I was in any trouble even though our fistfight had caused the jack to fall. But the stealing of the cattle was another matter. Would Pete demand that I stay employed at the ranch so he could keep his eye on me making sure I wouldn't talk? Would Ray, in some perverted way, want to do me harm for what had happened last night. Maybe they would both blame me for Dale's death. I sat drinking coffee, and all kinds of scenarios began to roll around in my head. The longer I waited the wilder my imagination became. Maybe I should get in my pickup and run. But then I imagined meeting Pete head on as he came driving back to the ranch. I imagined him running me down. At times I was almost frozen with dread, and then I would get a hold of myself and think I was exaggerating everything.

I waited and nothing happened. Several times I started to leave and then forced myself back down into the chair. I fell asleep in the chair and then woke up and then fell asleep a second time. I was miserable, and then I waited some more.

About twelve thirty midday, I heard vehicles coming. I got up and looked out of the window and saw Pete and Mitzi driving up, and behind them was Jimmy Duncan driving his official pickup with the big black stars painted on the doors. Riding with Jimmy was Ray. I watched from the window as Pete got out of his pickup and walked back to Jimmy Duncan's truck while Jimmy and Ray got out, and they all stood there talking. Mitzi got out of the passenger side, walked around and got in behind the steering wheel and drove off toward her and Pete's house. After about five minutes Jimmy Duncan got in his government-issued truck and drove away. Pete and Ray turned and looked toward the bunkhouse for a minute and then turned the other direction and leaned against the picket fence that made up the horse corral, and I could tell from a hundred fifty yards distance that they were talking. Should I go out and meet them outside? I decided, no, I would make them come to me.

They turned and headed toward the bunkhouse, and I stepped back away from the window. I pulled my hat down tight on my head as if I was about to make a bronc ride and walked over to my chair and sat down. I laid my right forearm on top of my Levi jumper that was covering the Ruger pistol. My heart was about to jump out of my chest. My mouth went dry as the door opened.

Pete came through the door first, slowly, and when he was half in, he paused looking around and then he saw me sitting there so he stepped on inside with Ray following. Pete took several steps toward me and stopped, "I see you're loaded up, Tommy. Where ya goin'?"

"I'm leaving."

"Yeah, well, where to? Why in the hell do you think you need to leave?"

"I don't know, but I'm leaving."

Pete stared at me for a while as if he was sizing the situation up. Ray stood off to the side and a step behind him. He looked absolutely horrible. His bad eye was swelled shut, and he had scabs all over his head. His lips were cracked, swollen and bleeding. He obviously had slept under a cedar tree somewhere and perhaps on top of an ant den. He was dusty and had grass and twigs in his hair and stuck in his collar and the back of his shirt. "One of these days I'm gonna get even with you, Peckerwood! I'm gonna kill you!"

"There ain't gonna be no killin' around here today, Ray." Pete lifted his left arm and held it up in front of Ray's face as a signal to stop talking. Pete continued, "Jimmy Duncan said that Dale's death was accidental. Is that how you saw it, Tommy?"

"I looked at the highway patrolman's report and that's what he wrote down, so it doesn't matter what I think."

"Well, there you go! It was an accident, nobody's fault! We all thought the world of Dale. Hell, he was as good a friend as I had in the whole world, but he's gone. It ain't your fault, Tommy! There ain't nobody blamin' you!"

"I didn't say they were."

"I'm blaming you!" Ray growled.

Pete lifted his arm again demanding silence. "Let me handle this, Ray!"

"So why are you leavin'? I thought we was gettin' along fine."

"We were, I guess, but now it's time for me to go, and I'm going! I would have already left, but I wanted to tell you to your face. I'm leaving."

"Dammit, kid, don't you realize that you got a whole truckload a' money comin' to you? It will be here tomorrow! I'll split Dale's part up between you and Ray!"

"I don't want it. Keep it!"

"Are you serious?" I thought he almost smiled. Smiled like a prosecuting attorney who had just squeezed a confession out of an innocent but very scared man. "Are you going to tell me, with Ray as my witness, that you are going to turn down all that money? Just walk away?"

"You can have all the money." They stood there staring at me and I sat staring at them.

"The trouble is, Peckerwood, you know too much. You'll talk to that church mouse, and we'll have the law and all of those holy rollers comin' after us. The trouble is, Peckerwood, you and I got a score to settle."

"He ain't gonna talk, are you, Tommy?" Pete said.

"No, I'm not talking."

"How can we be sure, Peckerwood?" Ray grinned as he said it.

"I give you my word." I said, and suddenly Pete stepped sideways to the left side of the room about three steps. Was he making room for Ray to beat on me?

"Your word about what?" Ray said.

"If you let me out of here alive, I am not going to say anything!" I realized that I had been reduced to begging.

Ray laughed and started to step forward, but I rose quickly with the Ruger Blackhawk in my hand. I cocked it and pointed it at Ray's belly. He froze. The black eye that was swelled shut, opened slightly. The other eye was open very wide. Pete stepped backwards and leaned against the bunkhouse wall and started laughing loudly and slapping his leg with his hand. "He's gotta pistol! Hell! He's gotta pistol! What do you think now, Ray? He's gotta pistol!" He roared with laughter "I think he might use it!" He continued laughing for a moment and then said. "Go ahead and go, Tommy Lee! We ain't gonna mess with a guy whose got a pistol! Get out of here before I change my mind!"

Ray said nothing as I walked way around to the right side of the room and backed my way to the door. "Tommy," Pete growled as I started to walk outside, "stop up there at the horse corral and throw Dale's Ray Holes saddle in your truck. He ain't got no kin, and he'd wanted you to have it. Take his spurs, too. Hell, I don't want 'em."

I backed Old Dirty up to the horse corral fence and quickly loaded the flower-carved Ray Holes saddle and spurs. I threw everything in, Navajo blankets, bridles, chaps, everything. I told myself they didn't deserve them.

I drove into Seligman and got there about three o'clock. I was hungry and stopped at the Copper Cart and bought myself a rib steak, medium well; that's the way Dale would have told them to cook it. I drank coffee and stared out at the traffic on Main Street, which was also Route 66. I looked at the Black Cat parking lot, which was empty. Nobody was about. The town looked dead. There were no clouds, and I wondered if it would ever go to raining. I wondered what Bevin was doing. I thought about going to see her and then told myself I couldn't. My rib steak came, and I ate it and thought of Dale. I wondered how in the world so much had happened to me in a mere six weeks. I sat there long after I had finished the steak and just stared out of the big plate-glass window and watched cars go by. I almost expected that she would come walking by and see me and would come and sit down with me. But she didn't come.

Finally I got up and walked to the counter and paid for the steak and then walked back and left a dollar bill on the table. A whole dollar! I told myself that I didn't want anyone in Seligman talking badly about me. As I walked out, I noticed the clock on the wall said it was almost five.

I drove down to the Conoco and pulled up to the pump and filled Dirty with regular gas, and the hillbilly with the dirty shirt was inside taking people's money. "Is Bevin in town?"

He looked at me, and after thinking about it for a minute, he replied, "In about an hour she'll be down at the Foursquare Church. They have two services on Sunday." He paused, grinning at me. One of his top front teeth was missing, and they were all tobacco stained. "But you don't go to church, do you?"

"No... I don't."

I fired Dirty up and headed east toward Ashfork on Route 66. I drove slowly, thinking about stealing from neighbors, from people you claim to be friends with. I thought about killing your best friend. I wondered if it was my fault that Dale was dead. I thought about Bevin, and in my dejected state, I slowed down to thirty miles an hour. People honked at me and gave me dirty looks as they passed. When I got to the Crookton Hill Road, I pulled off to the side and parked and stared straight ahead toward Bill Williams Mountain. I wanted to see her.

I turned around and drove back into Seligman and drove around until I found the Foursquare Gospel Church. I parked and got out and walked across the gravel parking lot toward the door. When I got close I could hear people clapping and singing.

> *In the name of Jesus*
> *In the name of Jesus*
> *We have the victory*
> *In the name of Jesus*
> *In the name of Jesus*
> *We have the victory*

I opened the door, carefully, not knowing what to expect. The music stopped, I didn't know if it was because the song was over or because the door hinges needed oil, and they made a loud offensive sound. It was virtually impossible to sneak inside. Everyone in the building turned around and stared at me making me feel like Cyclops or Jack the Ripper. Bevin was directly in front of me on the left side of an aisle that split the benches, one half being on the right and the other half to the left. She was on the left at the end of a pew four rows in front of me. She had turned around and was staring at me like everyone else.

For a moment it was eerily silent, and I looked around the room and could see that there were about thirty people present, scattered about. I noticed Bevin's mom and dad sitting off to the right side, and then I saw Jimmy Duncan, the cattle inspector, sitting with his wife off to the left against the wall. When I recognized him, he was staring at me, and then suddenly he jerked his head forward and stared straight ahead.

"Come on in and join us, son. You're welcome! Everyone is welcome! Have a seat." It was a woman talking. She was standing in front of everyone and had a Martin guitar held up by a strap over her neck. She began playing and singing.

> *Throw out the lifeline across the dark waves.*
> *There is a brother someone should save.*
> *Somebody's brother! Oh who then will dare*
> *To throw out the lifeline his peril to share?*
> *Throw out the lifeline! Throw out the lifeline!*
> *Someone is drifting away.*
> *Throw out the lifeline! Throw out the lifeline!*
> *Someone is sinking today.*

The lady played in the key of D, and everyone started singing and clapping except Bevin. She stared at me, saying nothing, and then turned around and looked straight ahead. I started to leave. But then she rose up slightly off of the bench and moved to her left about three feet making room for someone to sit there, so I walked down the aisle and sat down beside her.